THE *Only* GOAL

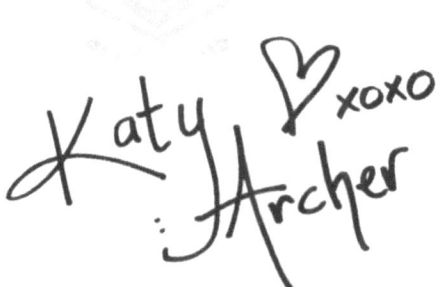

KATY ARCHER

THE ONLY GOAL
Nolan U Hockey #5

© Copyright 2024 Katy Archer
www.katyarcher.com

This is a work of fiction. Names, places, businesses, characters and incidents are either the product of the author's imagination or are used in a fictitious manner. Any resemblance to actual persons, living or dead, actual events or locales is purely coincidental.

Cover Design © Designed with Grace

ISBN: 978-1-991138-24-8 (Kindle eBook)
ISBN: 978-1-991138-27-9 (paperback)

Archer Street Romance
www.katyarcher.com

CHAPTER 1
TAMMY

I can't wait to get home.

Ugh. After an entire week in Gladstone, anyone in their right mind would be eager to leave that place in their rearview mirror.

I grip the wheel, feeling bad for thinking it. Some of my friends still live in Gladstone. It was nice to see Grace. She's a sweetheart and probably the least gossipy person in my hometown, but...

I've moved on. I never thought it'd be possible, but it turns out that three years of living in the city was enough to make me realize just how small Gladstone is. Just how narrow-minded and stuck in their ways they are.

It's like taking a trip back to the 1950s, and every time I visit, I always drive past that green sign with the yellow writing that says *Gladstone—Population 512—Mighty glad to be here* with a nostalgic smile.

And within an hour of being back, my smile is gone, and I'm inhaling air that's more like toxic gas, forcing pleasant smiles I don't feel, nodding at statements I don't agree with, and wishing to be anywhere else.

My parents are pissed that I bailed early.

I made up an excuse about Hudson needing me home. Mom bought it in a heartbeat, because apparently that's what good little wives do. They drop everything to be at their husband's beck and call.

My stomach knots, and I glance in the rearview mirror, checking on Kai. My precious boy is sleeping in his booster seat, looking angelic as ever. Because he is. Even when he's awake, he's an angel. My little shadow.

I smile, my heart melting in my chest. He's the only reason I survive places like Gladstone. He's the only reason I go back to visit. I can't deny my parents or my in-laws access to their grandchild... even if I do spend the entire time trying to justify why they don't have any more grandchildren yet.

"Kai's four now, Tamara. If you wait too long, the gap will be huge, and then they won't get along. You want them to be friends, don't you?"

I nearly bit back, "Oh, you mean like Karan and me?" I barely speak to my sister these days. And even when we lived in the same house, we didn't get along. We were like aliens to each other. We had nothing in common, and it still surprises me that we came from the same parents. She's a year older and left for college the minute she could. She'd always had her eyes set on the highway out of town, and she never looked back. She left before the summer was even done.

Left before I met Hudson.

Before he knocked me up... and then put a ring on my finger.

She was so disgusted by the fact that I was getting married at eighteen, she refused to come back for the wedding.

My parents haven't spoken to her since... I don't think.

That's probably why all the pressure's on me. I'm the good girl. The one who does what she's told. I'm their only path to more grandbabies, so why the hell am I not popping them out faster?

Gritting my teeth, I sniff and focus on the long stretch of highway.

Truth is, I can't bring myself to try for more. Hudson is so busy at work. Ever since we made the big shift to the city, he's been on a mission to prove himself and bring home the bacon. He got a job working for his uncle's company. Because we were such young parents, we both skipped college, and he worked for his dad in Gladstone for a year—had to pay the bills somehow, right? Then he got offered this chance in the city, and he took it. He didn't even ask me, just came home one night all excited. I didn't fight him on it, because I was suffocating, and the out sounded good.

But it wasn't as easy as I thought it'd be. City life is so

different, and I suffered culture shock for the first year as I tried to navigate my way with a one-year-old on my hip. We survived somehow and found a happy rhythm. Hudson worked his ass off, rising through the ranks with speed and constantly striving for more.

He seems to thrive in the business world. He comes home electrified and talking about investments that I don't understand. Something to do with stocks and bonds. It's a foreign language, but I nod and smile anyway while he eats his dinner. Then he leaves me to it, disappearing back into his office to deal with client phone calls. His laughter is muffled by the walls between us, and all I can do is gaze at Kai and wonder if his father will ever ask him how his day was.

"That's why, Mom," I murmur. "That's why I'm not popping out babies. Because I'm raising the one I've already got by myself. And the guy who can give me another one doesn't seem to mind the sex... but I don't think he'd be too happy if I stopped taking the pill."

Changing lanes, I glance to the west, my lips turning upward at the stunning sunset. The sky is drenched in gold and amber tonight, and I wish I could stay out in it, but our exit is coming up, and I need to get Kai home to bed.

I should text Hudson and let him know we're on our way back. He'd probably appreciate the warning, but it's not like he'll be having a raging party or anything. He's not like that anymore. He's not the party-loving senior I first fell for. He's serious now. A businessman. And businessmen don't play silly games or do silly dances. They wear expensive suits and talk about politics and market capitalization.

He'll no doubt be watching a game while drinking his bourbon. Maybe he'll have his feet up, but his laptop will be open, and he won't be able to help himself—working away while he "relaxes."

I snort and shake my head. The guy is addicted. But I guess I should be grateful that he brings in the bucks. We live in a gorgeous two-story house. I never have to worry about money—budgeting for groceries and taking a calculator to the supermarket like my mother used to. I drive a nice SUV that's only a few years old. I can buy whatever clothes I want, and Kai has the best of everything.

It's a good life.

I love being a mom, and sure, Kai starts full-time kindergarten next year and I have no idea how I'm gonna fill my days, but I won't start worrying about that yet.

Right now, I just want to get my boy home, shake off Hell Week in Gladstone, and enjoy a glass of wine with my man.

Thirty minutes later, I'm turning left onto my suburban street. The houses are all the same—like the developer couldn't be bothered coming up with anything original and just built a bunch of Lego replicas one after the other. I pull into my driveway, the garage door opening smoothly before I glide into my spot. Hudson's Audi R8 is in its usual place, which means he's home. I was expecting him to be, being Saturday night and all, but it's still nice to know he's not at the office for a change.

Kai's still in dreamland, so I leave him be, slipping into the house to make sure his bed is all set up. Hopefully, I can make it a smooth transition for him.

Slipping off my shoes, I pad into the house, ascending the carpeted steps and veering right when I hear the shower running. I'll say a quick hi to Hudson so I don't scare the crap out of him when he turns off the water and hears movement in the house.

I glance at our unmade bed, the sheets a tousled mess, and roll my eyes. Of course he wasn't going to make it while I was gone. That's a woman's job, right?

He'd never actually say it, but I know he's thinking it. He grew up in the same kind of house I did. Women did all the domestic chores while the men went out and worked. Honestly, I thought we were done with that bullshit, but I've gone and slipped right into this life without argument.

Because I was young and pregnant, and I didn't know what the hell else to do.

Closing my eyes, I draw in a calming breath.

You have a good life here, Tammy. He provides for you. He could have left you with a kid, but he married you, and you need to be grateful for that. Everything you need is in this house.

I repeat my usual mantra as I walk toward our en suite.

My fingers are just touching the door to push it open when I hear a moan. At first I think it's Hudson. *Is he masturbating in the shower?* The thought makes my lips quirk, and for a second, I wonder if I should join him... but then I hear that moan again...

And that is not a man.

"What?" I whisper, pushing the door open and assaulting my senses.

The glass might be steamed up, but I can see enough.

Painted nails, hands splayed on the tiles, boobs bouncing back and forth... my husband's hands gripping her hips as he thrusts into her from behind.

"Yes, baby," she gasps, more pornographic noises popping out of her mouth as he grunts and glides his hands up her body, pinching her nipple, then squeezing her breast.

She bites her bottom lip, tipping her head as he grunts again, his ass cheeks smushing up against the glass. I stare at them—so taut and muscular. How many times have I held those in my hands, dug my fingers into them as he thrust into me. I thought those grunts of pleasure were mine and mine alone.

But obviously not.

A sick bile swirls in my stomach, my chest starting to hurt as I stand there watching my husband and whoever the hell she is.

I need to go. To flee. To stop staring at this. But I'm frozen in shock.

Hudson's cheating on me.

He's—

The woman's eyes pop open, and she lets out a strangled gasp when she spots me gaping at them.

That's what I'm doing.

Gaping. My mouth seems incapable of closing. I definitely can't speak.

All I can do is stare.

The shower clunks off, and Hudson spins around, his dick still standing to attention, her juices coating the hard shaft.

Her juices.

Not mine.

Hers.

"Tam." He chokes out my name, and it jolts me out of my stupor.

The shower door swings open, and I blink at him, then do the only thing I can.

Spinning on my heel, I bolt out of the room.

"Tamara!" Hudson shouts after me, but I keep going, thundering down the stairs and back out to the car.

I forget my shoes, but like hell I'm going back for them.

Kai's still mercifully asleep, blissfully unaware of the shit show unfolding around him.

Pushing the button, I start the engine, begging the garage door to open faster as I hear my name once more.

"Tamara!" Hudson bolts into the garage, a towel clutched around his waist. Droplets cascade down his body. A body I've licked and kissed and made my own.

But it's not just mine anymore.

I can't even look at him.

Turning with a growl, I fire out of the garage, my tires screeching when I hit the road and make a quick turn, accelerating away with a fury I've never felt before.

CHAPTER 2
BAXTER

Laughter bounces around the old walls of the dining room as I share a meal with the girls at Ponderosa Countryside Villa. They've all come over to watch the hockey game together. The guys start in about half an hour, and we'll move into the parlor to watch their game against Providence. Can't believe I live in a place that has a parlor. It's more like a TV room/library thing, but Rachel insists that we all say parlor because it sounds fancier, and when guests start arriving later in the year, she wants to make a good impression.

So, parlor it is.

"I'm telling you, the new goalie isn't half as good as you." Caroline points at me, her red curls flying when she flicks them over her shoulder.

I smile at her. "He's pretty good. He's gonna have a great season."

"I don't know." She frowns, clearly concerned. "I just think Falco should be starting the game."

"Falco isn't as good as Tyrell."

She blinks at me like I've lost my mind. "He's better!"

I shake my head. "The kid might be fast, but he lacks the experience. Tyrell has been subbing for me since last year, and he's gotten really good. He's gonna be great this season. You just wait. Now that I'm out of the way, he has a chance to really shine."

Mick nudges me with her elbow. "We'd rather have you, dude."

"Hey, I'd rather be playing with the guys," I agree. "But watching the game with you ain't so bad either," I finish in a mumble, and Rachel makes this sweet little "aw" sound before starting to collect the empty plates.

"Let me help." Jolie jumps up from her seat, the nervy little freshman looking relieved to have something to do. She showed up about an hour before dinner and spent most of it in the kitchen, I think. I was hiding away out back, keeping busy in the maintenance shed. As much as I love the girls, when they're en masse like this, it gets a little intimidating. I didn't really need to tidy the shed. It's all straight and looking super safe and professional, just the way Vanessa wants it. She's the lady Mick's dad hired to make sure we're checking all the boxes. Every time she stops by, we're all on edge, but at least she said my shed was looking passable. Probably because I spend so much damn time in there. It's quiet. I like it, and Fezz does too. I've put a little doggy bed in the corner for him, and he'll often follow me out there for a nap.

But I couldn't stay out there all night, so I put on my big boy pants and joined the girls for dinner. Ray would have been gutted if I'd just taken a plate to my room. These ladies are missing their men, and I think they like having me around.

The guys flew out on Thursday and should be back tomorrow. The house is so much quieter without them around, but I'm happy that their season is finally kicking off. They've been desperate for these first games, and last night's was a winner. Hopefully, tonight will be one too.

Damn, I wish I was with them.

Not hitting the ice this season has sucked.

I mean, I've been on the ice, but not in a way I ever thought I'd be. Coaching Mini Mite hockey has been an experience, that's for sure. It's not so bad. The kids are cute and only a little annoying. Their enthusiasm makes up for their inability to listen and follow instructions... most of the time.

I can't help a small grin as I pass Jolie my plate. I'm thinking about my little team, but she doesn't know that, and I glance away from her blushing, twitchy smile so she doesn't think I'm flirting with her. That's the last thing I need.

Jolie's been hanging out here a lot since school started. She's obviously struggling to fit in at Nolan U. Caroline's helping her out. They're cousins or something, and Casey's cherry girl has gone full-blown mother hen looking after her. Like Caroline, Jolie's in the dorms, but I don't think they're in the same building. I'm not sure of all the details, but the snippets of conversation I've heard make it clear that Jolie's not sure if this is the right place for her.

Caroline's desperate for her to stay and throwing out suggestions whenever she can.

"Why don't you join the school paper? You love writing, and that'd be a chance to meet some new people."

Jolie nodded at that one, but she seems to nod at everything, so I wonder if she'll go for it. I hope so. I think Caroline would be a little heartbroken if her cousin bailed after only a month or so here. She was so excited to have her join us.

Jolie's lucky, you know. When I started at Nolan, I knew exactly zero people. That kind of thing didn't bother me too much, I guess. People are tiring, and it's easier to stick to myself. I don't mind my own company, and it's better than navigating a minefield of conversations and social mixers. That's why the second Asher showed up in my sophomore year and started talking about this place his uncle had hooked up for him, I had to get in. Thankfully, he agreed, and I finally got my own room. Living in the dorms my freshman year was a nightmare. As soon as I moved to Hockey House, I found my mojo and never looked back.

Space. Quiet. A place where I can hide away.

That's all I'll ever need.

The sound of sweet laughter echoes in the back of

mind. It doesn't belong to any of the girls here. That melody is a memory from my past. It hurts, and it soothes, and it makes me ache and pine in ways I'll never recover from.

I miss my girl.

Even though she belongs to someone else, she'll always be mine. Well, she'll have my heart anyway. Not a day goes by when I don't think about her. It's an undeniable torment.

Tammy Tan.

I wonder what she's doing right now.

She'll have a kid. I'm guessing around four, if my calculations are correct. I try not to ask Dad for deets. I know he'll have them. Gossip and Gladstone are synonymous. He knows everything… he's just wise enough not to tell me.

I don't want to hear that she's happily married, living in the city (he let that one slip) and being mother of the year.

She would be.

Damn, she'd be an amazing mom—fun-loving, kind, playful, organized, invested. She'd love that kid with everything she has, because that's Tammy.

I just wish she could have loved me.

Chosen me instead of him.

Maybe if I hadn't shut down so quickly after—

I snap my eyes closed, not wanting to think about it.

Pushing back my chair with a loud scrape, I wince and jerk up straight when everyone glances at me.

"I'm just gonna…" I point over my shoulder and feel my muscles tighten at Lani's astute gaze. "Take Fezz for a walk."

His ears perk up at the word *walk*, and he trots around to my feet, his tail going a mile a minute.

"You're not going to watch the game with us?" Caroline's bright eyes fill with disappointment.

Shit. Why did I say I would?

Because you want to watch the game, dumbass!

I clear my throat, my pulse quickening at that gnawing in my chest, which I can't seem to shake. I just need to walk for a second, get her out of my head… then I can focus on the game.

Rachel eyes me up with her soft, green gaze, her lips twitching before she quietly murmurs, "I'm sure Fezz would love that. You'll be back in time, right?"

Her wink does me in, and I agree before I can stop myself.

"Sure," I mutter, walking out through the kitchen and grabbing the lead from the mudroom. Fezz is prancing at my feet, his excited bark cute and adorable. "Calm down." I grin at him. "Now sit."

He does as he's told, his little body quivering with eagerness. I chuckle and pat the top of his head before clipping on the lead.

"Raf-raf!" He tells me it's time to go, and I walk him out the door, the cool night air kissing my skin.

I should have grabbed a jacket, but I'm not going back in again.

I just need me a minute.

A long, quiet one.

Gazing up at the stars, I'm transported back to those summer nights when Tammy and I would sit on the back lawn, pointing out constellations to each other and making up funnier stories of what those Greek gods really got up to on Mount Olympus. She'd have me in stitches every time.

Will I ever hear her laugh again?

Not like that.

Not like the way it was—all carefree and unchecked.

She's a married woman now. A mother.

Things will never be the same.

I lost her.

And it kills me.

CHAPTER 3
TAMMY

It's raining by the time I find a motel and get Kai settled for the night. My bare feet get frozen and saturated, but that doesn't seem to matter. Seriously, wet feet are the least of my worries.

"Where are we?" Kai's sweet little voice and confused expression nearly breaks me, but I manage to paste on a smile.

"We're having an extra-special adventure. Just the two of us."

He's smart enough to know something's off, but he gives me a small smile and snuggles against my chest as I dash through the rain and up the motel steps. I could hold on to him forever. He's my teddy bear. My comfort. I want to sob against his soft hair and cling to him.

But I can't do that. Because his needs always come before my own.

So I put on a brave voice and somehow find a smile. "Look, Kai. You get this whole big bed all to yourself."

"Wow!" He scrambles onto it, and I let him jump and bounce around because I need to hear his laughter.

Then he takes a bath while I order pizza. I let him splash, and he giggles at the droplets running across the tiles. We eat while watching *Octonauts*, because that's his favorite.

Somehow, I find the strength to read to him without crying. Thankfully, our bags were still in the car from our trip to Gladstone, so I have everything he needs on me. He loves my old Curious George books, and his delighted face as he taps his little finger on the page and laughs, "Silly George," melts my heart.

I kiss his hair and smell his sweet scent.

You can do this, Tammy. You can be strong for him.

But as I'm tucking him into bed, he whispers something that makes my eyes glassy with tears. "Where's Daddy?"

"Um... he's still at home." I try to swallow and nearly choke on the boulder lodged in my throat.

"Working?" His sad, resigned pout is a killer, but I nod, because I can't exactly tell him what else Daddy's been up to.

My stomach clenches into a knot so tight, it hurts.

That bastard!

That cheating slimeball.

Anger rages through me—a sudden hot flash of it

that's unexpectedly strong and vehement, but it's quickly followed by a wave of heartache.

He's cheating on me.

My husband is having sex with another woman.

I can feel the rain clouds building inside me—a brewing, black depression that's going to drown me.

You can't let Kai see that!

Clenching my jaw, I run my fingers through my son's black hair and will my voice to come out soft and easy.

"You know... Daddy's gonna be real busy for the next little while, so we might stay away for a little longer. How do you feel about that?"

Kai nods, his big brown eyes so innocent. So trusting. He'll believe anything I tell him, because I'm his mommy, and he knows I'll never hurt him or let him down.

But I will. It's inevitable. It doesn't matter how hard I try, I'm going to let him down.

My soul hurts and aches in ways I didn't think possible, and it's making these tears even harder to fight.

"Where are we gonna go?" His voice is so sweet.

"I'm not sure yet. Mommy's going to come up with a plan while you sleep." I try to smile, but I don't know what the hell my mouth is doing.

Kai's face folds into a frown. His short little fingers touch my cheek, and he strokes my face. "Don't be sad, Mommy. We'll have fun just you and me."

Oh, my heart.

It's melting and hurting and bursting with love all at the same time.

My smile turns genuine as I lean down and kiss his forehead. "Yeah, we will, kiddo. We're gonna have the best time."

He wraps his arms around my neck and gives me a tight squeeze before he finally rolls over and settles down.

I kiss him one more time, tucking the covers up around his shoulders before shuffling to my bed.

My phone buzzes with yet another message from Hudson. He's been calling incessantly, and I haven't answered once. Because I can't right now. He needs to leave me the fuck alone so I can process this shit.

Jumping into a hot shower, I stand under that spray and relive what I saw. I don't want to, but my mind is cruel and uncontrollable. I see her boobs rocking, watch him pinch her nipple.

I hate that feeling. I never liked it when he tried to pinch me. It hurt, and I wasn't into the whole pain and pleasure thing. He tried a few times, spanking my ass and nipping my skin. He even shoved his finger up my butt once, and I shot off the bed like he'd burned me.

I told him I wasn't into that, and he sighed and pulled me back onto the mattress, returning to the soft caressing I enjoyed.

Is that why he's cheating on me?

Because I'm not adventurous enough in bed?

I press my palms against my nipples, then squeeze my boobs. Boobs he's licked and sucked. But not the only ones he'll ever enjoy. My body starts to shudder with these dry sobs, and my legs crumple. I land in the hard bathtub with a soft thud. Curling into a ball, I let the water rain over me and finally let it out.

I don't want Kai to hear me, so I press my mouth against my knee and let those sobs rack my body in agonized silence.

What the hell am I gonna do now?

Where am I gonna go?

I can't go back to Gladstone. My parents will probably scoff at me. "How could you let his eyes wander? Why weren't you a better wife?"

Grace, Miranda, and Kelsey will shake their heads and be sad for me, sure... but then they'll no doubt start up with the whole "So, he strayed a little. Get over it. Forgive him. You can't walk out. He's your security. Look at the lifestyle he gives you."

Hudson's parents will tell me that their boy is a fool, but I can't go taking his child away. "You're a family. You do whatever it takes to stay together."

I heard his mother say that once, in that clipped way of hers. You don't argue with Mrs. Clark. That woman is always right... apparently.

"Like every other mother in that damn town," I mutter while drying myself off.

The towel is rough and scratchy, but I hang it up nice and straight on the rail before creeping into the bedroom to unearth my pajamas. They're soft and silky, the pale purple fabric shimmering.

Hudson bought these for me. I hold them up,

tempted to rip them to shreds. These surges of anger are surprisingly strong, but they're followed very quickly by a wave of overpowering sorrow... and then I'm tripped up by this blinding fear.

What the hell am I supposed to do now?

My phone starts vibrating on the bed. I automatically reach for it, then growl when I noticed Hudson's name on the screen. Throwing it down, I get dressed, checking on Kai one last time before crawling into bed.

The phone screen lights up again.

Hudson: Just tell me you're okay. Where are you? Where'd you go? Are you back in Gladstone?

I cringe and shake my head. Is he worried that I've shot back to our small hometown and run his name through the mud? Damn, that would kill him. He's always cared about appearances.

I still remember the first time I saw him.

My carefree, wonderful summer with Baxter had ended in disaster, and I hadn't really spoken to my best friend properly since that afternoon by our secret swimming hole.

He'd gone away to visit his grandparents the week before school started, and I couldn't wait for him to get back so we could patch things up. But then my parents introduced me to Hudson at church that weekend... and he offered to drive me to school the next day. I don't know why I said yes. I should have told him that I always catch a ride with my best friend, Baxter. But the word just popped out of my dazzled mouth.

He was so cool and handsome. He played guitar and wore a leather jacket. There was this swagger about him... this confidence that was so appealing.

New and mysterious, he had this smile that made my instant attraction impossible to deny. With his soft brown hair and sparkling blue eyes, I was a goner.

"Hey." That was all he said, but it was enough to have butterflies dancing through my stomach.

"Hi." I smiled up at him, no doubt blushing.

I couldn't help it. He was looking at me like I was the prettiest girl he'd ever seen. His gaze was this mix of awe and adoration that made me feel like a queen.

He asked me what grade I was in as I fidgeted with my hair, and then he wanted to walk me out of the building and all the way to Dad's car. It was the sweetest thing... and so...

Well, it was a compliment. Out of all the girls in church, the new, cool, superhot guy with the trendy shades chose me. He wanted to drive *me* to school, and in that moment, I forgot all about patching things up with Baxter.

Hudson swept me right off my feet, and I was helpless to stop myself from falling hard and fast. He always knew what I needed to hear. He wooed me like I was under his spell, and life changed. The gap between

Baxter and me grew so wide, we practically became strangers.

We tried every now and then, but our conversations became more stilted. We weren't besties anymore. I was dating Hudson... and then I got pregnant.

A chill runs through me as I relive the terror of reading that positive pregnancy test. Baxter was the first person I told.

Closing my eyes, I dip my chin and remember that hideous conversation.

"Baxter," I rasp, tears burning my eyes as I rub my thumb over my phone screen.

I wonder where he is now. What he's doing with his life.

He went to Nolan U in Colorado to play hockey, but he would have graduated by now.

I hate that we lost touch. After his mother died, he took off, and he wouldn't reply to my messages. I tried for weeks... months... but then I gave birth to Kai, and my world became all about my little boy.

As the years passed, Baxter's been stored away in the back of my mind, only popping out when I'm feeling sad or nostalgic.

Right now, he's clear as day—his shy smile and soft gaze. I always used to love the way he studied the world. He was so quiet and thoughtful about everything. The way his ears used to turn fire-engine red when he got embarrassed always made me laugh.

I can't help a soft snicker as I see him all over again. My favorite person in the world. My best friend. My BB.

My throat swells as I remember him. As I think about what could have been if we hadn't—

If I hadn't—

Snapping my eyes shut, I set a few tears free. They trail down my cheeks as my memories fade and reality comes back with a chill so cold, I actually shiver.

Burying myself under the covers, I settle my head on the pillow and wonder again where Baxter might be.

He wouldn't judge me for taking off and not replying to Hudson's texts.

He never seemed to like the guy much anyway. I didn't understand why. Everyone else loved him, but Baxter was always frosty.

Maybe he saw something the rest of us couldn't.

Or maybe he was just annoyed that Hudson was stealing all my attention.

Baxter used to get it all. He was my safe place, the one I'd run to with a new joke or an angry rant or a sad confession. He always listened to me. And he heard me. He was my best friend.

My insides crumple, and that old familiar ache rises inside me again.

I want to see him.

I want to run to him right now with my sad news. I want to blubber on his doorstep. And he'd stand there and let me get it all out, then say something soft and sweet... or nothing at all. He'd just let me in and let me be.

My lips curl into a soft smile.

I should find him.

But what if he's married or has a girlfriend or—

So what if he does? I'm just looking for a place to stay until I'm ready to deal with this Hudson bullshit. I just need a place to hide for a few days and lick my wounds.

Scrambling for my phone, I work in the dark, opening a new search window and seeing what I can find on Baxter Brown—the small-town boy from Gladstone who became a star goalie for the Nolan U Cougars.

"What are you up to right now, BB? Make it something obvious so I can easily find you."

CHAPTER 4
BAXTER

I stand on the ice, trying not to laugh as I watch an argument between two Mini Mites.

"I'm taller than you!"

"No, I'm taller!"

Their little sticks bang on the ground while the rest of the team skates around them like ants, oblivious to their disagreement.

"I'm older, so I'm taller!" Marty starts to shout, his gloved hand trying to prove his point by banging between their two helmets.

"Don't hit me." Shelby pushes his padded shoulder, and I pick up my pace and move toward them.

"Hey! You two! Get skatin'." They jump a mile, Marty hitting the ice before scrambling back up. Shelby grabs his sleeve to help him, and I can't hide my grin as they tear off around the outside edge of the rink while Ethan and Liam stand on the sidelines cracking up.

I bet those two were just like that at this age.

I know I was.

Or, well, actually... I was probably more like little Josh, studiously working on my stick skills in the middle of the rink.

"Good job, kid." Casey claps and skates forward, directing Timmy around the course we set up so they could practice their dribbling.

I give him a thumbs-up, glad he's on the ice with me today. He didn't have to come down, but when the guys saw me leaving with all my gear, they jumped off the couches and followed me. Casey was offering to help me out before we'd even pulled away from Ponderosa.

It's nice having them around. No one usually practices on a Sunday, but a space came free, and I had some parents asking, so I put out a last-minute invite, and most of the team showed up.

We're running all the best drills—the ones the kids love—and we'll finish with a friendly game that will no doubt be adorably cute and heinously inconsistent of good hockey play. The kids can't help themselves. They see that puck, and they go for it—who cares about structure and effective positioning, right?

I snicker, shaking my head as I come to a stop next to Milo and Claudia, who can't seem to stay on their feet today.

"Come on, you two." I grab a hand each and haul them back up, making sure they're steady on the ice before I let them go and direct them toward Ethan and

Liam. "Go and give those two big guys a high five for me and get back here as fast as you can."

I watch them take off, studying their glide and stance. Claudia needs to work on her balance; she's throwing too much weight to her right, and it's making her wobbly. Milo isn't extending his legs far enough either, doing these short, choppy moves that are slowing him down.

The kiddos high-five the giant hockey players, then skate back to me, and I take a knee, explaining what I saw in a way that they'll hopefully understand. I even get up and demonstrate what I mean, but by the time I'm done, they're both distracted by the scuffle breaking out between Shelby and Marty.

"I'm taller!"

Seriously? They need to let that shit go.

Casey's already over there, but I skate across and join him, gently tugging the kids apart. Bracing my hands on my knees, I get down to their level and tell it to them straight.

"There is always gonna be someone taller than you. And there's always gonna be someone shorter than you. It's just the way it is."

"But she's a girl, and I'm older. I should be tallest!" Marty's distress is endearing.

With a kind smile, I wrap my arm around his shoulders and lean in to whisper, "Dude, you're totally gonna be taller than her. Just you wait. But for now, she's got half an inch on you. Deal with it. She's your best friend, man."

The boy lets out a heavy sigh and gives me a withering look before holding out his fist.

Shelby scowls at him before finally pounding knuckles.

"You might be taller, but I'm faster." The boy grins, taking off while Shelby sputters and chases him.

"No fair, you started early!"

I bulge my eyes and share a look with Casey, who's already laughing. "Hey, you agreed to this shit show."

"I didn't mean to," I mutter, leaning against the side of the rink for just a minute and letting the chaos reign. I can already feel it bubbling and escalating, so I'll cut it short soon, and we'll run a quick game to finish.

Checking the clock on the wall, I make sure my timing's good, then watch Casey skate off to instruct Josh on his stick work. My gaze tracks back to Marty and Shelby, still playing chase and now laughing together.

She careens up behind him, checking him against the wall, then laughing hysterically until he grabs her ankle, and she hits the ice with a squawk. The sound that comes out of her cracks them both up, and they're soon lying on that freezing-cold ground, laughing the way only best friends can.

And my mind shoots back ten years... to a different ice rink. To a girl with brown eyes, black curls, and dimples to die for. She'd hold my hand, squealing and wobbling on her skates while I forced her to do my favorite thing with me.

She was always a good sport about it... as long as I

then went with her to the nail salon afterward. Yeah, I've had my fair share of pedicures thanks to TT.

My insides shimmer as I remember her sweet face and the way she smiled at me.

She was the prettiest girl I'd ever known.

She probably still is.

And like always, whenever I think about her, I hear that warning in the back of my mind—*you'll never love another.*

So, what the hell does that mean for me?

She's with someone else.

She can never be mine.

Does that mean I'm destined to a life of solitude?

Sure, there's some appeal to that, but when I see my friends with their ladies, I can't help aching, because I want that too.

The problem is... I only want it with Tammy.

CHAPTER 5
TAMMY

Sunday was a write-off. After a terrible night's sleep, I was groggy and grumpy... and I took it out on poor Kai. He basically stopped talking, which is what he does when he's stressed, and that made me worried and miserable.

Hudson texted incessantly until I lost it and sent back:

CAN'T YOU JUST GIVE ME SOME FUCKING SPACE? I DON'T WANT TO TALK TO YOU RIGHT NOW! YOU CHEATED ON ME! I CAN STILL SEE YOU IN THE SHOWER WITH HER!

He went dark after that. It's been a nice reprieve... but also unsettling. I've never felt more alone in my entire life. That isolation ate at me throughout the day. Kai watched way too much TV and turned into a demon child by the afternoon. I managed to get my shit together enough to take him to a playground so he could burn off some steam, and then we ate in a run-down diner with crappy decor and the best food. Too bad my appetite was nonexistent. I forced down half a sandwich and a few fries. I really hate wasting food, but my stomach just couldn't take it.

And now we're on the road again. After a second shitty night, I got up this morning and made the call I'd been too afraid to make.

The phone rang three times before a gruff voice answered, "You got George."

"Hey, Mr. Brown. It's Tamara Tan. Do you remember me?"

He chuckled. "Of course I do, kid. I still live next door to your parents."

I winced, feeling like an idiot, wondering just how badly my voice was shaking. Did it match the trembling in my stomach?

"I was just thinking about Baxter and wondering what he's up to these days."

There was a pause that made my nerves burn. "Really?"

"Well, yeah. I mean, he was my best friend through middle school and... high school." My voice went wispy, and I had to clear my throat. "I'm on a little road trip with Kai and thought if he was still in Nolan, I might swing past and say hello. But he would have graduated by now, right?"

"Yeah. Finished up college this year."

"Oh, okay." My head started to pound in time with my heart. "So, where'd he end up, then?"

Another pause.

I held my breath.

"He's still in Nolan. Doing some building at the Ponderosa Countryside Villa."

"Oh, wow. Building. He always used to love working with you in the summer." I couldn't help my smile. Baxter had always been good with his hands.

A memory flashed through me, and I cut it off before it could fully form. I couldn't think about his hands in that moment.

Shit, I probably shouldn't have even been calling.

But I did.

And now I'm on the road, driving my son to Ponderosa Countryside Villa and second-guessing myself the whole way.

But where else can I go?

This desire to see Baxter is overwhelming. Growing up, he was always my safety net. And then he was gone, and I mourned him. Shit, I grieved when he left Gladstone. Hudson thought it was because of the unexpected pregnancy and processing that... which, sure I was. But it was losing Baxter that killed me more than anything. I should have known he'd go. He'd been pulling away from me long before I got pregnant. I just didn't think I'd permanently lose him. I thought we'd find some middle ground somewhere, that I'd still see his quiet, sweet smile when I crossed the street.

But he moved to Nolan and never looked back.

Why are you doing this to yourself?

Common sense has been my earworm since I turned off the expressway, but do you think I've taken my foot off the gas or even once entertained the idea of turning around?

Nope.

I'm going to see Baxter. Even if it's just for a little minute.

Or a lot of minutes.

However long it takes to figure out what I'm supposed to do now that I know my husband likes to have sex with other women.

Shit, was it just that one?

Or has it been many?

Is he in love with Shower Girl? Or was she some fling... or worse... was he paying her to be there?

Bile surges in my stomach, and I grip the wheel, so caught up in rocking boobs and pinched nipples that I nearly miss the turnoff.

Braking sharply, I swing the wheel right and check the rearview mirror.

"Sorry, buddy. Nearly missed the sign."

Kai gives me a quiet look, then turns to gaze out the window. He's clutching his little panda bear like his life depends on it, and I know he's unsettled right now.

Of course he is.

His mother's acting crazy. Taking him into this foreign territory, crying into her morning coffee, and having shaky phone calls with a man he doesn't even know.

George Brown might still be my parents' neighbor, but I never pop over to see him. Since his wife died, he's really lost his spark. There's no more friendly waving over the fence or popping around with freshly baked cookies to share. It must have been so hard on him, losing Kylie that way and then having Baxter leave for college only weeks later. What a lonely life he must lead.

My chest hurts, and I rub at my collarbone, recalling the end of our conversation.

"Tammy..." He made me stop midsentence.

"Yes?"

"I'm not sure why you want to see my boy again, but please..."

"Please what?"

"I..." He lost his words after that, so I quickly filled in the awkward space.

"I just want to say hi. Catch up for old time's sake. It's no big deal, Mr. Brown. Really."

"It'll be a big deal for him. You were his best friend, TT."

TT.

My heart wept as a wave of nostalgia hit me with a strength I wasn't counting on.

I wanted to tell him that it'd be a big deal for me, too, but I couldn't find the words. Instead, the last thing I expected popped out of my mouth. "If you could not tell my parents about this, I'd really appreciate it."

He sighed. "I know they never liked my boy."

I winced.

"I barely speak to your folks these days. They're quite involved in the church, and well... you know how it is."

"I do," I croaked, hating his underlying tone and all it meant. I didn't want to think about my parents and what they'd have to say about any of this.

Kylie Brown was a free-spirited hippie in their eyes. They didn't like the cavalier way she embraced life and raised her child with no obvious rules or restrictions. They didn't like that her son was my best friend.

They didn't like a lot of things.

They still don't.

Which is why I'm in no rush to tell them that I'm traveling all the way to Nolan, Colorado, to see my old friend. To maybe even seek shelter with him while I try to figure out what to do with their daughter and grandson.

I brake at the intersection to let a car through before turning left and heading down the country road. It's pretty with the mountains looming in the background— tall, grand, and so majestic. My heart smiles, but it's not enough to get my lips moving.

Two minutes later, I'm pulling into a freshly paved driveway and stopping outside a grand old villa. It's been done up; you can tell by the fresh coat of paint and the new sign.

Grand opening coming soon! is plastered across the edge.

Turning off the engine, I spin to look at Kai. "You ready to explore this big ol' house with me?"

He looks out the window, assessing it in that quiet way of his before nodding.

"Okay." I force a grin, trying to act chipper and upbeat as I stride around the car and help him unbuckle.

He wants to be carried, and I don't fight him on it. I need him in my arms for this.

My legs are shaking as I climb the stairs, my heart now lodged firmly in my throat. I open the front door and struggle to call out, "Hello? Anybody here?"

The entrance is empty. There's a shiny reception desk just in front of me, the wood gleaming with new polish. I run my hand across it and turn to scan the space. Behind me is a large archway that leads into the dining room, and on the other side of the entrance, a wall has been opened up, heading into what looks to be a spacious living area. Plump couches and chairs angle out toward the window, curving around a coffee table that's meant to look old but is obviously new. Everything about this place smells clean and fresh and new.

"Hello?"

I can't hear any bustling feet and suddenly start to worry that no one is here.

But why'd they leave the front door unlocked?

Kai's grip around my neck tightens, and I try one more time before bailing.

"Hello?"

"We're not actually open yet!" a deep voice calls down from upstairs.

I turn to take in the stairwell with its pretty carpeted strip, then lose the ability to breathe as a large, tall man with sandy brown hair and a beard to match freezes on the landing.

Baxter.

Holy crap, he looks good.

He's grown even bigger, broader. That shaggy beard is a trip. I've never seen him like that before, but I know it's him. Those eyes that are drinking me in right now, staring at me like I'm a ghost... I can never forget that gentle gaze.

My heart swells with affection, nostalgia rushing through me in a wave so strong, I'm surprised I don't sway on my feet.

"Baxter Brown." A smile stretches across my face. I can't help it. It's so good to see him, I want to giggle like a schoolgirl.

I want to run over to him, jump into his arms, and give him the tightest squeeze. He gave the best piggy-backs when we were kids. I always jumped on him any chance I could... and he caught me every time.

He walks down the last part of the stairs, stopping on the final one and gripping the railing. I can't tell if he's happy to see me, and it kills that euphoric buzz in my chest.

"Hey, Tammy."

His voice. Oh my gosh, it's so deep and manly now.

What do I say to him?

Why can't I form words?

I want to scream and do the happy dance we came up with in seventh grade.

And I also want to curl into a ball and weep.

Baxter finally moves off that last step and inches toward us. He points at Kai in my arms. "And who's this guy?"

"This is Kai." I smile at my son, lightly brushing his nose. He looks a little scared and uncertain. I won't force him to say anything just yet. This is all quite overwhelming. I get it.

"Hey, buddy." Baxter waves at him, and Kai proves my point by gasping and burying his face in my neck.

Maybe it's Baxter's beard. He does look like a bit of a mountain man with that unkempt thing.

I try to come up with an excuse that won't offend anyone. "He's shy." My voice breaks, tears glassing my eyes as I admit, "It's been a rough couple days."

Baxter's expression crumples with a frown as he walks toward us.

"I'm sorry to just show up like this." Great, now I'm crying. I didn't know what I was expecting, really. I just wanted to see a familiar face, and it's taken all of two minutes for me to slip into confession mode. How does Baxter get stuff out of me so easily? He doesn't even have to try.

With a sniff, I keep blubbering, "I can't go home. You

know what Gladstone's like. My parents won't understand, no matter what I say... and none of my friends will get it either."

"Tammy, what's going on?" His voice has shifted to that soft, gentle lilt, and I'm done for.

I forget about the fact that Kai is still in my arms. I forget the great divide that formed between Baxter and me all those years ago.

Suddenly, it's just him and me and my personal nightmare.

"Hudson's having an affair."

Baxter's eyes darken, his expression turning hard. I look away from it. He never liked Hudson. I've thought of myriad reasons why, and I've never been able to settle on one. I didn't want to think about what all those reasons could mean, so I just ignored them. Pretended like it wasn't a big deal.

But it was.

Biting my lips together, I will myself to stop crying. "I just need somewhere to lie low for a few days while I figure this out. You were my best friend in high school, and I know we..." My gaze dips to the floor, memories flashing through me like flying photographs. "I mean, we... well, we lost touch... after..." I clear my throat, heat racing through me. "But... I don't know where else to go."

Baxter looks up, his eyes catching mine before he reaches out and brushes the tears off my cheek. The move is so natural. So familiar.

I ache in ways I can't even explain.

"It's okay," he whispers. "You can stay here for as long as you need. We'll find a space for you."

We'll...

I wonder who he means. I wonder if she's pretty and nice and everything he deserves.

My soul feels crushed and wounded as I nod and force a smile. I'm grateful. I really am. And if he's with someone, that's awesome. If anyone deserves to be happily in love, it's him. I just hope she doesn't mind me hanging around.

It won't be for long.

I just need a day or two. Just a small reprieve before having to decide what to do with my life now.

Do I forgive Hudson and head on home?

Or am I about to venture out into this great big world as a single mother?

A young single mother with no money, no work experience, and only a high school diploma to her name.

CHAPTER 6
BAXTER

Tammy's here. Holy shit, Tammy's here!

She's standing in my house—on my turf—needing my help.

Saying no was an impossibility. I didn't even hesitate. She needs me, and shifting back into that role is the easiest thing in the world.

"Do you have any bags or anything?"

She sniffs, her lips trembling into a smile. "Ah, yeah. In the car."

"Okay." I give her arm a light squeeze and head out the front door.

She trails behind me, still carrying Kai, who's clinging to her like a bear cub. And then his little arms practically choke her when a yapping dog comes racing around the side of the house.

"Ah!" he yelps, his legs hooking around her hips even tighter.

"It's okay, sweetie. It's just a little doggy." Tammy rubs his back, her fingers splaying across his shirt.

Her hands are still the same.

Not that they'd change, but... there's just something so familiar about them that I freeze for a second, mesmerized by the shine of her nail polish and the memory of the way they used to hold a pen when she doodled on my homework, or gripped my shirt when we were roughhousing, or drew letters on my back that I had to guess.

Shit. So many memories. I'm struggling to breathe.

Fezzik's excited bark pulls me back to the present, and I blink when I hear Kai whimper into Tammy's neck.

Casey and Caroline's black-and-white ball of fur bounces around Tammy's feet before resting his paws on her knee and desperately trying to say hello. His shaggy tail is going nuts.

"Fezzik," I warn him. "Come here."

The dog lets out another happy yip before trotting over to me while I pull two small suitcases out of the trunk.

"Don't go scaring the kid." I try to put my stern face on, but it's pretty hard to stay mad with the pup. He's freaking adorable. "You need to be polite to our guests." I crouch down, lightly patting the Shih Tzu's head. "I know you're excited." He rests his paws on my knee. "But you need to chill out and... where have you been, anyway?" I swipe my hand across his dirty muzzle. "I hate to know what you've buried. It better not be anything out of Rachel's kitchen."

I glance up, and Tammy is blinking like she's fighting tears again. It kills me to see her this way. I need to get her inside, set her up in one of the guest rooms, and try to distract her from that asshole of a husband. I can't fucking believe he cheated on her. Why? Why would you ever want to cheat on a girl like Tammy? She's always been perfect. How could Hudson not see that?

I give her a gentle smile, gripping the bags and walking back toward the stairs. She turns to follow me, and Fezzik dances around our feet, still letting out the odd bark.

"He's really harmless," I assure her. "The guy just loves meeting new people. If you want me to keep him outside, though..."

"No, that's okay. Kai needs to experience new things, and he's never really been around dogs before. This will be good for him."

Kai makes a little grunt of protest, and Tammy smiles as she rubs his back and rests her cheek against his head. Wow. She's a mama all right. And looks to be a good one too. Of course she was going to be. She's sweet and kind and fun.

I look away from her, my swallow thick as we ascend the stairs. "We're trying to decide what to do once this place opens up to guests, you know? Rachel won't let him in the kitchen, so he's pretty good about that, but he's been roaming the rest of the house like he's the king of the manor, and I'm not sure how guests will feel about that. We might have to start restricting him to certain areas, and it's gonna be pretty hard to train him when he thinks this place is his castle."

Tammy follows me down the hallway, and I open the first door on my right.

"None of these rooms have been used yet, but I'm sure Rachel won't mind." I wink at Tammy, and Kai has finally lifted his head to look around. As soon as we make eye contact, he gasps again and buries his face away.

I wince at Tammy, who smiles and shakes her head, then scrapes her bottom lip with her teeth. "So, Rachel, huh?"

Placing the bags down at the foot of the bed, I glance at Tammy and nod. "Yeah, she's gonna be in charge of looking after guests, as well as the kitchen. We kind of need to find someone else to assist her, but we're doing a soft opening so we can ease into it, you know? I'll be around to help when I have to, but she's way better with people than I am, so I'm really hoping I won't have to do much. I'd rather be peeling potatoes in the kitchen than greeting a bunch of strangers." I scratch the back of my neck, trying to figure out that look on Tammy's face.

"How long have you guys been together?"

The question stumps me, and I frown. "Together?"

"Yeah." She glances around, walking over to the bed and brushing her hand across the soft duvet. "It must have been a while if you're running this business. Are you guys married or...?" She turns to face me, and all I can do is gape at her and then blink like an idiot.

"Married? I..." A laugh punches out of me before I can stop it. Tammy's perfectly shaped eyebrows pucker, and I rub my forehead. "We're not..." I shake my head. "Rachel's not my girlfriend, or wife. I don't..." I'm still shaking my head. "I'm not..."

Tammy's eyebrows rise, her big brown gaze so expectant.

Blowing out a short breath, I manage, "Rachel's with Liam. He lives here too. A bunch of us do. We used to live closer to campus. We all roomed together, but then that house fell through, and we got this place. I decided to stick around after graduation and help get it off the ground. Since Rachel and I are the only two not in college, we're kind of running it."

"Oh." Tammy's head bobs. "Okay. So, how many of you—"

"Baxter?" Rachel's voice shoots up the stairwell. "There's a car I don't recognize in the driveway."

Fezzik's ears perk up, and he lets out a little bark before racing out the door to say hi to her.

"Yeah, uh... coming!" I call down.

Tammy looks nervous all of a sudden.

"Hey, it's okay." I give her a reassuring smile. "Let me go down and explain the situation."

She winces, and I feel my heart breaking for her. "I

don't have to say anything about... Hudson. I'll just... mention that you're visiting."

"Thanks," she whispers, her lips trembling into a smile.

"She won't mind at all." I grin. If anything, Rachel will be stoked. She can test out her hostess skills on Tammy and Kai. She'll love it.

Brushing my hand down Tammy's arm, I slip out of the room and am just closing the door when I hear Kai's voice.

"Mommy?"

"Yeah, baby."

"Are we staying here for long?"

"Not sure yet. But... is that okay?"

"Yeah, I guess." His voice is soft and sweet.

"You know the puppy's not gonna eat you, right? He just wants to sniff your butt, probably."

The boy snorts and starts to giggle. "Mommy!"

"What? That's what dogs do, right?" He laughs some more, and Tammy giggles too. Then her voice gets warm and motherly. "It's gonna be okay. Baxter was my best friend growing up, and he's really nice. He'll take care of us while we're here."

"He looks scary."

"You think so?"

"Yeah."

"Is it the beard?"

"Did he have that when you guys were kids?"

Tammy's laughter is soft and melodic. "No, he didn't. I've never seen him with a beard before."

"It's big."

"And wild and bushy. He looks like a mountain man, don't you think?"

"Or a big, scary bear."

Tammy growls, and Kai squeals, then bursts into fits of laughter. She's probably tickling him by the sounds of things.

I ease away from the door and creep down the corridor, rubbing my beard and figuring I'll be shaving it off tonight. Don't want to go scaring the poor kid.

Rachel meets me halfway up the stairs, holding Fezzik and looking worried as she strokes his head. "Do you know who parked in our driveway?"

"Yes." I nod.

"What's going on?"

"A friend of mine from high school showed up unannounced. She needs a place to stay for a few days, and I said she could. Hope that's okay."

"Of course it is. Where have you put her?"

"In the Juniper suite. She's got a kid with her, so I figure they could use the space."

"Good idea." Rachel looks around me, like she's itching to get up there and make sure they have everything they need. "I'll get some fresh towels for them. Did you check the en suite to make sure there's enough toilet paper and shampoos? Soaps?"

"No." I shake my head. That hadn't even occurred to me.

Rachel tuts and is walking past me before I can stop her.

Two minutes later, she's standing in the room, hugging Tammy and welcoming her to the Ponderosa Countryside Villa. As soon as Rachel hears Tammy's name, she spins to give me a look that makes me want to die of embarrassment—why did I ever mention anything about my past to her?—but thankfully, she doesn't say anything.

She really is the hostess with the mostest. She's treating my little TT like a VIP guest and then crouching down to welcome Kai too. She gets a smile out of him within seconds, and he's soon nodding happily when she asks if he likes to read books and play games.

"We have a bunch I'm sure you're going to love. Let me get you a stack of books, and I'll bring them up here so you can read on the bed while Mommy gets freshened up, okay?"

"Okay." His eyes dart to me as I loiter in the doorway, and his smile is quickly replaced with a cautious frown as he inches closer to his mother and wraps his arm around her leg.

She brushes the top of his black hair while she chats with Rachel, and I ease out of the room, giving them the space they so obviously need.

My chest is swelling and aching at the same time.

It's so damn good to see Tammy again, but it's

different now. She's not the mischievous, playful girl I grew up with. Life has toughened us both up. Loss, heartache, and now betrayal teaching us that joy and security can be fleeting.

She's a mama now. All grown up.

A hurting mama who's trying to be strong for her son while her heart breaks over a husband who never deserved her in the first place.

CHAPTER 7
TAMMY

Rachel is an angel. There is no other way to describe her. Not only did she get a smile out of my very shy son, but she also brought him snacks, books, games... and even managed to get him petting Fezzik. The little dog sat, his tail wagging, while Rachel coaxed Kai away from my leg.

"That's it." Rachel grins. "I'll hold his collar, and you can pet him here or here." She points at the dog, and Kai reaches forward, then jumps back when Fezzik whips his head around to sniff him.

Rachel laughs. "It's okay. He just likes to sniff *everything*." She bulges her eyes, making a face that pulls a laugh out of my sweet boy. "Come on. You can do this."

Kai inches forward again, crouching down this time and holding out his hand. Fezzik gives it a quick sniff, his black nose twitching as he investigates this new person. Then he gives Kai's thumb a lick and lets him stroke his fur.

"He's soft."

"I know, right?" Rachel beams at him, staying low until Kai is obviously comfortable, then rising to talk to me again. "Please let me know if there's anything else you need. We're not officially open yet, but I'm going to treat you like my first VIP guest." She winks at me, and I fall just a little bit in love with her.

It takes everything in me not to start bawling on the spot. Her kindness is too much, yet exactly what I need.

Her gentle green eyes soften as she reaches out and rubs my arm. "I'm not sure exactly why you're here, and you don't have to tell me, but just know that we'll take really good care of you."

"Thank you." I nod.

Rachel steps back from us, pointing down at the dog. "If you want him gone, just order him to go find Baxter and he'll shoot out the door in a hot minute. He loves the guy."

I can believe that. Baxter always had a way with animals. His mom used to joke that he was better with animals than he was with humans.

Watching Kai jump on the plush armchair and beckon Fezzik up beside him, I have to wonder if my son's the same. Sure, he was scared at first... but that's only because he's never had pets in his life. I should get him a dog.

When we get back home, I—

The thought cuts off, and I cross my arms, shrinking in on myself and fighting the urge to throw up. When we get back home? Is that my plan? To return to Hudson after I've had a chance to cool off? Or is this it? Is my marriage over and then... what? Am I a solo mother now? Do I have to find a job and support my son? What if Hudson decides to fight me for custody or something? What if—

"Tammy? Are you okay?" Rachel's soft voice slices through my panic, and I blink at her, barely able to nod.

After a thick swallow, I manage to rasp, "Yeah. All good. Just tired after driving all this way." Lamest excuse ever.

"I'll leave you to get some rest, then." Her smile is kind, yet somehow all-knowing.

I look away from her, crossing my arms and digging my fingers into my biceps.

"You're welcome to join us for dinner later, or I can deliver it up here to your room. Just let me know." She walks for the door, gripping the handle before turning back to smile at me. "You're safe here. I don't know what's going on, but Baxter's pretty protective of us girls."

"Us girls?" I frown, wondering if this is some kind of harem situation or something. Baxter said a bunch of them live here, but is it just Rachel's boyfriend, Baxter, and a bunch of females?

"Yeah. I mean, all the guys are protective, but... I just know that Baxter will make sure you're safe. If that's the issue."

I shake my head with a wobbly smile. "It's not. It..." I wince, not even sure how to word this.

"Okay. I'm sorry. I don't mean to pry. I just want to make you feel better."

My laughter is short and more of a scoff as I shake my head and feebly reply, "Thanks for trying, but I'm..." I shake my head again.

Rachel just nods with a smile and leaves the room.

As soon as the door clicks shut, my shoulders deflate, and I slump onto the bed. I don't know what to do with myself. Baxter had to go to a hockey practice. He didn't say much before he left, but I felt bereft when I knew he wasn't in the house anymore. Thankfully, Rachel appeared with books, games, and food to distract us, but now she's gone, somewhere inside this big villa, and I don't know when Baxter will be back.

Wrapping my arms around myself, I glance over my shoulder at Kai. He's happily pointing at pictures and making up stories. He knows some of the words on the pages but not all of them. I love his singsong whisper as he talks to himself, unaware of the world around him.

My phone buzzes, and I glance at the screen. It's Hudson again.

Where are you?
Tell me that you're safe. Please.

I asked for space, and he gives me less than a day. He's relentless! I find it so frickin' ironic when he'll go days at work, barely checking in, but as soon as I leave, he needs constant contact.

With a huff, I quickly reply.

We're safe, and I'm not telling you where we are, because I'm not ready to see you right now. I asked for space, Hudson. You owe me that. Please, stop texting me!

You're my wife! Of course I'm going to text you and make sure you're okay. Especially when you won't answer your fucking phone!

I'm not answering because I don't want to talk to you right now. And I might be your wife, but you definitely weren't acting like my husband two days ago!

I'm sorry, okay? I'm sorry! If you'll just pick up the phone, I can actually say it to you. You can't just run away. We need to fix this.

I scowl at the screen before dropping the phone and listening to it buzz while Hudson sends through another chain of texts. He won't let this go until he knows where I am. But screw him. I'm not saying anything right now.

That's why I turned off my location tracker. I don't want him hunting me down and showing up here. Not until I figure out... what? I don't know what I need to figure out; I just know I can't face him yet. It's too painful.

My phone buzzes again, and I let out a little screech, snatching it off the bed and turning the thing off. Not just silent but freaking *off*! Slamming it back down on the soft duvet, I pinch the bridge of my nose and sniff.

"Mommy?" Kai's voice is soft and full of worry.

Shit. I'd forgotten he was sitting right there. What is wrong with me?

Forcing a smile, I look across the room at him. Fezzik is curled up by his side, his chin resting on Kai's little thighs. They look adorable together, and I should take a picture, but I don't want to touch my phone right now. "What's up, sweetie?"

"Are you okay?"

"Uh-huh." I nod, biting my lips together, knowing he can sense my lie.

His light brown eyes drink me in. He's watching me in that quiet way of his. I love his cute face so much. His serious, thoughtful expression. My heart is bleeding with affection... and also pain. I never wanted him, but as soon as I held him in my arms, he was mine, and I loved him with a fierceness I never thought I was capable of feeling.

"Do you miss Daddy? Is that why you're sad?"

The question stumps me for a second, and I work my jaw to the side as I try to answer him. Eventually, I settle for a deflect. "Do *you* miss Daddy?"

He shrugs, his lips turning down at the edges.

As much as I hate to do it, I pick up my phone and hold it out to him. "You can call him if you want." It should be safe enough. Kai barely speaks anyway, and it's not like he'll tell Hudson where we are. I do run the risk of him telling Hudson about the dog and possibly talking about a scary man with a beard, but I'll be right here to monitor the call.

As much as I don't want it to happen, I can't deny Kai access to his father... even if his daddy is a shithead.

Guilt pinches me.

I feel bad for calling my husband that, but... dammit, he is!

He cheated on me!

The thought is like a punch to the stomach, and I feel the pain hit me with a force so strong, I nearly buckle.

I've been a good wife. Loyal. Supportive.

And he's screwing blondes with big boobs in my freaking shower!

It hurts. This pain is like nothing I've ever felt before. It makes me want to crumple to the ground and weep... or maybe scream. I don't know. I hate this onslaught of black-and-blue emotion so much.

"Um..." Kai bites his lip, staring at my phone like it's a snake.

I can't help a soft grin. "Still scared to talk on the phone, huh?"

He wrinkles his nose, and all I can do is laugh at his cute expression. "Well, if you change your mind, you just have to ask, okay?" I swallow the rock in my throat and grit out, "I'm sure Daddy would love to hear from you."

He glances at the phone, then back at Fezzik, and then his eyes track to the stack of books Rachel left for him. He doesn't reach for one, and my insides spasm. Does he want to keep talking? Is he going to ask me why I left or what an affair is?

Shit. I shouldn't have spoken so freely around him.

He opens his little mouth, but before any words can pop out, I jump off the bed.

My quick move startles Fezzik, and he sits up, perking his ears and then barking once before leaping to the floor and racing out of the room.

Kai jolts and gapes after him—a mixture of disappointment and curiosity.

"Shall we go see where the little dude's going?"

"Okay." Kai jumps down and scampers after him.

Relief floods me as I chase him out the door. Awkward conversation averted. But I can't expect that to last forever. At some point, he's going to want the truth, and somehow I have to explain it in a way a four-year-old will understand.

I'm on borrowed time here. Hudson won't just let me get away with ignoring him. And Kai will eventually want to talk to his dad. I'm a good mother, and I have to put Kai before my own emotional nightmare, which means later today, I need to find the courage to turn my phone back on and set up a video chat with Kai and his dad.

"Fezzik?" Kai softly calls, following him down the stairs, then jerking to a stop with a quiet yelp.

I hurtle down the stairs, wondering what's got him spooked, until I spot the tall, muscly guy in the entrance. He glances up the stairwell and looks at me, confusion buckling his expression.

"Can't fucking believe Coach ended practice with that bullshit drill. What the fuck?" Another guy walks in, rubbing his shoulder and cursing some more, until the first guy nudges him with his elbow.

He shuts up immediately and glances my way, spotting Kai peering through the railing. I edge up behind him, resting my hand on his chest while we both gape at the group of giant men who are now piling in the front door. Their bags land with thuds on the shiny wood floor.

"Yeah, well, that new assistant coach is a piece of fucking work. He's gonna make us sweat blood in training, I'm telling ya." The man with dark hair frowns when he notices his two friends staring at us. Then his gaze inevitably tracks to the staircase, and now I'm nervously smiling at what I can only assume are hockey players.

Big, burly hockey players with foul mouths who look like they could squish us in a heartbeat.

Do these men all live in this house together?

Shit. What have I done bringing Kai here?

He leans back against my legs, his white-knuckle grip on the railing making me want to race back upstairs and pack our bags.

But then Baxter appears at the bottom of the staircase. Fezzik yaps at his feet, then rushes to the guy with messy blond hair.

"Hey, buddy!" He bends down, a wide smile dominating his face as he scoops up the dog in his arms and gets excited puppy kisses.

Mr. Tall is still studying me along with Mr. Dark Hair. It's unnerving. I glance at Baxter, who gives me a reassuring smile, so I wave at the guys. "Uh... hi."

"Who are you?" Mr. Tall crosses his arms and narrows his eyes at me. It's not a mean look exactly, but he obviously wasn't expecting some strange lady and her kid invading their turf.

"This is Tammy." Baxter speaks before I can. "She's a friend of mine. We grew up living next door to each other, and she's just swung by to say hi and stay for a couple days." His soft explanation leaves no room for argument, and the guys all relax, their smiles turning friendly. "And this is her son, Kai. He's... four?" He glances up the stairs for confirmation, and I nod.

"Yeah." I squeeze Kai's shoulder. "Say hello, please, kiddo."

He swallows, and I give him another soft nudge. Eventually, a greeting that sounds more like a mouse squeak pops out, and it causes the one with the puppy to laugh, then call up to him. "Nice to meet you, man. Welcome to our castle." His wink and grin are downright adorable, and I feel Kai relax beneath my fingers. "Don't be shy, dude. Come on down. You met my puppy yet?"

"He's yours? I thought he was Baxter's dog?"

"What?" The incredulous expression is hammed up, and it makes Kai giggle. "I bought this little dude for my girl, and he's ours. Baxter just looks after him for us when we're at school."

"You go to school?" Kai's face buckles in confusion as he starts walking down the stairs. "Aren't you too old for that?"

My mouth drops open. Kai is talking to strangers. He's having an actual conversation. Using words. His little voice ringing out loud enough to actually be heard.

"We're in college."

Kai stops on the fourth step from the bottom as the man approaches him. Fezzik is starting to squirm, and he places him down so the dog can dance up the stairs and sniff Kai's feet. The man crouches down so he's level with my son.

"College is like school for big people. And I've only got one year to go. Then I'm gonna get me a contract with a professional hockey team."

Kai bobs his head, his wide eyes drinking this man in.

"I'm Casey, by the way." He sticks out his hand. Kai stares at it for a second, and Casey laughs. "Slap me some skin, little man."

After a cautious pause, Kai does as he's told, and Casey laughs, then points out the other men in the entrance. "That tall one over there, that's Ethan. He's our captain this year. Pretty decent guy most of the time."

Ethan gives him a dry look, crossing his arms and muttering, "All the time. I'm decent all the time."

Casey ignores him. "And that shorter one over there is Liam."

My eyes dart to the man who is waving at Kai with a kind smile. That must be Rachel's boyfriend.

"And Mr. Cool back there with the dark hair... that's Asher."

"'Sup." The man lifts his chin, and Kai gives him a shy smile.

Casey leans in with a stage whisper. "Don't let his charm fool you. The guy's a total dork."

Kai giggles while Asher rolls his eyes, then gets nudged aside by another player.

"Don't forget me." He waves his hand, moving to the front of the pack and grinning up at me. "Hi there. I'm Connor."

CHAPTER 8
BAXTER

Connor's smile is in full flirt mode, and my insides simmer as he grins up at Tammy. Thank God I arrived back from coaching at the same time these douchebags did.

I glare at my friend, then glance up at Tammy. She smiles down at Connor with two dimples that make my heart hurt. She's so pretty. She always has been. Even when we were kids, she stood out from the rest. And then after puberty... holy shit, she was a knockout. I'd fallen for her long before then, but after that, I was so attracted to her, I could hardly stand it.

I'm still attracted to her. Desire pulses through me as I watch her glide down the stairs. She shakes Casey's hand, then greets the other guys.

"I hope you don't mind us crashing for a little bit."

"Of course not." Casey grins. "Mi casa es do casa."

"It's mi casa es *su* casa, dumbass," Liam grumbles, giving him a pitiful frown.

"Don't mind him. He gets a little cranky when he hasn't had his afternoon nap." Casey winks at Kai while Ethan snorts and shakes his head.

But before Liam can even respond, he gets distracted by Rachel. His entire face lights up with appreciation as she walks into the room. "Hey, cariño." Wrapping his arm around her waist, he pulls her in for a kiss, then whispers something in her ear that turns her smile mushy. They rest their foreheads together and look like a freaking Hallmark couple as they whisper-chat, melting into the background for a little privacy.

I turn back to check on Tammy, who is watching them with a wistful, crestfallen look on her face. Instinct tells me to move into her line of sight, distract her, let her know that she deserves that kind of love and adoration. She deserves all the attention and kindness and—

"So..." Connor sidles up to the stairs. "How long are you two staying?"

"Uh, not sure yet. We're just visiting Baxter." Her dimple appears as she whips a look at me before grinning at Connor. "Don't worry. We won't overstay our welcome."

Connor's eyes dance with appreciation as he eyes her up and down. "I don't think that would be a problem for a pretty thing like you."

I want to punch him.

Right in the mouth.

What the fuck is he doing flirting with my girl?

She's not your girl, Bax.

A chill sweeps through me, and I grit my teeth, watching Connor shift into full charm mode. It reminds me of Hudson when he first showed up at Gladstone High. I will never get rid of that image—him leaning against Tammy's locker, tucking her hair behind her ear and smiling down at her with the grace of a fucking movie star. She stared up at him, all wide-eyed awe and wonder. He'd say something saccharine and irritating, and she'd blush and giggle. I'd never seen her act like that before. She never did that kind of thing with me.

Probably because I was never going to be more than a buddy. I was friend-zoned for life, and I felt helpless to change that.

Hudson made everything worse, and I instantly hated him. The feeling only grew as he dragged her further into his world and far away from mine. Then he knocked her up and fucking married her.

Tammy was my girl.

Except that she wasn't. He proved that.

And now Connor's doing the same thing. Talking to her like she's the only person in the room, his smile flattering, his perfect words and smooth voice enough to capture anyone.

Fuck!

I'm never gonna catch a break... not even when she

shows up out of the blue because her fuckwit husband cheated on her.

"Actually..." Tammy's voice cuts through my maelstrom. "I'm married." She flicks her fingers in the air, and we all spot the ring.

It's still on her finger.

My gut plummets while my brain tries to remind me that... of course it is.

Hudson may have cheated on her, but she obviously hasn't decided what to do about that yet. I don't know the full details, but it clearly wasn't a case of her ripping that ring off and throwing it in his face.

She took off to regroup.

And she wants to regroup here. With me.

But that doesn't mean she's gonna stay.

That doesn't mean she's suddenly mine now.

Her expression washes with sadness that she only just manages to hide behind another bright smile.

Shit, is she gonna forgive that douchewad and go back to him?

I don't think I can stomach that.

I lost her once... and I can't go through that again.

Slipping from the room, I head to the shed out back. I'm sure it needs tidying or something, right?

I just need a little distance. Some space to remind myself that Tammy's just here for a minute. I'll take care of her, make sure she's safe and supported, but I can't go letting my heart get in the way.

She's not mine.

Maybe she never was.

I'll be her friend... just the way she wants me to be.

And then I need to prepare myself to let her go.

CHAPTER 9
TAMMY

Baxter was there one minute, and then he was gone.

While Connor was trying to flirt his ass off and impress me, I looked for an out, hoping Baxter would step up and muscle his way through all these players. Maybe he could stand by my side and make some joke about me needing space.

But when I turned to look for him, he wasn't there, and it hit home like a mallet to my face.

Baxter always liked to retreat. I knew this only a few short months into our friendship. We got into a fight over something stupid. I can't even remember what it was now, but rather than shouting back at me, he gave me a quiet frown... and ran away. It took me hours to find him, and eventually I spotted him down by the creek, throwing stones into the water with annoyed little grunts.

I stood beside him, not saying anything until the silence got too much for me. So, I punched his arm and told him he wasn't allowed to go running off. It didn't matter if we disagreed on something, we could still be friends.

He turned and looked at me. Then, without a word, he held out his hand and passed me three stones. "The target's that tree branch in the middle. You see it?"

"Yeah, I see it."

"First person to hit it three times gets to choose what movie we watch tonight."

I grinned and threw those stones like my life depended on it.

We ended up watching the first Star Wars movie... so it's safe to say I lost the whole stone-throwing thing. But I won my friend back, and at the time, that was all that mattered.

Biting my lips together, I brush my hand across Kai's shoulders as he steps aside to let the big boys tromp upstairs. They haul their gear out of the entrance, and I trail Kai, who has darted into the living room to chase after Fezzik.

"Here, why don't you go into the yard and throw this for him." Rachel appears with a plastic toy, and Kai looks to me with a hopeful expression.

"Of course. Let's go."

Heading out through the mudroom, we step into the crisp, fall air. Colorful leaves have been dropping from trees for a few weeks now, and the yard is covered. It makes me smile watching Kai run through them, laughing and throwing the toy for an excited Fezzik while yellow and orange leaves spray up around them. He kicks a small pile and laughs, dancing through the debris. Fezzik jumps and yaps, running through the leaves with a doggy smile. Kai chases him, and they run in circles, laughing and barking together.

Wow. Kai's certainly gotten over his fears quickly.

If only adults could do the same.

Digging my hands into my pockets, I lean against the railing and watch my son play—so carefree and trusting. He still believes the world is a good place. I think he's aware that people can hurt each other, and that makes him cautious, but he doesn't understand the depth of that pain yet.

Thank God.

I never want him to, but I know that's unrealistic.

You don't get through life that way. You have to burn. It's a rite of passage, right?

You have to get hurt, sometimes do the hurting yourself... and then you grow and heal and...

What if that part never comes?

What if you hurt someone you really care about, and then you *don't* deal with it? You let this precious thing slip through your fingers because talking about it's too awkward. And then this new guy comes along and steals all your attention, and you're too stupid to realize what you were leaving behind.

Then when you finally worked it out... he was too hurt to let you find him by the creek and throw stones with him.

Running my hands through my hair, I rest my elbows on the rail and feel the pain ride through me.

Baxter was my best friend. That's why he took me in today without hesitation. But the way he walked out of the room just before... it was a good reminder that we will never be what we once were.

He's not my man out to protect or claim me.

I'm already taken.

"Apparently," I mutter, twisting my wedding and engagement rings around my finger.

My insides are raw and hollow. My soul feels fragile, on the brink of shattering, and for some reason, all I can think about is that summer by the swimming hole.

That summer I believed my friendship with Baxter would last forever.

Until we started making out in the sunshine, and then I went and ruined it all...

CHAPTER 10
BAXTER

The summer before senior year...

"Ah! Stop it!" Tammy laughs, lifting her hands to cover her face as I push another wave of water at her.

As soon as I stop, she retaliates, and the water fight continues until we're both spluttering and wiping droplets out of our eyes.

"Okay, truce! Truce!" I call it, swimming over to her and lifting my hands so she knows I meant it.

She laughs, coughs up some more water, then jumps on my back. Her slippery legs wrap around my waist, and I try not to notice how hot her boobs feel squished against my back as I swim us to shore.

It's the perfect summer afternoon.

We have the swimming hole all to ourselves. The sun

is shining, the sky cloudless, the breeze just cool enough to make the heat bearable. I couldn't have picked a better way to spend my last afternoon before I go visit my grandparents out of state.

I'll be gone for nine whole days.

I moaned and complained about spending my last week of the summer break that way, but Mom wouldn't let me get away with it.

"You can leave Tammy for one week!" She'd thrown her hands up and gotten all exasperated. "I told you she can come with us."

"Her parents won't let her." I'd frowned and gotten a sympathetic smile.

"You two can survive without hanging out. Knowing you, you'll be texting each other the whole time anyway. Or messaging or snapping or whatever it is you do."

I didn't try to correct her, still too caught up in being annoyed that my grandparents lived so far away.

"You'll see her the night before school goes back and then drive her in the next morning." After that, she cupped my cheeks and got all mushy. "My big boy, your last year of high school. I can't believe it."

I endured the attention, because I'm an only child, and I knew Mom needed to lavish me with all her motherly love. It also got me out of lunch with the Johnsons and meant I could spend the afternoon chilling with my favorite person.

"Where do you want to go, TT?" I ask over my shoulder.

"Over there." She points to a patch of grass just below the boulder we like to jump off.

I breaststroke until my feet hit the bottom, then keep her on my back. Water cascades off our bodies, the breeze making her legs ripple with goose bumps.

Placing her down, I plonk beside her when she takes a seat and stretches her body out. She's gotten taller, leaner, yet curvier in the last year. Her boobs have popped. It's impossible not to notice, and it takes maximum effort not to stare at them any chance I can get.

The blue bikini she's wearing is so not helping. I mean, she's definitely not as big as some of the girls in our grade, but those triangular bits of fabric are housing some pretty sweet melons. Or mangoes. That's what Heston called them at junior prom. I thumped him with the back of my hand and told him to stop being a dick.

"So fucking protective all the time," he grumbled, straightening his jacket and giving Tammy one more look before frowning at me. "It's not like she's your girlfriend."

But I wanted her to be.

Oh man, I've wanted that ever since I've been old enough to understand the concept.

Do you think I've found the courage to do anything about it, though?

I hate what a coward I am, but I can't risk losing Tammy. She's my best friend—my only real friend—and I'd be lost without her. I can't go making a move and screwing things up.

"Aw, man, I want this day to last forever." Tammy tips her face up to the sun.

I follow the line of her neck, rolling to my side and leaning on my elbow so I can pick grass blades and look at her.

She's stretched out like a swimwear model, and I snap a bunch of mental pictures that will no doubt keep me company in bed tonight.

I want to skim the pads of my fingers up her glistening leg, wipe the last of the water drops away, and then suck the end of my finger. Maybe then I'll know what she tastes like.

Would she freak out if I did that?

We touch each other all the time, but it's always just a friendly hug or playful tussle.

Although, this summer has been a bit more... I don't know... flirty?

Our hugs have lasted a beat longer than they used to. Our excuses to bump into each other or brush hands seem to be more frequent. Or am I just imagining it?

Sucking in a breath, I try to still my racing heartbeat.

"What time do you have to go?"

"Not sure." I shrug. "I don't even know what the time is... and I don't care."

She giggles, popping her eyes open and looking at me. "Doesn't it feel like we're the only two people on Earth right now?"

"Imagine if we were." I lie back, gazing up at the trees above us. The leaves are rustling in the wind. It's a gentle music—a lullaby that could rock me to sleep. The sun is a lazy drug heating my skin, but there's no way I'll fall asleep. Not with Tammy beside me in that blue bikini. Not with my pulse racing and my senses heightened to her softest breath and smallest movement.

"Well..." Tammy wriggles her butt down so she can lie next to me. "I guess we'd eventually have to find ourselves some food."

"I brought snacks," I murmur.

She laughs, nudging me with her hand. "Where's the fun in that? I think we should make ourselves a bow and arrow and go hunting."

"A bow and arrow?" I give her a skeptical frown. "Okay, let me just whip one of those up for you."

"Thanks." She giggles again. "And I'd like deer for dinner."

"You don't even like red meat." I snort and nudge her back. "I'd have to hunt this forest for some kind of chicken."

"Or we could go fishing."

"Or catch you a frog or lizard."

"Ew!" She sticks out her tongue. It's perfect and pink, and I want to suck it between my lips.

The image makes me flush. I dart my eyes away from her.

"I know they eat that stuff in France, but can you imagine how slimy and gross they are to prepare?"

"Fish can be slimy."

"That's why you'd be catching it, deboning it, and cooking it for me. I'm not touching raw fish."

"Oh, really? And what are *you* going to do?" I sit up on my elbow and mock-glare down at her. "Work me like some slave while you sit there getting a tan?" Without thinking, I rest my hand on her flat belly, then give it a very light slap.

She gasps, sitting up with a jerk and trying to slap me back. I laugh and catch her wrists, and so begins one of our standard wrestling matches.

She tries to knee me, so I roll over her, parting her legs so those lethal knees don't get me in the gonads. She wriggles beneath me with a little grunt and fights a giggle while I loosen my grip and let her push me back over. Before I know it, she's straddling me, and then I'm staring up at her body, my mouth hanging open when I notice that her bikini top has shifted and I can see her right nipple.

I should tell her, but won't that be awkward?

I swallow, wondering if she can feel me growing hard beneath her.

If she does, she doesn't say anything.

In fact, I don't know what the hell is going on right now, because she's still holding my wrists and giving me this weird look.

Breaths are punching out of both of us, like all we're capable of doing is breathing. Her brown eyes dart across my face, her eyebrows dipping together.

What? The word is on the tip of my tongue, but I can't

seem to say it.

Because now her eyebrows are rising, her expression opening with a look I can't decipher. She's leaning closer to me, her wet hair brushing my chest as her mouth inches toward mine.

Closer.

And closer.

Her breath skims me, and I lose the ability to think.

Then my brain short-circuits completely when her soft lips brush over mine, then return with a delicate pressure that is...

I don't know what it is, but holy shit!

Tamara Tan is kissing me.

What do I do?

What do I—

The question slips away as instincts take over and I tentatively part my lips.

The tip of my tongue skims out for a taste, and that's when I finally get to live out one of my longest running fantasies.

Her tongue greets mine in a tentative touch, her grip on my wrists tightening. Then she lets out this soft sound, her tongue thrusting forward with an energy that's easy to match. I shake my wrists loose and cup the back of her head, leaning into the kiss and, for the first time in my life, experiencing what it means to make out.

After all this time, I know what Tammy tastes like. I know what she feels like pressed against my body.

And I want more.

CHAPTER 11
TAMMY

The summer before senior year...

Baxter's tongue is soft and delicious. The second it skimmed my lips, I opened my mouth. It was an instinctual move, like my body told my brain it's not required for a while because... *I got this.*

And I'm happy to let it, because this feels so good.

I don't know what possessed me to do it.

Curiosity, maybe?

Baxter's gotten uber hot this summer. I don't know how it happened, but one minute he was kind of long and gangly, and then over the winter, he bulked up bigtime. I nearly lost my mind the first time I saw him shirtless this summer, and it's taken everything in me to play it cool and not let my attraction show.

But right now, I can't help myself. This is our last day of summer together, and when he was lying beneath me, looking at me like I was the sun and he would happily spend his life orbiting me, I just had to test my "can we be more than friends" theory.

I could feel him all hard beneath me, and it sent this terrifying, yet addictive, thrill right through me. I obviously turn him on, and I want to know where this leads. I've never done it with a guy before. I'm curious, but I've never met someone I wanted to go all the way with.

Could Baxter be it?

I mean, he'd be a safe bet, right?

If I was going to lose it to anyone, why not him?

He's my best friend. We care about each other.

But do you love him?

Of course I do!

I mean, like that. Do you love him romantically?

I'm not sure. Although my body would suggest otherwise.

Our breaths are growing short as we deepen the kiss again. I skim my hands over his shoulders, curling my fingers around the back of his neck and letting my tongue take the lead on this.

He tastes amazing. I love the feel of our tongues gliding against each other. Long licks, then short swipes, then another lick that pulls a moan out of my throat.

Baxter's hands are skimming my back, the pads of his fingers sending tendrils of pleasure across my skin.

I want him to undo my bikini.

The thought catches me off guard for a second, but I know it's true. My body is yearning for pure skin on skin, and before I can stop myself, I'm reaching back and doing it for him.

"Tammy, what are you...?" His words trail off as I sit up and let the fabric slip off my shoulders.

His face is the picture of awe, his eyes drinking me in like I'm the eighth natural wonder of the world.

"You're beautiful," he croaks, trying to sit up.

I shuffle back to give him room, and he reaches for my chest, then stops, his hand in midair as he checks my face.

"It's okay." I grab his fingers. "I want you to." Placing his palm over my right breast, I catch my breath when he gives it a light squeeze.

"Holy shit," he breathes, his lips flirting with a smile as he curls his hand behind my neck and pulls me forward for another deep kiss.

His hand is still massaging my breast, and it feels new and tantalizing and so freaking good. Then he lets his fingers explore, brushing over my nipple—a delicate study of my sensitive skin.

My tongue falters in his mouth, and I sit back with a gasp. "That feels good," I manage, staring down at his fingers on my nipple.

He cups the side of my breast and runs his thumb lightly over the nub. I can't help a soft whimper. Biting my lower lip, I relish this buzz of energy running all the way through me. It charges down to between my legs, tingling and begging for more.

I don't even have to ask him before he's reaching for my other breast, teasing the other nipple as well until I can feel this intense pressure and heat pooling at the top of my thighs.

I've never felt like this before.

I've made out with guys when we played spin the bottle at parties. I've done seven minutes of heaven in the closet with Ricky Tolson at his fourteenth birthday party, but that was just heavy kissing and some over-the-shirt action.

This is something else.

"Bax," I whisper, fisting the back of his hair and angling his mouth to mine.

Our kisses turn deep again. Deep and desperate. He starts to groan, too, and my hips can't help but rock over him.

He groans again, squeezing my breasts and letting out a soft whimper.

I can feel his hard shaft skim my inner thigh, and oh man, I want to see it, touch it.

Ripping my mouth from his, I stare down at his tented board shorts. He's breathing hard, his face the picture of desperation. Is the pressure too much for him too?

"I want to touch it."

"Tammy." He breathes my name, but I don't give him a chance to say anything else.

Skimming my fingers into the waistband of his shorts, I ignore that flash of trepidation and pull them down. His dick springs free, and now it's my turn to gaze in wonder at this thing. It's hard and long with this glistening drop at the end of it. I've never seen a penis before—only cartoon images in puberty books.

This is... "Wow," I whisper.

He groans, tipping his head back like he's about to orgasm, but I haven't even touched him yet.

"Tammy," he moans.

I reach for him, curling my fingers around that shaft and gliding my hand up and down.

"Oh, wow," I breathe, barely able to hear past the hammering in my heart. This feels amazing. How can something be so hard and yet the skin around it be so delicately soft and smooth?

He groans as I skim my thumb over the end, marveling at this new discovery. No wonder people always make sex sound so great. The sensations skipping through my body right now are overwhelming. This heady zing, this aching need between my legs.

Swiping that bead of moisture off the top of his dick with my thumb, I grasp him again and run my hand down until Baxter jerks, his eyes popping wide and his body convulsing.

"No, wait," he rasps, jolting on the grass, his legs spasming beneath me as a spurt of white cream shoots out of his dick and lands directly on my cheek.

CHAPTER 12
BAXTER

Present day...

Rubbing a hand over my clean-shaven face, I gaze in the mirror and shake my head. Shit, I look so much younger without a beard. I may be twenty-three now, but I still feel like a kid sometimes. A clueless boy who doesn't know how to navigate this great big world.

That feeling grew a million times worse when I lost Mom, but it started that day I lost Tammy. I mean, I guess I didn't lose her with the brutal swiftness that Mom was taken from us, but it felt like the beginning of the end somehow.

Sadness sweeps through me, weighing down my bones and making me feel small.

I can't let it win.

I've got hockey in forty minutes, and my Mini Mites need me sharp and enthusiastic.

Resting my hands against the sink, I let out a heavy sigh, and that's when the door squeaks behind me.

I glance over my shoulder and spot a little pair of brown eyes. They bulge when our gazes connect, and then he disappears.

A soft chuckle rumbles in my chest. I was just like that as a kid.

Shit, I couldn't talk to anyone. My mom freaking *made me* say hello to any guest who walked in the front door. It was always torture.

But I loved to stand on the edge of a room watching.

It felt safe somehow. Like I was hidden in the shadows but could see everything.

Wiping down the sink, I throw the towel in the hamper and head down to my room. I live on the top floor with Asher, Ethan, and Liam. The next two floors down are for guests, and Casey has been relegated to the pool house thanks to the stench of his shits and Fezzik's early morning barking and bathroom breaks.

He was pretty pissed about it at first, but he lost the vote fair and square.

Now the only thing to disturb my sleep is Liam and Rachel's sex life. Those two are noisy, and they're in the room right next to mine. Thankfully, Ethan and Mick are on the quieter side, but I still hear the odd moan coming out of their room if I happen to pass at the wrong moment.

Asher's room is down at the end of the hall, so I don't hear much from him. Lani sleeps over occasionally, but she's mostly in her dorm, especially when he's gone for away games. She's pretty into her studying, and now that she's a junior, the workload has intensified that much more.

I don't mind when she stays. She's neat and organized and respects everyone around her. Just quietly, she's one of my favorite hockey girls. There's just something about her that I warm to. I feel more protective of her than I do the others. Maybe because I know what she's been through. Maybe because I let her in on my secret love for Tammy.

Who knows.

But we're tight, and I always love it when she's at Ponderosa.

Padding down to my room, I walk in and dump my stuff before grabbing out my hockey gear.

The door squeaks behind me, and I glance over my shoulder to spot those brown eyes again.

He gasps and disappears behind the wood.

"It's okay, Kai. You can come in. I'm just getting ready for hockey practice."

He doesn't respond, and I assume he's run back to Tammy... until I hear the door creak once more.

I move slowly, keeping my expression casual and my gaze off his face as I pack my bag for practice. I have a few extra sticks to take—they rattle together as I dump them in the open bag.

Kai eases into the room, and I keep ignoring him, not wanting to scare him away.

He's been here for three days now, and although he's still super quiet, he's getting a little braver. Chasing Fezzik around is helping with that. That pup can get Kai's giggles going, and he sounds so much like his mother when he laughs that it always trips me up.

Tammy's been quiet but calm as she potters around, helping Rachel with cleaning and whatever else needs to be done around this place. Yesterday, I caught them swooning over menus and cooking ideas.

I think Rachel's fallen for Tammy as fast as I did.

It's hard not to. She's sweet and funny, and although she's not as lively as she used to be in high school, I can see that spark lingering. At least I think I can. If she wasn't hurting so badly over what Hudson did to her, I'm sure she'd be filling this house with laughter and mischief. She couldn't help herself when we were younger. She was always after the fun, talking me into crazy shit just for a laugh.

Clenching my jaw, I crouch down by my hockey box and sort through a few pucks, throwing them into the bag as Kai shuffles up to my bed. Resting his elbows on the duvet, he cups his cheek and watches me work.

Not saying anything is becoming harder and harder, so eventually I give in and quietly ask, "No Fezzik, huh? He sleeping?"

Kai nods, the left side of his mouth dipping.

"Your mom said you're not allowed to wake him, huh?"

He nods again, and I can't help a snicker. "I guess you just have to think about how much energy he'll have when he wakes up. He'll be busting to play with you."

Kai doesn't respond to that, and I wonder if I said too many words this time.

It's obvious that he doesn't like to talk much, although Casey seems to be able to get the words out of him. When the guy's home, Kai follows him around like a puppy. Casey cracks jokes that make the little guy smile, and he even growled and turned himself into a bear last night. I thought that would scare the shit out of Kai, but he just squealed and took off running, his laughter bouncing off the walls as Fezzik and Casey chased him. Caroline was over, and she got all misty-eyed for a minute as she watched them. Casey nabbed Kai and threw him in the air, catching him and tickling the poor kid until he nearly peed his pants.

Rachel got up and gave her a kiss, murmuring something soft that I only just caught the end of. "...great dad one day. When the timing's right."

Caroline smiled and mouthed, "Thank you," then went back to watching her boyfriend play.

I shared a look with Tammy, who was smiling and crying all at the same time as well.

It broke my heart a little, because I knew it was for different reasons. Caroline still mourns her miscarriage every now and again... as far as I can tell.

Tammy's mourning the fact that her husband is a disloyal shithead... I think.

She's definitely torn up, and I don't know what to do about it... or how to help her.

Clearing my throat, I stand and watch Kai step back from me.

"I'm not gonna hurt you, kid." I smile down at him, then rub my cheeks. "I even shaved off the scary beard for ya."

His nose wrinkles. "You did that for me?"

"Yeah." I nod.

The boy eyes me up, his lips twitching like he wants to smile, but maybe he's just a little afraid to do it.

Shit. What was his home life like?

Hudson may be a douche, but he never struck me as the kind of guy who would scare his family. He was always so charming and cared too much about appearances to be anything other than cheesy.

But was that plastic veneer hiding a darker side?

Part of me wants to ask, but I'm worried Kai will take off if I do. Maybe Tammy will tell me, if I can get her alone for long enough to talk to her. This house is way too busy sometimes, and when everyone's at school, she's always with Rachel.

Crouching back down by the bed, I get eye level with Kai and see if I can coax a proper smile out of him. I have no idea what to say or how to relate to a kid this age, but...

Yes, you do. You coach Mini Mite hockey.

I reach for a stick and pull it out of the bag.

"You like hockey?"

Kai eyes the stick, his right shoulder hitching.

"You ever watched a game?"

He shakes his head.

"Okay, well, it's my favorite sport. Casey loves it too." Even the mention of the guy's name makes Kai's eyes light up. "And do you know what I do two afternoons a week?" I wait to see if he'll respond. When he just keeps staring at me, I hold out the stick to him. "I coach kids about your age how to play. Here."

I jiggle the stick, and he cautiously takes it off me.

"That's it." I grin, standing up and grabbing another stick. I look ridiculous because it's so small compared to my own, but I bend down and get my stance about as good as I can. "Now, you want to hold it here and here." I show him where his hands should go and then move around behind him to correct his stance. "Good job." I copy him and demonstrate. "Now, you swing back like this and then hit through like... this." I swing the stick, hitting an invisible puck and holding my stance for a second before looking down at him.

He assesses me for a long, slow beat before trying to mimic what I did.

"Yeah. Yeah, that's good." I correct his elbow, then crouch down and ask him to show me again. He executes it pretty damn well, and I grin, searching the room for something he can hit.

One of Fezzik's soft toys is just under my bed where

he left it, and I snatch it out, placing it on the ground and instructing Kai to hit it.

He misses the first time, only skimming the top. His little face pulls into a frustrated pout, which makes me laugh.

"It's okay. Try again."

His eyebrows dip together, his tongue poking at the side of his mouth, as he lines himself up and let's rip.

The toy goes flying, spiraling across my room and thumping against the wall before dropping back to the floor.

"Yes!" I hold up my hand for a high five, and he gives me a hesitant look before grinning and jumping up, slapping his little palm against my open hand.

It feels like the win of the century.

CHAPTER 13
TAMMY

The kitchen smells amazing as Rachel and I test out one of her latest recipes. She wants to perfect her high tea menu. Right now, we're working on her scone recipe. We've made them small so they'll fit onto the tiered plates she's ordered, but trying to get the texture "just right" is turning out to be quite the mission. The counter is crowded with baking trays of various designs—from plain scones to ones with dates and another with cranberries.

I nibble on the apple and cheddar creations that have just come out of the oven.

"Oh my gosh," I groan. "The flavor is so great."

Rachel's nose wrinkles. "But the texture is still pretty crumbly. I want them to feel like they're biting into a fluffy cloud, you know?"

"These are not far off," I assure her. "I think you're being too hard on yourself. Seriously, I could eat this whole tray. In fact, these would be great made bigger as like a one-off order. There'll be some people who just want a little bite and a drink, you know? You could have a glass cabinet with a bunch of yummies on display."

"That's true. I've been thinking about that, actually." She pulls out a notebook and starts flipping through the pages. "I've been jotting down ideas of one-off items, but I'm liking your thoughts on the glass display cabinet. We could make it look so pretty." Her eyes start to dance, and I can't help but get in on her enthusiasm. What she's trying to achieve here is so cool.

And in just a few weeks, the place will open for the first round of guests and visitors.

Mikayla's father and step-grandfather are already working on the soft launch. From what Rachel's told me, their marketing team has been emailing constantly with details of what they're promoting and how it's all going to go down.

There's a giveaway running for exclusive weekends in November, and apparently entries are flying in. Plus, on November first, the doors to the café will open for high tea. Rachel is putting together a warm, wintery selection that will be the perfect escape from the icy winds outside. She's got this whole spiel the marketing team have been helping her with.

I'm just stoked to be along for the ride... for now. It's a good distraction. These guys are letting me stay here for free, and I want to pull my weight. I've been cleaning and making sure the renovated villa stays spotless. Baxter is still working on finishing third-floor rooms, and I've been trying to keep Kai and Fezzik out of his hair and away from the fresh paint.

It's been three days living like this, and it's surprising how normal it all feels. Kai seems to like the hockey bros. They're fun and friendly—especially Casey—bringing out a side of Kai I've never really seen before. The girls are lovely too. I've met all of them but Lani, and so far, they're awesome. Mikayla cracks me up. She has no problem telling us exactly what she thinks, and Rachel's the biggest sweetheart. Caroline, with her shock of red hair, is adorable, and the way Casey smiles at her melts my heart every time.

I honestly don't know if Hudson has ever gazed at me the way these guys seem to gaze at their women.

There's a lot of love in this place, and it makes it warm and inviting.

It also makes the thought of going back home to my husband and mess of a marriage so much harder. Guilt constantly niggles. I know I should make contact with him. It's my responsibility as his wife to at least hear him out, right? If I love him, then I should.

But... I don't want to right now.

My house in Chesterfield feels cold and lonely compared to the warmth of this old villa. I know I can't stay here forever, but this is the first place to make me feel this way since... I used to hang out at Baxter's house. His mom would be in the kitchen, creating some kind of healthy option which she swore tasted great but totally didn't. Cookies without sugar don't work. It didn't matter, though, because we'd all laugh and tease her, and she'd pull hidden treats out of the pantry and throw them at us.

"Go watch a movie or something, you cheeky monkeys!"

We'd laugh and scamper off, then snuggle under her handmade quilt and watch TV or play video games.

I miss those days.

They were simple and sweet and—

My phone buzzes, and I tense. Eyeing it up like it's made from hazardous materials, I'm tempted to ignore it, but Rachel's gazing at me. Snatching it off the counter, I check the screen, my shoulders relaxing a little when I see that the message isn't from Hudson. It's from one of the moms in Kai's swim class.

Does Kai want to come over for a play? Max is driving me insane. He's got so much energy I think he's going to explode! He's like a human tornado today!

I grin, picturing poor Lisa as she tries to manage her wild child. To be honest, Kai doesn't like him that much, but out of politeness, I force him to go there sometimes. It's good for him to learn to interact with all kinds of people —even the slightly annoying ones. I always go with him, though. Which is probably what Lisa is hoping for as well —a little adult company to break up the day. She's a full-time stay-at-home mom like me, and the days can be long sometimes.

Wincing in sympathy, I text her back, unable to ignore my relief as I type:

We'd love to, but Kai and I are still out of town. Thanks for the invite, though.

I hold my breath as little gray dots appear on my screen. I'm hoping she's not going to ask for details and the reason why I'm staying away longer than I originally planned.

Sad face! I hope you and Kai are having a wonderful time. Let's catch up when you get back.

She ends her message with a string of emojis, and I respond with a simple thumbs-up and a love heart. My fingers are shaking as the words *when you get back* pulse on the screen in front of me.

When I get back?

A panic that is becoming all too familiar slices through me. I try to cut off the emotion and focus on the positive fact that I don't have to explain myself yet. I can only imagine what the mothers and nannies at Kai's various playgroups and activities are going to say.

Ugh, I don't even want to think about it.

Placing my phone back down, I grip the edge of the counter and bite my lips together.

"So, I really love having you here." Rachel grins at me, obviously trying to make me feel better. "It's nice to have a cooking buddy. Have you always enjoyed working in the kitchen?"

"Not really." I shake my head. "My mom was the kitchen queen, and whenever I tried to make something, she'd always take over under the guise of helping." I roll my eyes. "I've had to learn how to cook all on my own, and I've had my fair share of disasters in the last few years. I'm getting better. Slowly."

Rachel laughs. "How about baking? You seem pretty good at that."

"Well, I definitely prefer it. I didn't get many chances as a kid, although I used to try at Baxter's house." I laugh as memories hit me from all sides. "His mom was a bit of a health nut, so it was hard to find the right ingredients for baking something delicious."

"Was she?" Rachel's face lights with curiosity. "Wow. I didn't know that. Baxter never talks about her." She lets out a soft snort. "He hardly talks at all, actually. The guy likes to stick to himself."

I watch her face, wondering if she'll give more away, but she doesn't say anything, and I can just imagine. I mean, when we were young, he didn't have a bunch of friends, but he definitely hung out with me any chance he could. But the day his mom died in that car accident, both Baxter and his dad shut down. It was like the light went right out of both of them. I was devastated, too, but didn't really have time to process it because I was trying to adjust to married life, deal with the fact that I was pregnant, and still get a good score on my SATs.

Seriously, it was crazy and all too much.

All I wanted to do was run to Baxter and hold him, comfort him... but I couldn't. And the day after graduation, he left.

"Hey, you okay?"

I jerk when Rachel's hand brushes my arm.

"Yeah, sorry. Just thinking."

"I know you've probably got a lot on your mind right now. I don't know all the details, but I'm a really good listener if you want to offload."

My shoulders slump with a sigh, and I plunk onto the kitchen stool. "I was just remembering my wedding and that time of my life."

"Oh yeah?" Rachel's expression turns sympathetic. "How long have you been married? Or is this too painful to talk about?"

"Not painful..." I shake my head and wince as though it is. "I was only eighteen. Our parents really wanted us to tie the knot before the baby was born. And Hudson's mom in particular couldn't bear the thought of me showing when I was walking down the aisle, so we had this little wedding thrown together in like three weeks flat." My throat grows thick. "We didn't have a honeymoon. I was at school two days later, going to class and trying to study for my SATs. We lived with his parents until after graduation, which was... *awful.*" I bulge my eyes. "I mean, they're not bad people, it's just not a comfortable way to start a marriage. I felt like I was under a microscope, and my mom was constantly calling and checking in as well." I huff and stick out my tongue. "That summer, his parents let us live in their rental, and I guess it got a little easier after that, but it just..." My shoulder hitches. "Wasn't what I'd dreamed as a kid, you know? Some shotgun wedding and then moving in with my in-laws. It..." I let out a humorless laugh and shake my head.

"Yeah, I can imagine." Rachel starts cleaning up the counter, throwing away eggshells and wiping up flour dust. "So, the fact that you're staying here for a while... does that mean your marriage is not in a great place or...?"

"I guess that's one way of putting it." My shoulders hitch with a hopeless sigh. "I caught him cheating on me."

"Oh shit."

"Yep." I nod. "They were doing it in the shower."

Rachel gasps. "You walked in on it?"

"Yeah." My eyes bulge, a shudder running through me. "And I have no idea if it was a onetime thing or if he's been seeing this woman for months. He works long hours in the city, so who the hell knows."

"Oh, sweetie. I'm so sorry." She means it. I can tell by her sincere expression and gentle tone.

I rest my elbow on the counter, cradling my chin with a sad pout. "I really don't know what to do other than ignore him for now. Though that's probably immature. I need to face this, but I just want to hide and pretend like it isn't happening to me."

Rachel nods, rinsing off the dishcloth before turning to face me. "Do you still love him?"

For some reason, the answer doesn't come quickly. It's not that I'm struggling to word things just right. I guess I'm just trying to figure out what I'm feeling.

Eventually, I nod and murmur, "He's the father of my child."

"But do you really love him? Do you feel it here?" Rachel taps her chest.

I close my eyes, thinking about my time with Hudson. We did have some good moments. When we first got together, I adored him. I was obsessed. He was everything. And then I got pregnant, and it was terrifying. Marrying him was the only option our families would let us consider, so we did, and I guess it was pretty good. His proposal was this big romantic gesture, and when I said yes, the whole school cheered. It felt great. But then Kai was born, and *he* became my world. We moved to the city and Hudson got that job, and we just turned into two ships passing in the night. He was desperate to impress his bosses and rise through the ranks. He did. Fast. Because he's so good at what he does. And I made my life all about motherhood and filling the spaces for Kai when his dad couldn't be there to play with him.

Do I still love Hudson?

A part of me always will, I guess. "He's the only guy I've ever been with," I admit out loud, then feel the heat rise through my body when I think about that summer with Baxter. Our swimming hole mishap will be forever burned in my memory.

I've wondered a thousand times what would have happened if we'd slept together that day. Would he have become my boyfriend? Would Hudson have not even caught my attention?

Would my life have turned out completely differently?

"That's why the betrayal hurts so much more." Rachel's voice is soft and kind. I glance at her, and we share a sad smile that gets disrupted by the oven timer.

She takes out the next batch of scones, and we eye them up like scientists until Baxter walks through the door.

I see him from the corner of my eye and can't help turning to face him. He's so big and powerful, yet those eyes are so gentle and—

"You've shaved." I state the obvious with a wispy voice as I'm hit with a battering ram of nostalgia. Without that beard, he looks like my best friend from high school. Sure, his face is more refined and manly, but there's my BB.

And he's one hot ticket.

The pulse of desire that beats through me is intensely strong, and I jerk my eyes back to the safety of the scones so I can catch my breath before daring to look at him again.

"Yeah." He rubs his face. "Sorry I didn't get to it earlier."

My eyebrows buckle. "Why did you do it at all?"

He glances down at Kai, who's hovering behind his legs. "Thought it was about time I stopped looking like a big, scary bear." He gives me a subtle wink.

And there goes my heart, melting to putty. Baxter has always been the sweetest, most considerate guy. That's why he was my best friend.

Kai steps to the left, and I notice the hockey stick in his hands.

"Whatcha got there, kiddo?" I ask, then laugh when he gives me that hopeful smile of his. "What's up?"

My gosh, he's so cute. Those big eyes and that adorable face. My heart starts bleeding as I think about the way he has his father's nose and chin. No matter what I choose to do over Hudson, a piece of him will always stay with me.

My son looks up at the giant beside him. They share a wordless conversation of some kind, and then Baxter chuckles and looks at me. "Do you mind if I take Kai to hockey practice with me this afternoon? He's never played or seen a game, and I thought he might like it. He's got quite the swing on him." He lightly ruffles Kai's hair, and my son's smile turns shy and proud all in the same second.

"Sure, I'm okay with that. I can get you his booster seat out of my car." Crouching down beside Kai, I squeeze his shoulder and quietly double-check. "You want to go?"

He bobs his head.

"Baxter will take good care of you."

"Yes, he will," Rachel pipes up. "Baxter's the best."

Now it's his turn to look all bashful and proud.

He always was adorable.

I look up at his handsome face and can't help grinning at him. His lips curl up at the corners, and I drink him in for a second.

I've missed you so much.

The words are right on the tip of my tongue, but I can't say them. Instead, I go to grab my car keys and sort Kai out for his little adventure into town.

With Baxter.

Wow. That's a shift from the day we arrived. It hasn't taken much for my son to defrost in this place. It feels miraculous somehow. Kai's always been a slow burn when it comes to people. He watches them carefully before sharing a smile. He studies from a distance and creeps into a game after he thinks he'll enjoy it.

And now he's willing to drive off with this man he barely knows so he can watch a hockey practice.

A man I trust, even though I haven't seen him in years.

As I walk up the stairs, I can't help asking myself that

question once more. *If I hadn't chickened out that summer, would things have been different?*

And yeah, I think they would have.

Sure, Kai wouldn't exist, so obviously I'd never wish to change what happened. But for a fleeting moment, I let myself imagine that Kai is Baxter's son. And it's impossible to deny that my little boy would be having a very different life if that were the case.

CHAPTER 14
BAXTER

The arena is loud, a cacophony of slapping sticks, flying pucks, and skates slicing through the ice. My kids are working hard today, surprisingly motivated for a Thursday afternoon. There's an energy in the air. I can't explain why, but it's buzzing and electric.

"Good job. Good job." I clap. The drill I'm supervising is dynamite, and I'm getting great action from my little skaters. "Control the puck, Marty. You can do it."

I put him in a different group to Shelby today, and it seems to be bringing out the best in him. No more "I'm taller" arguments distracting the friends.

With a grin, I skate backward, giving him room to whip around the cone and head back for the goal.

"That's it! Nice!" I shout, lifting my arms as he fires and hits the back of the net.

He whoops, skating back to his line like he's just

scored in a Stanley Cup Finals game. It's impossible not to laugh as I high-five him, then turn my attention to the next player.

Rescuing a flying puck from the drill behind me, I flick it back and check on Kai. He's bundled up in the stands with my jacket wrapped around him. He looks kinda cute engulfed by my clothing with just his little head popping out the top.

Those big brown eyes, just like Tammy's, are gonna do my heart in, I swear.

I watch him studying the drills with fascination and decide I need to give him some ice time before taking him back to his mama.

Checking the clock on the wall, I bang my stick on the ground and holler, "Two minutes! Go hard. Go hard!"

The energy in the rink picks up another notch as we rush to the end of practice. Then I gather in the group of puffing, exhilarated kids.

"You guys were awesome today." They grin up at me, their tired little faces splitting into cheesy smiles. "Now, we have a game coming up this weekend, and I know you're all pumped for it. I'll figure out the roster and make sure you all get equal ice time and get to play a mix of positions. You need to be here half an hour before game time so you can get suited up before we hit the ice. Any questions?"

A little hand shoots up at the back.

"Yeah, what's up, Toby?"

"Do you know my grandpa's coming to watch me?"

"That's awesome."

"My dad's coming!" Shelby shouts.

"My mom too. And my sisters." Cora jumps in on the action, and soon everyone is telling me who's attending the game. The student coaches at the back start laughing, and I shut down this shout fest by raising my hands in the air.

They all copy me, shutting their little pieholes and giving me their attention.

"I'm stoked that we're gonna have lots of support for the game. And if you don't have anyone sticking around to watch you, don't worry about it. I'll be cheering you on, okay?"

Mike, the scrappy little kid near my right foot, nods and gives me a sad smile.

I wink at him, then point for the exit door. "Get going. Don't leave the locker rooms a mess or you'll be skating laps next practice." They scramble up to their skates and head off the rink. "And be good to your parents!" I shout after them, the same way I always do.

They laugh and wave while I skate the rink and start collecting up cones and gear. By the time I'm done, I can see the next group arriving for their practice and skate over to talk to their coach.

"You're not starting for another fifteen, right?"

He looks at the clock, giving me a friendly thumbs-up.

"Just want to give my kid a little minute on the ice if that's cool. He's never skated before."

The guy gives me a confused frown but nods. I don't know what that look is about until I jump into the stands and realize I just said *my kid*. I don't know how the hell I made that slipup. I guess it was just easier to call Kai mine than try to explain that I'm looking after a friend's kid.

That wouldn't have been hard to explain, you idiot. And now that guy thinks you've got a kid who's suddenly appeared in your life, and you've never taken him skating before!

I mentally kick myself for the faux pas and try to put on a friendly smile as I take a seat beside Kai.

"Hey, you want a turn?" I point to the rink.

He looks kind of scared, gripping the stick he hasn't let go of since I handed it to him back at the house.

"I'll be with you the whole time. It's definitely one of those things where it looks scarier than it actually is."

"I can't go fast," he murmurs.

"You don't have to."

Reaching for the skates I found him before practice, I crouch down and start loosening the laces.

"Let's take your shoes off and put these on. We're only gonna have ten minutes anyway, so you only have to try for a short second."

After a long beat, he finally mumbles, "Okay," and rips his boots off without untying them properly.

I grin and help him into his skates, then walk him down the stairs. He wobbles and nearly trips trying to adjust to the blades under his feet, so in the end, I lift him up and rest him on my hip, carrying him down to the ice.

As soon we hit that hard, cold surface, I feel that familiar sense of comfort. My dad got me on the ice when I was three. He gave me my first stick when I was four, and I've never looked back.

"Okay, buddy." I set him on his feet, and he flinches, digging his little fingers into my arm. "I've got you. Hold my hands and I'll skate you around."

With a nervous frown, he takes my hands, and I skate backward, gently gliding him around the ice. He wobbles at first but starts to gain confidence by the end of our first circuit. His lips are twitching like he wants to smile, but he's kind of too busy concentrating.

"Do you want to try on your own or keep holding my hands?"

He glances up at me, then, after a little consideration, loosens his grip and lets me go. I move back, giving him some extra space and slowly skating beside him while he inches across the ice.

"Try to glide if you can."

I show him how to push off, and he copies me, doing a half-decent job. "That's it. Now this foot... Good... Good... You got it."

A small dimple appears in his left cheek. I think of Tammy, wishing she was here to see this. Slowing down, I watch Kai pull away, imagining Tammy against the wall, clapping and cheering him on. Or maybe she's beside me, beaming as she watches her sweet little boy trying something new.

A dreamy smile tugs at my lips... until Kai lets out a short gasp and starts to fall.

It happens so fast that I can't reach him in time, and for reasons I will never understand, rather than cushioning the fall with his hands, he decides to hit the ice face-first.

"Oh shit." I dash toward the crunch, skidding to a quick stop and crouching down to help him up.

He's shaking, his eyes wide with shock as I get him back on his feet.

Brushing the ice off his face, I notice that it's already starting to swell up, his lip getting fat and purple before my eyes.

I hiss with a wince, and that's when his eyes start to tear up.

Oh shit, please don't cry on me, kid.

My internal begging goes unheeded as Kai's lips start to tremble, and then this pitiful whimper that's gonna shatter my heart pops out of him.

"It's okay. You're okay. You hit that ice pretty hard, and I bet it hurts, but you're gonna be just fine."

"Mommy," he wails, and I'm quickly feeling like the worst human on the planet as I scoop him into my arms and skate for the edge.

"Is he okay?" One of the moms stops to check as I race up the stairs.

"Yeah, we're good," I bark, probably sounding like an asshole, but I don't need a fucking audience for this.

Sitting Kai on my lap, I undo his skates with quivering fingers while he cries in my ear.

Fuck.

Tammy's gonna kill me for this.

I was supposed to be looking after her kid, and I'm bringing him home a bruised, wailing mess.

CHAPTER 15
TAMMY

"Tammy!" Baxter shouts my name, and I jerk at the panic in his voice, racing out of the kitchen and into the entryway.

I reach the reception desk and spot Baxter cradling my son like he's a precious porcelain vase. His large hand is cupping the back of Kai's head, and the worried look in his eyes makes my heat lurch.

"What happened?" I race across to them, catching Kai as he launches himself into my arms. "Oof."

"He hit the ice." Baxter runs a hand through his hair, looking as beat-up as Kai's face. "I was trying to teach him how to skate, and I should have stayed closer to him, but I thought he had his balance and then bam. Face crunch."

I brush Kai's hair back to check him out, giving him my sad smile as I take in his swollen lip and cheekbone. "Ouch, buddy. That ice really did a number on you."

"It hurts, Mommy." He lets out a hiccupping sob and rests his head against my shoulder.

"I know." Kissing his forehead, I rub his back and murmur, "Should we get you some ice?"

He jerks up to give me a horrified frown. "More ice?"

I can't help a soft laugh, which he is *not* impressed by. "Sorry. I mean like an ice pack. It might help with the bruising."

"I don't want it." His bottom lip sticks out, and then his chin bunches before he launches into a cry that looks to be breaking Baxter's heart.

"It's okay." I squeeze Baxter's forearm. "He's gonna be just fine."

"I'm so sorry. I was supposed to take care of him, and I... I..."

"You did a great job."

"What?" His voice breaks. "I did the worst job."

"No, you really didn't." Clutching my sobbing child against my chest, I pivot and walk into the kitchen, where Rachel is already waiting with an ice pack and some candy. With a little coaxing, we subdue Kai's tears, and he ends up falling asleep on my chest, the lollipop he's halfway through sticking to my shirt.

With a soft laugh, Rachel throws it out for me, and I carry Kai up to our room, settling him into bed and gently kissing his face.

His lip has already started to go down, but he'll have a nice little shiner on his face for a few days. Poor guy. I wonder if I'll ever be able to get him back on the ice. I was so touched that Baxter wanted to do that with him. Kai doesn't have many men in his life who will play sports with him. My dad's a book nerd and seems allergic to sweat. Hudson's dad has thrown a baseball with Kai a few times, but Hudson was more of a rock star than a jock... and now he's a businessman who doesn't get home before Kai goes to bed.

With a soft frown, I pad out of the room and go in search of Baxter.

I find him on the third floor, carefully painting a window frame with an unhappy scowl on his face. An old, familiar affection blooms within me. I've seen that look before. It's the one he wears when he's annoyed about something. And right now, I know he's super pissed with himself... even though he did nothing wrong.

"Hey." I capture his attention by waving my hand in his direction.

He jerks, pulling the pods from his ears and turning off his music. "Is he all right?"

"Yeah, he's sleeping. I don't know how long he'll nap for, and it's going to screw up his night routine, but..." I shrug.

"Tammy." My name sounds raspy coming out of his mouth. "I'm so sorry."

He looks tortured, and it's breaking my heart.

Stepping into the room, I take the paintbrush out of his hand, dropping it in the can before capturing his wrists and turning him to face me. "You didn't do anything wrong. You took Kai skating, and he fell over. It happens. Kids fall all the time. It was an accident."

"But I was supposed to be taking care of him. It just happened so fast and—"

"It always does. You can't catch them every time." I smile up at him, rubbing my thumb over the fine hairs on his arm and failing to ignore the strength I'm holding on to. He's pure muscle and power. I can only imagine what his body looks like under his T-shirt, but my stomach swirls with a wanton desire that's unnerving.

I swallow and focus on his face instead, and my heated yearning turns to something else. Affection scatters through me again, and I can't help smiling. I'm pretty sure I'll do anything to make him feel better right now.

So, I share a secret I've never dared to tell another soul... not even Hudson.

"I remember once, when Kai was about two... I was trying to bake in the kitchen, and he was tottering around, getting in my way. He wasn't trying to be naughty, but I was flustered and tripping over him. He was having a clingy day, and when I wouldn't pick him up, he went all quiet and sulky. Anyway, at one point, I pulled the pantry door open to grab something, and I flicked the door shut behind me—way too hard, because I was feeling frustrated—and heard this chilling scream." I close my eyes and shudder.

Baxter hisses. "You jammed his fingers in the door."

"Yep. Poor kid."

"Ouch." He winces.

"I felt so bad. It took me weeks to get over it, even though he didn't lose any fingers. I mean, they bruised up pretty good, but they didn't break, and they were back to normal before I knew it."

Baxter's shoulders relax on a sigh.

"My point is... kids heal fast, and they forgive even quicker."

"Thank God for that," he mutters.

I run my hands down to his fingers and squeeze them, loving how long and strong they are. "The trickiest part is going to be getting him back on the ice."

"He won't want to."

"Doesn't matter." I shake my head. "We have to make him or his little mind will turn what happened today into this big, terrifying thing, and it'll hold him back. Maybe next time I'll come with you, and we can do it together."

"Next time," Baxter whispers, his eyes starting to smile.

"Yeah, and sooner rather than later. Maybe we can go this weekend or something."

"My Mini Mites have a game this weekend if you want to come watch."

"Yeah, for sure. That'll be great. Kai can see kids falling over and getting back up again."

"There's definitely a lot of that." Baxter laughs, and I grin up at him, impulse taking over as I dive for his chest and wrap my arms around his waist.

"Thank you," I whisper into his shirt. "Thank you for letting us stay here."

"Of course." His large hand lands on my back, rubbing a slow line from the base to my neck and back again.

I close my eyes, sinking into the feeling of him holding me. It's so secure and warm in this place. I splay my hand across his back and hold on a little tighter, wondering if I can just stay here forever and forget the world outside this paint-fumed room.

I'll take this toxic scent for a decade if I can just keep hugging Baxter like this.

He leans down, resting his chin on the top of my head, just the way he used to. And those gentle caresses up my spine somehow become something different.

I don't know how or when the shift happened, but I sense the heat before I fully recognize it. He's not doing anything differently; it's just my body responding in ways it never has before.

Well, it did once.

At that swimming hole.

A breath catches in my throat, and suddenly Baxter jolts, letting me go like my body is literally on fire.

Could he feel it too?

Can he sense the way I'm burning for him?

When he steps back from me, I sway on my feet, feeling his loss with a powerful ache I can't define.

"I should, uh... get back to it." He points at the window frame, and all I can do is nod.

I don't know what just happened, but my cheeks feel like an inferno as I head for the door. When I reach the frame, I spin back to... I don't even know... just watch him for a second.

His ear pods are back in, and he's concentrating on his job. I think he can tell I'm watching him, but he refuses to look.

I want to know what he's thinking, but maybe I don't.

Maybe he felt a charge between us too.

Maybe he didn't.

Or maybe he stepped back because he remembered that I'm married to Hudson.

Shit, I'm married to Hudson.

The thought sits ugly inside me for a second.

My cheating spouse. Are we still married?

I don't even know.

All I do know for sure is that every time Baxter pulls away from me, it hurts.

Gripping the frame, I want to ask him why he's doing it again. I want to demand that he tell me why he walked away from our friendship back in high school.

I wanted to save it. Why weren't you there when I desperately needed you? Why'd you tell me to go? Why'd you not tell me I was wrong that day?

CHAPTER 16
BAXTER

The summer before senior year...

I've never felt humiliation like it.

This can't be happening.

I gape at my semen on Tammy's face. I gape at her surprised look of horror.

Oh fuckity-fuck!

Swiping at her cheek, I desperately try to get that white goop off her skin but accidentally push some of it into her mouth.

Shit!

She makes a gagging noise, wiping at her lips while I try to clean my hands on the grass. She's still straddling my legs, her boobs heaving as my dick gets limper by the second.

This is a nightmare. What do I say? What do I do?

I'm so fucking embarrassed!

Do I say that to her? Just own this shit or...?

She reaches for her bikini top, scrambling off my legs and turning her back so she can retie it. Her hands are shaking. So are mine. I wrestle my shorts back up and can't think of one fucking thing to say. My mouth keeps opening to fill this awkward silence, but no words are coming out.

"Um..." Tammy glances over her shoulder, her smile tight and fake. "We should probably get home soon, right? Before it gets... dark." She looks up at the sky, and we both cringe. Sunset is hours away. Neither of us are due home anytime soon. She's bailing—as fast as she can.

I want to make it easy on her, but then I also don't.

We should talk about this.

But... I still can't think of anything to say. My throat is so swollen, I'm struggling to swallow, let alone form words.

Our eyes connect, but only for the briefest second.

I stare at the water, wanting to dive back into it and hide beneath the surface.

"I'm, ummm... damn, this is so awkward." Tammy covers her face, then runs a hand over her head. "I think maybe I'm not ready for this."

"To talk?" I mumble.

"No. Sex. I'm not ready for sex yet. I don't know what came over me just then. Maybe curiosity or..." She points to the swimming hole behind her. "Maybe there's something in the water." Her laughter is soft and pitiful. "I just think... well, you and I are probably better off as friends, you know?"

She rests her hand on my leg, and I flinch away from her touch. I didn't mean to—it just happened.

Curling her fingers into a soft fist, she rests it on her knee and stares at the grass. "We shouldn't cross that line into something more. It won't work. You're too good of a friend, you know? I don't want to lose that."

"Yeah," I croak. It's all I can manage. I want to tell her she's wrong, that I've loved her for years and it could totally work. We don't have to have sex yet, but I could be her boyfriend. Can't I just hold her hand and call her mine? That would be more than enough.

I've wanted that for so long, and now is the perfect chance to tell her that we can be friends *and more*.

But I can't do it.

She wants out of this awkward situation.

She wants friendship and nothing more.

I'm gutted.

It makes it impossible to look at her as we pack up our stuff. Thank God I'm going away tomorrow.

As much as I love her company, I want to get as far from her as I can right now.

Shit. I came on her face.

I'm such a fucking idiot.

It just happened before I could stop it, and now I've ruined everything between us.

We could have gone all the way if I'd been able to control myself.

My insides shrivel as we walk back home not saying anything to each other. It's the longest march of my life. When we reach our houses, there's no standard high five or secret handshake. We just give each other one long, last look and don't even say goodbye.

CHAPTER 17
TAMMY

The summer before senior year...

Baxter left this morning, and I didn't even see him go. I stayed buried under my covers, listening to his family car pull out of the driveway. I cried myself to sleep the night before. I didn't know what to do with all the emotions coursing through me.

He touched my boobs. No one has ever done that before. He kissed me like I was his oxygen. His tongue was warm and delicious. The feel of his strong arms around me, his hand cupping the back of my head, the way his breaths mingled with mine. The hardness of his muscles... and his dick.

It all felt so amazing. Like nothing I've ever experienced.

But then it got awkward.

I've swung from hating myself for kissing him to wishing I'd had the guts to wipe his cum off my face and ask him to touch me some more.

It was a compliment that he came so fast, right? It means I turned him on.

But that thought terrifies me too.

We've been best buds since we were kids. Going all romantic and sexual changes things between us. Suddenly, I was afraid we'd lose what we had and that broke my heart. So I told him I wasn't ready and that his friendship means more to me than anything else.

But I've texted him twice since his car pulled away, and I still haven't heard back from him.

Is he icing me out because I wouldn't put out?

The thought made me rage for a second, then had me crying all over again. Baxter isn't like that, is he?

He's my friend.

My BB.

It's not until after dinner that I finally hear back from him. It's just a boring informative text telling me he's arrived at his grandparents' house. I text back a lame:

Have a good time.

What the fuck?

That's not who we are. All formal and—

My thumbs hover over the phone screen, trying to think of something cool and funny to stay, but all I can picture is his ashen face as he tried to wipe semen off my skin and then his look of horror as some went into my mouth.

Sure, I didn't love the taste and texture, but that's because it was like nothing I'd tasted before. That gag reflex was more of a shock than anything. I'm not exactly up to the play when it comes to things like sex. Mom isn't open about the topic, my sister and I aren't very close, and my girlfriends get the giggles whenever we talk about blow jobs or orgasms. They're as clueless as I am.

And there's no way in hell I'm telling them what went down with Baxter.

I just need to figure this out.

Everything's going to be okay. I'll leave Baxter alone while he hangs with his grandparents, and then when he gets back, we can put this whole awkward thing behind us.

That's my plan, anyway... until my parents introduce me to the sexiest guy I have ever seen at church on Sunday morning.

His name is Hudson Clark, and he's got a smile to die for. He gazes down at me like I'm pretty and then asks me if he can give me a ride to school the next morning. I say yes without a second thought, and it isn't until I get home and see Baxter's car in the drive that I remember I usually ride with him.

Feeling kind of bad, I text him to welcome him home

and then tell him I'm catching a ride with a new friend who wants me to show them around.

I don't know why I feel bad about that, but somehow there's this guilt that burns when I press Send.

Baxter doesn't reply that night. I don't know why, but it hurts, so I get into Hudson's car the next morning and focus on his beautiful smile and the way his eyes track my body.

He makes me feel pretty and wanted. Like I'm something special.

We listen to music on the way to school, and he tells me all about his big shift to Gladstone and how his mother wanted a break from the city. His father is in finance and can work from anywhere, so they made the move.

"Sure, it's hard leaving all my friends for just the last year of high school, but family first, right?"

He beams at me, and I feel my heart swelling and pulsing in time to the beat of the radio. He's so gorgeous and dreamy and obviously sweet.

We end up spending the day together. I walk him to the office so he can finish his registration, and then I volunteer to show him around the school. I introduce him to all my friends. They instantly love him.

Except Baxter.

He shakes Hudson's hand but doesn't smile.

He nods at Hudson's introduction but doesn't offer anything about himself, and it pisses me off.

Why does Baxter always have to be so shut off all the time?

I frown at him behind Hudson's back, and he just gives me a sad smile and walks out of the cafeteria without a backward glance.

I can't even describe the emotions running through me right now. On the one hand, I've just met a guy who's giving me major butterflies and love bubbles. On the other, I'm watching the person I thought would be my friend for life walking away like I mean nothing to him.

CHAPTER 18
BAXTER

Present day...

She means everything to me. That's why I'm hiding away upstairs, painting and not engaging with her.

Yes, it seems idiotic, but that hug yesterday—that one simple hug—was enough to remind me why I have to keep my distance.

I'm still in love with her.

I've known this all along, but now that she's here, it's so much more potent. Watching her with Kai, seeing her interact with my friends. She may have changed some, but she's still Tammy at her core. And I love that woman.

Being around her is wonderful and heartbreakingly painful at the same time.

I want to grab her in my arms and beg her never to go

back to Hudson. I want to promise her that I can take care of her and love her the way she deserves.

I want to tell her how I feel, but that's so unfair, right?

How can I dump that on her?

She's got enough to deal with and doesn't need my emotional angst on top of it all.

I have to stay strong and silent, just the way I did in high school.

Hudson captured her right from the start, and I didn't want to get in the way of her happiness. Her smiles around that guy were full beam. The look of adoration on her face every time he walked into a room. Being around them was torture, so it made keeping my distance a little more motivating. But I didn't just do it for me.

Hudson would have seen me as a threat. I could tell the second I met him that he was a territorial prick. But Tammy wanted him so badly, and I had to back off.

Maybe I backed away too far, I don't know.

I've never been an expert at relationships. Any kind. Talking is hard. Opening up and being vulnerable? I don't even know how to do that shit.

It's easier to stay closed off and mind my own business.

I did it in high school; I can do it again.

Tammy needs a safe place to stay while she figures out what to do about Hudson. I can give that to her. And I won't go messing with her head sharing everything I feel. She doesn't need that pressure.

And if I'm honest with myself, I doubt I'd ever be able to find the words.

I couldn't back then.

I didn't even know what to text her while I was sulking at my grandparents' place.

When I got back, I looked in the mirror and told my reflection that I needed to get the fuck over myself. I promised I would talk to Tammy as I drove her to school the next day. I was geared up. Terrified but willing.

Then she texted to say she was catching a ride with someone else.

I got to school, saw them flirting by her locker, and I knew it was the end of us.

There was no point in trying to say anything after that. So I backed off.

But now could be your second chance!

The voice in my head is urgent and desperate and... insane.

She's married.

She's come here for a safe place to lick her wounds, not finally find out that I'm so far gone for her that I've never even slept with another woman.

Dipping the roller in the paint tray, I practice the perfect technique YouTube taught me and come away with just the right amount of paint. I'm about to touch it to the wall when I hear a scampering outside the door.

Shit!

Whipping around, I'm seconds away from barking a few swift orders at Fezzik—Stop! Sit! Stay!

But instead I find myself staring at a curious face with pale bruises on his cheek and lip.

I wince, wondering how many times I have to apologize before I start to feel better.

His little fingers curl around the door handle.

"Fezzik still downstairs?" I gently ask.

He nods.

"You know not to let him past the gate, right?"

He nods again.

"I just don't want little puppy paws painting the hallways, you know?"

His big brown eyes stare me down, and I try to smile but give up with a sigh. Pointing at my cheek, I then point to his and ask, "Does it still hurt?"

Those little shoulders shrug, and I don't know what to say next, so I do the only thing I can think of.

Grabbing the spare roller, I hold it out to him. "Wanna help? I can show you how."

He tips his head, hesitating, until I crack a grin.

"There's no ice involved. I promise."

This gets his lips moving, and he gives me a cautious smile while creeping into the room.

"Okay. Here we go." With gentle prompting, I show him how to dip the roller and wipe off the excess paint. There's a strong chance that he'll screw up this wall, but I can just paint over it, right? We can spare a little so this guy can have some fun.

"And now we roll it on the wall. Like this." I hold his

hand, guiding the roller up and down the flat surface with clean strokes.

He giggles, reminding me of his mama, then shows off his dimples.

"Good?"

He nods, more enthusiastically this time, and sets about painting the lowest part of the wall. I paint above him, enjoying the rhythmic sounds of our rolls and then smiling when Kai dips his roller again, forgetting to wipe off the excess and splattering a massive blob on the wall. He gasps and scrambles to fix it, desperately trying to right his wrong, and I can't do anything but laugh.

Sweeping my roller down, I catch the drips, then lightly paint his arm.

He spins around with a shocked gasp, and the sound that pops out of him next takes me back to my childhood in a heartbeat.

His laughter rings out loud and clear, his dimples on full display as he dances around the paint tray and tries to get me back.

CHAPTER 19
TAMMY

"Tammy, this is unacceptable," Mom barks in my ear.

My muscles are so taut, I'm surprised they're not snapping. Talking to my mother always has this effect on me. "It's not up to you."

"He is my grandchild, and you are my daughter. I won't let you do this."

I grit my teeth and try to stay calm. "I can make my own decisions. I'm an adult now."

"Well, you're certainly not acting like one!"

"Mom!" I snap. "He cheated on me."

"So you just leave him?"

My mouth drops open. "What do you expect me to do?"

"I expect you to at least talk to him. You don't just walk away without a word. He's been losing his mind trying to reach you, and you cut him off at every turn. He was in tears last night talking to your father."

My insides pinch into such a tight knot it's painful.

"If he loves me so much, why'd he sleep with someone else?"

Mom sighs. "Because he made a mistake. He's very sorry. And you would know that if you just talked to him. This is why I hate texting! Cell phones are a design of the devil."

I roll my eyes, tempted to tell her that she's talking to me on my cell phone right now.

"They're just an excuse not to communicate properly."

"Mom—"

"No. Don't you cut me off again."

I hold my breath, letting her say her piece. I want to hang up, but my inner child wouldn't dare. The wrath of Mrs. Tan is a fierce one.

"I know he hurt you, and you have every right to be mad. But you have a son together, and you can't just turn your back on your marriage. Go to counseling. Figure it out."

"What if I don't want to figure it out?" The question takes me by surprise, and I blink at the wall. Huh. I did not know I was feeling that way.

"Tamara, don't talk nonsense."

I ignore her and keep going, the revelations coming to me as I say them out loud. "Why can't I experience life without him? Why do I have to stay married to him?"

"Tamara," Mom grits out. "You're not seriously going to divorce him. That is absolutely shameful."

"People get divorced all the time."

"Not in Gladstone, they don't!"

I roll my eyes. "Yeah, well, I don't live in Gladstone anymore." *Thank God!*

"We still do! Think about our reputation. The shame your sister has put us through over the years with her drinking and partying."

"She was a teenager cutting loose, Mom."

"She got arrested once."

"For jaywalking!"

"That's not the point. You father will never live down the embarrassment of having to collect his child from the police station. Don't you dare be like her. Don't put your father and me through this. Please."

"Officer Dawson didn't have to arrest her. He was being completely over the top trying to make some stupid point because he didn't like her. People know that. You can't keep carrying that around with you. It's ridiculous."

"Oh, *I'm* being ridiculous? I'm not the one planning on leaving a perfectly good marriage!" Mom snips. "Now, tell me where you are. I'll come and get you myself."

I clamp my teeth together, struggling for calm as I repeat this part of the conversation yet again. "I don't want to tell you where I am. I don't want to tell Hudson where I am. I just want some space to think and breathe!"

"But you're not thinking clearly."

"Maybe I am." I square my shoulders, lifting my chin and knowing full well that if my mother were standing in this room, I would not have the courage to be so bold.

"You're not being practical. How are you supposed to support yourself and Kai? You have a child to feed and raise. You're denying him his father. And a safe, secure life."

"He's safe and secure with me, and not once have I denied him access. If Hudson ever asked to speak with him, I'd hand the phone over in a second."

"Yet you won't tell him where you are."

"I don't want him showing up here unannounced. He needs to respect what I'm going through right now."

"Yet you won't respect him."

"He cheated!" I shout. "He doesn't deserve anything from me!" My hand flies into the air, slapping back against my thigh as I let out an exasperated scoff.

Mom's sigh is heavy. I can feel the weight of it from miles away, and my shoulders slump without my say-so. "I know he made a huge mistake. But Tamara, he's your meal ticket. You live in a beautiful home that most people would give anything to spend one night in. You can buy whatever you want. You don't have to take a calculator to the grocery store, and Kai has a good, secure life. He will go to the best schools, and you don't have to be a working mother. Do you have any idea how lucky you are?"

I close my eyes, hearing the pain in Mom's voice, knowing all the things she sacrificed over the years by marrying a man who would never earn much over the minimum wage. She went back to work full-time when I was just one, and she's always envied the time and attention I've been able to give Kai. She would have done anything to be a stay-at-home mother. But there were bills to pay and two daughters to feed. That's why I spent so much time at Baxter's house growing up. That's probably one of the reasons she didn't like Mrs. Brown. She was jealous, and it's only in my adulthood that I've been able to understand it.

"If you choose this solo-mother path, you'll be working all the time. You'll never see Kai. You'll be too stressed and tired to play with him and give him the attention he deserves. I don't want that for him... or you."

"But you're happy for me to be in a loveless marriage?"

"You love each other." Her voice pitches with disbelief. "Of course you love each other. So he strayed a little. He wants you back. That's love, darling. You forgive. You work through it. You move on."

My soul feels gray and depleted as I plunk onto the end of the bed, fighting tears. Guilt wraps its talons around my heart, squeezing until my chest starts to hurt. I rub the spot below my collarbone, but it does nothing to chase away this aching disquiet.

Mom lets me sniffle in silence for a few moments before softly murmuring, "I know this is hard and I'm hurting for you. I am. But you need a voice of reason in your life right now. A little practicality to speak over all this emotion you're battling."

I fist my flowy dress, crinkling the fabric beneath my fingers.

"You can't just run away. Your friend Baxter always used to do that, and it solved nothing."

My blood runs cold at the mention of him. If Mom knew he was the one I'd run to, she'd hit the roof.

"Do you remember? He'd run and hide when he was upset, and you'd get so frustrated with him."

I bite the inside of my cheek.

"And now you're doing the same thing to Hudson. Things don't get resolved this way. They fester and turn nasty."

My swallow is thick and audible. She knows I'm listening, and so she keeps torturing me.

"Be smart about this. You're not the only person you have to think about. Kai deserves a stable life. And you can't deny that Hudson is stable. He'll provide for you. I know you're probably sitting there second-guessing yourself, wondering if you should have married him. You probably felt a little forced into things because of the baby, but it's a good match. I never would have wanted you to end up with someone like that Baxter boy. As soon as things got a little too tough, he would have been out the door, hiding away and leaving you high and dry. You don't deserve that."

I don't deserve infidelity either.

"Tamara, are you listening to me? You haven't said a word."

I let out a dry laugh and shake my head. There are so many things I could say right now, but I'm not ready to do everything she's telling me. Maybe it's immature, but I don't really care right now. I'm not ready to go back to Hudson... and so I take the easy out. "I heard every word, Mom. And I appreciate that you care so much about me and Kai, but I'm not ready to fix this. I don't want to go back to a man who cheated on me. How am I ever supposed to trust him again?

"Now, I'm safe. Kai's safe. He's fed. He's watered. He's happy. And I feel... free." I blink, realizing it for the first time. I *do* feel free, and I can't even explain why.

"So, it's divorce, then? Without even trying?"

"Yeah, Mom." My voice quakes. "It's divorce."

"But—"

"I'll talk to you later." I hang up before she can argue with me and drop the phone on my bed.

Splaying my fingers, I stare down at my wedding and engagement rings, twisting them around my finger and feeling a deep sense of sadness. My fingers start to shake as I sink my teeth into my bottom lip and wriggle the rings off, fisting them in my right hand while I stare at the tan lines on my naked ring finger.

Am I really doing this?

"Shit." I close my eyes and set my tears free.

I hate that Mom spoke so practically about everything. I hate that she's got some really solid points.

I can't just sponge off Baxter and his friends. Guests will be arriving soon. Kai and I will have to move out, find a place. I'll need to get a job. Kai should properly start preschool soon to prepare for kindergarten, and I'll need to figure out where we're going to live.

It's all so overwhelming.

Can I do this?

Or should I just crawl back to Hudson and accept what he has to offer—a stable life with a side of mistrust? Because how can I ever really trust him again? Every time he calls to tell me he'll be home late… how will I know he's not hooking up with another woman?

For that reason alone, divorce makes so much sense. I let that bubbling anger surge through my stomach as I slump back against the pillows and stare up at the ceiling. My insides start to ache as I imagine my life as a solo parent—working, rushing around, stressed. Do I seriously want to put Kai through that? His needs have to come first, right?

But do they always?

Don't you deserve a little love too?

Someone who puts you first and makes you feel like you're the only woman in the world?

Closing my eyes, I shake my head to rid myself of that fanciful thought. Does anyone ever really get that?

The way Casey watches Caroline zips through my head, followed swiftly by the joy that washes over Liam's face every time Rachel enters a room.

Maybe that kind of love does exist.

But could it ever exist for me?

What are my chances of meeting someone when I have a kid in tow?

If I divorce Hudson, there's a strong possibility that I'll be single for the rest of my life.

That's harrowing. I rest my hand on my stomach, gripping my dress again and resisting the urge to throw up.

Glancing at the bedside clock, I check the time and am surprised by how late it's gotten. Kai will probably be after a snack by now.

Actually, where is he?

I bolt upright, searching the room in case he quietly snuck in while I was distracted by my phone call.

"Kai?" I softly call out.

Getting off the bed, I place my rings on the nightstand and stare at them for a long beat before walking out of the room and hunting the second floor.

I reach the gate that's blocking the stairs for Fezzik and figure Kai wouldn't have climbed over it, but then I hear his laughter and I pause.

"Kai?"

What's he doing up there?

Oh no! I hope he's not getting into the paint! Baxter's been working way too hard and—

Another laugh reaches me, and I recognize it straight away.

Baxter?

Climbing over the gate, I run up the stairs and follow the sound of their voices.

Moments later, I'm peeking through a half-open doorway, and my heart melts on the spot.

My little guy is painting the wall, his ragged, untamed lines so chaotic compared to the perfectly neat ones

Baxter is doing above. BB doesn't seem to mind. He's moving behind Kai and painting over his work like it's no bother at all.

Music is coming from a speaker in the corner, and Kai trots back over to the paint tray, dipping the roller in, then looking up at Baxter with a cheeky grin.

"Don't you do it." Baxter laughs.

Kai's giggle is adorable as he runs the roller up Baxter's jeans before jumping over to the wall.

Bax makes a big show of his displeasure while Kai giggles and squeals, leaning away when Baxter comes after him with his own roller. I can see the paint on his arms already and figure this must have been going on for a while.

They haven't noticed me yet, and I'm glad, because I just want to stand here for a minute and watch them.

My son is getting to experience the awesomeness that is Baxter Brown.

I remember that time we painted my room. I didn't tell my parents we were doing it, and they threw a fit when they got home and found Baxter and me caked in bright orange paint. The walls of my room were jarringly vivid, but I loved them. Baxter's proud smile was everything, until my mother and father yelled him out of the house and told him to stay the hell away from me.

Thankfully, he ignored them, and we snuck to our few secret hiding spots until Mr. Brown managed to smooth things over a week later. Baxter was allowed back under very strict conditions.

At first, I was worried that my parents would totally screw up my friendship with Baxter, but they never could.

No, I left that job up to me and my stupid mouth that just had to kiss him.

My insides clench.

It wasn't just that afternoon that pushed him away.

And it wasn't like I pushed him that hard. I nudged, and he ran a mile. After that, the distance between us just got bigger and bigger.

Then when I needed him the most, he was too far away to reach.

My heart starts to cry as I think about that night I went to him in tears and the despondent look on his face when he told me to leave...

CHAPTER 20
BAXTER

The night Tammy found out she was pregnant...

Tammy's tears have always been my undoing.

Knowing she's upset kills me.

And even though we're not really friends anymore, I can't ignore what I've just seen.

She's sitting on her bed, sobbing into her hands so loudly that I can actually hear her.

As usual, her parents aren't home, and she's all by herself. Her sister's away at college now, and even if she was around, she probably wouldn't bother to check on her.

Where the fuck is Hudson? Shouldn't he be there comforting her?

Unless they've broken up. Is that why she's so sad?

Hope sparks. Selfish, desperate hope.

Edging to the window, I open it all the way and call through the space between our houses.

"TT. What's the matter?"

She keeps her face covered, but I see the way her shoulders ping. I know she's heard me.

Resting my elbows on the frame, I lick my lips and try again. "Come on. You can talk to me."

Her red-rimmed eyes appear—so glassy and puffy. My heart hurts watching her like this. "Can I?"

The question, said with such stony coldness, makes my stomach writhe. "Of course you can."

She shakes her head, slashing tears off her face and sniffing.

"Please. I hate seeing you like this. What happened?"

"I can't tell you."

"Come on. You can tell me anything."

With a huff, she gets off the bed and walks to her window. For a second, I think she's about to close the curtains on me, but instead she slides the window open and stares at me with this desolate frown. "I can't tell you this."

My lips pinch with frustration, and more than half a year's worth of regret piles on me—hot and smothering. Before last summer, we had zero secrets between us. At least I think we did. Now she's living this whole other life with Hudson and her friends, and I'm on the outside looking in. Watching her laugh and have fun while I stand in the cold, unable to interact with her because every time Hudson touches her, I want to break his fingers. And every time she smiles at him like he hung the moon, my own heart shatters into a thousand pieces.

Gripping the frame, I try one more time. "Did Hudson... hurt you or something? Did he dump you or—"

"No," she snaps, her frown deepening.

"Then why are you so sad?"

"I'm not sa..." Her voice peters out, her body slumping like she can't bear this weight by herself. "I'm just... scared."

The word jolts me, my protective instincts shifting into overdrive. "Of what?"

She bites her lips together and shakes her head.

"I'm coming over." I move away from the window.

"No, don't." She holds out her hand, but I ignore it, grabbing my phone and shoving it into my pocket.

"If you're scared, I'm gonna be there with you. I don't care what the problem is. You shouldn't be alone right now."

"I don't need you to sit with me." Her voice squeaks, fresh tears spilling out of her eyes when I move back to the window.

"Tammy," I whisper, and her shoulders start to shake.

"I can't be here." Her voice pitches. "I can't do this."

She's not making sense, but I'll do anything she wants

me to right now. I have to help her. I have to stop those tears from falling. "Tell me what you need. I'll do it."

"I don't know. I just…" She shakes her head, looking more lost than I've ever seen her. It's so unnerving, I end up taking charge.

That's not usually my role, but she's falling apart right now.

"Put on a jacket, grab a flashlight, and meet me at your back gate. Let's go to the treehouse, okay?"

My suggestion surprises her enough to stop her shoulders shaking. She looks up at me and then nods. "Okay."

And five minutes later, we're tramping through the darkness toward the edge of the forest. We started building the treehouse when we were eleven. We wanted it ready by the summer and spent every spare weekend we could finding bits of wood and adding it to the structure. My dad found out about our project a few weeks in and came to check on it… and basically rebuilt the thing so it was up to code. He'd get home from work and disappear for a few hours, and it took me three days to figure out where he was going. By the time I showed up, he'd completed the structure, and then Tammy and I filled it with all our shit. She called them treasures, while most people would call it junk. To us, we were kings of the realm. Tammy didn't want to be a queen or a princess; instead, we were warriors, guarding our keep and fighting off imaginary trolls and dragons. That was the best summer.

Even as we grew older, we'd keep using it, although we haven't been here since senior year began. And as I climb the rickety ladder, I seriously have to wonder about its safety.

I've grown even bigger this year, my hockey training contributing to my strength and muscle weight gain. But it gives me the ability to pull Tammy up with ease and make sure she's secure on the solid floor before closing the hatch.

She sets the lantern on the table and plunks down on the huge pillows Mom made for us. Dust billows up around her and she coughs, waving her hand through the air.

"Wow," she splutters. "You haven't been here in a while either, huh?"

I run my flashlight beam across the walls and nod. "Not since last summer." I can't help a soft laugh. "Remember how we did that sleepover and a frickin' woodpecker decided to have a night rave?"

She lets out a watery laugh. "That's right. I don't think I got any sleep. Plus, I was paranoid my parents would figure out I lied about going to Grace's house instead. They would have killed me if they knew I was out here with just you."

My laughter dies, my tone getting serious without me meaning to. "Still a good night, though."

"Yeah." Her voice is so wispy, I barely hear it.

Switching off my flashlight, I let the lantern take over and stare at her through the soft glow. Half her face is cast in shadow, but I can still see her chin bunching as she fights off even more tears.

"Tammy, what is it?"

She sniffs, pulling her knees to her chest and hugging them tight. "You can't tell anyone. *I* haven't even told anyone."

"You know your secrets are always safe with me." I try for a smile. "I never talk anyway, right? And who am I gonna tell? I've got like no friends this year."

Shit, I didn't mean to say that.

I clench my teeth and look away from her.

This sad silence seems to fill the air, and I don't know how to get rid of it. Threading my fingers together, I grip them so tight it hurts.

She sucks in a shaky breath. "I'm pregnant."

The world falls out from beneath me. Everything plummets, like the treehouse has just given way and there's nothing to stop me from falling to my death.

"What?" I stare across at her, unable to hide my shock.

She sniffs again. "I just took a test. Actually, I took three, and they all say the same damn thing."

"But..." My chest caves in, the air rushing out of me in a heavy whoosh. "You and Hudson are sleeping together?"

Her expression buckles when I glance at her, and she nods.

"For how long?"

Closing her eyes, she lowers her chin and mutters, "A few months. We... started just after New Year's."

"New Year's." I nod, my jaw clenching so tight I think my teeth might crack under the pressure. "I thought..." I swallow, my voice coming out hard and low. "I thought you weren't ready for sex."

CHAPTER 21
TAMMY

The night Tammy found out she was pregnant...

It's impossible not to miss the angry hurt in his voice.

His simple statement speaks volumes. His shock over the fact that Hudson and I have been sleeping together makes my insides curl and writhe. He's not asking how I'm going to cope with this or how the hell I'm supposed to tell my parents. No, he's trying to deal with the fact that I—who said I wasn't ready for sex—gave myself to Hudson when I wouldn't give myself to him.

Seriously?

Part of me wants to scream at him for being a selfish prick, but he looks so wounded right now that all I can do is stare at him.

And that's when I start to realize something I never thought of before.

That afternoon by the swimming hole... maybe it meant more to him than I realized. Maybe it wasn't just the curious fascination I'd been feeling.

Holy shit, was it more?

Had he been hoping we'd become a couple or something?

Why didn't he say anything?

My emotions are so fragile and strung out right now, I don't know whether to be touched, furious, or blindsided.

"Bax, did you—" I don't get a chance to ask my question because he talks over me.

"What are you going to do?"

"Huh?" I blink.

"About the pregnancy. You're gonna have to tell people." His sharp tone snaps me back to the problem at hand, and all I can do is stupidly nod and agree with him.

"Yeah."

"Who are you going to tell first?"

"I don't know."

"You should probably talk to Hudson. You know, because he's your... boyfriend and... the father." He grits out the words like they hurt him, and I can't believe I never truly noticed this before.

"Bax." I reach for his arm, but he shifts before I can touch him.

"You know, you should probably get back. Your parents are due home any minute, and they'll wonder where you are." He's looking anywhere but at me. "You should go."

A stone lodges in my throat, and I stare at his shadowed face, so set and emotionless. He's staring at the wall ahead of him, and I'd do anything to have him glance at me, flash me his sweet, lopsided smile.

I stare at him, silently begging him to look at me. But he doesn't.

"Are you coming with me?" I finally ask.

"I'll help you down." He nods.

"But you're not coming with me."

The muscles in his jaw clench, and I'm pretty sure he's never going to look at me again, let alone talk to me.

I want to ask him why he's doing this.

I want to hear him fucking say it.

Tell me why this is hurting you so badly!

Tell me why you're being a jerk and not supporting me when I need you!

But I know he never will.

Baxter's a closed book, and since I got together with Hudson, he's a freaking locked diary.

I'm not breaching those walls anytime soon, and if I'm honest, I don't have the energy to. I've got bigger problems right now, and I don't need to add Baxter's angst to my list.

Clearing my throat, I try to lift my chin, try to nod and be brave, but my courage is flailing. My soul is gasping for air, panic working through me as I inch toward the trap door. As soon as I leave this tree fort, I'm going to be vulnerable and exposed. I'm going to have to go home and call Hudson—ruin his night as well.

Then I'll have to tell my parents and... oh shit, my mom's gonna kill me.

It takes everything in me not to throw myself at Baxter and beg him to take me away from this. But I'm not his problem anymore.

I chose Hudson, right?

The trap door creaks as it opens, and Baxter's strong hand catches my arm when I start to descend. For a second, I think he's trying to pull me back up, but he's just helping me down. When I hit the ground, I lift my lantern to spot his face, and I swear I see tears in his eyes.

My lips part in surprise, because Baxter is not a crier. He keeps those emotions in check. Always.

But not tonight.

His eyes are glassy as I gape up at him, and then that trap door snaps shut... and I know we're done for good now.

The thought is devastating, and I stagger my way home, sobs working through me until I reach my back door and slump on the grass in the yard.

Dad finds me out there when he gets home. He's mystified by my weird behavior and doesn't know what to do. Wrapping me up, he guides me inside, and I'm forced to tell my parents the truth.

They're pissed at my reckless, ungodly behavior and immediately call Hudson's parents. Then the two of us are soon sitting on the couch being yelled at by four irate adults who have obviously forgotten what it's like to be a teenager in love. They're each taking turns, and all we can do is stare at each other. He's going into shock and so am I, but then his fingers thread through mine, and I know I'm not completely alone.

His thumb rubs over my knuckles as his parents inform us that we have to get married immediately.

I'm so numb, I can't even fight them on this.

The four parents are in agreement, and we just have to go along with it, because this is Gladstone, and teenagers out of wedlock are not allowed to have sex.

"You haven't told anyone else, have you?" Mom's sharp glare makes me shrink.

I lie and shake my head.

"Good." Mrs. Clark nods. "Well, it's settled, then. We'll throw together a wedding and get you two hitched before she starts to show."

My father rolls his eyes. "People in this town aren't stupid. They're going to figure it out."

"Yes, but we're doing the right thing," Mom retorts. "So we won't be judged as harshly."

Nausea rolls through me, the weight of all this feeling like too much as our mothers go into planning mode and start picking out a date.

"They have their SATs soon. Let's get this done before that starts," Mrs. Clark murmurs, her head bent over her diary, while my mother checks the calendar on the wall like we're booking in a family dinner or something.

Shit, I'm getting married.

And by the end of this year, I'll be a mother.

Shit. Shit. Shit!

I feel like my world is crumbling around me and I'm helpless to stop it.

As I sit there on the couch, holding Hudson's hand, all I want is Baxter. I want him to walk through the door and take me away from this.

But he's never gonna do that.

Because I chose Hudson.

And without meaning to, I lost my best friend.

The thought brings on a fresh wave of tears, and I start to cry all over again. Hudson seems to snap out of his shocked reverie and pulls me close, kissing my forehead and murmuring that he loves me... and that everything's going to be okay.

But it's not.

Nothing is ever going to be the same again, and I mourn my childhood like I'm attending its funeral, weeping for what was and what I can never have again.

CHAPTER 22
BAXTER

Present day...

"Fezz, c'mere, boy." I click my fingers and beckon him back to me.

His little ears perk up and he trots back through the grass, having to jump over longer patches. It's going to be snowing in the next month or so. That's gonna be fun to see. The little guy hasn't really been around too much snow yet. He was only a puppy at the end of last winter, and I can just picture him jumping into the backyard and disappearing in a mound of white powder.

It makes me laugh. We'll have to keep a close eye on the little guy.

I crouch low, petting his body while his tail wags. His little paws land on my knee, and he gives me a doggy smile. I really do love the guy. I know he's not mine, but I'm stoked to be one of his faves.

And I think Kai is fast becoming one too.

It's been a week since he smashed his face on the ice, and I was so relieved that I managed to get him back onto it. They came last Saturday and watched my Mini Mite game. It was pretty cool having them there, cheering on my team and watching me coach the chaos. My team lost, but the way Tammy and Kai cheered, you'd think we'd won a major final. I stared across the rink, loving her dimples and the way the pom-pom on her beanie danced when she pumped her arm and clapped. Kai got into it, too, his little legs swinging, and for just a second, I imagined they were mine.

I let myself pretend that we'd gone all the way that summer. That Tammy had become my girl and married me instead. Kai was ours, and Hudson didn't exist. We were the Browns. Baxter, Tammy, and Kai Brown.

Damn, I wanted that to be true in ways I could never express.

But it never will be.

Kai is Hudson's son, and nothing will ever change that.

Reality slaps me upside the head, and I focus back on Fezzik, picking up a small stick and hurling it through the air. With a happy bark, he chases after it, and my mind takes me back to Sunday, when Casey got Kai back on the ice. Seriously, the guy's a miracle worker. For someone who thought he couldn't be a dad, he's pretty fucking awesome with kids.

Kai whined and worried as Tammy laced his boots.

"It's going to be fine. There are four of us here to catch you, and even if you do fall again, you're not going to land on your face this time, because you're gonna put your hands out like this." She showed him once more, and he scowled at her.

But then Casey cajoled him, and then Caroline fell over, landing on her butt and laughing her head off. Casey helped her back to her feet, holding her and rubbing her ass with a playful grin.

Kai watched them having fun on the ice, saw the way she got back up and didn't cry.

He inched to the edge of the rink.

I jumped onto the ice and skated circles around Casey and Caroline while Tammy held Kai's hand and tried to encourage him.

"Come on, kid. You can do it." Casey skated across, held out his hands, and Kai took them.

We then spent the next hour building up his confidence, and by the time Tammy's teeth were chattering, Kai was skating between us, launching himself from one set of arms until he fell into the next.

It was pretty triumphant, and I bought us all ice cream to celebrate. Tammy seemed really grateful but only picked at her sundae. Casey ended up finishing it for her, and I sat there worrying that she was looking pale.

She'd seemed a bit off, and I was desperate to talk to

her about it, but once we got back to Ponderosa, she lightened up and has been relatively happy since.

Rachel's been keeping her busy, and she even met Vanessa yesterday. The uptight woman gave her the once-over. Tammy handled it like a pro and even responded politely when Vanessa told her that she would be moving out of that room before November first and needed to arrange other accommodations.

Tammy got super quiet after that, but I told her I'd help with it.

She gave me a tight smile and nodded. "I know you will."

Then she walked out of the room. I shared a glance with Rachel, who looked kind of pained. "I think she's starting to realize that she needs to earn some money, and she's really not sure how."

"We'll look after her."

"I know you want to, Bax." Rachel's eyes shone with understanding. She knows what Tammy means to me. I told her and Lani about it months ago. Of course, I didn't expect Tammy and Kai to show up when I was sharing that shit, but here they are and... I still haven't done anything about it.

What am I waiting for?

I guess I wanted to know for sure that Tammy had left Hudson.

Well, it's been two weeks, and she still hasn't said one word about returning to him. Plus, I noticed she's not wearing her rings anymore. That means it must be over, right? Which means I could probably tell her how I feel and that I'd do anything to keep her and Kai safe. I want to provide for them, give them a home.

But would that just freak her out?

I shake my head with a huff, wishing I could be more decisive over this, have more courage. But there's so much at stake. If I bear my soul and she's not interested, that will be so awkward, and I don't want her to feel like she's gotta leave… and I don't want to be in this house trying to avoid her either.

It's better that I just keep things as they are.

Kai's doing great. He seems to love it here.

Tammy's settled… most of the time.

"Hey, Baxter!" I turn at the sound of her voice. "Sorry to bother you, but do you know where Kai's panda is? We're about to start story time, and he can't find Mr. Beans."

"Yeah, I think I saw him in the den. He was watching TV this afternoon."

"Okay, thanks."

She disappears back through the door, and I wrap up the stick-throwing with Fezzik. We get back inside, and the little pup shakes off before trotting toward the entrance. He's no doubt wanting in on story time, and I grin as he fires up the stairs.

The house is so quiet this evening.

It will be all weekend.

The guys have an away game, and the girls decided to join them for a change. They left after classes yesterday and won't be back until Sunday evening. Since they've gone to the effort of flying to Arizona for the game, they figure they might as well enjoy Sunday there as well.

I was invited to join them but didn't want to leave Tammy and Kai alone. And even though Mick suggested they come, too, I knew Tammy would feel the pressure of paying for flights. She might have access to money, but I get the sense that she doesn't really want to use it. Because it's not her money... it's Hudson's.

I really should ask her how things are going there and if she's made any official moves to end it with him. But I don't want to make her feel uncomfortable. She'll talk to me when she's ready, right? No point forcing the words out of someone.

Although I'm dying to know what's going on.

Surely Hudson will be missing his wife and son.

Surely he's tried to reach out and contact them.

Is Tammy keeping their location a secret?

Could she get in trouble for doing that?

Worry eats away at my insides while I clean up the dishes from dinner and make sure the kitchen is spotless. Rachel's not back until tomorrow night, but still. I feel compelled to keep her space as clean as she likes it... even when she's not here.

By the time I'm done, Tammy is padding into the kitchen. She's in bare feet and a little cotton nightdress that makes my heart hitch. It comes to her knees, and she's wearing a flimsy sweater over the top of it. The house is nice and toasty thanks to the underfloor heating

Mr. Hyde insisted we install, and I'm grateful for it as I watch Tammy's smooth legs approach me.

My gaze trails up her body, but then I flinch when I see that she's watching me check her out.

"Uh…" I clear my throat. "Kai all settled?"

"Yeah, he was asleep before I even finished the book." She grins, reaching for a mug and filling it with water. "Thanks to you, that kid is sleeping like a log most nights. You sure know how to tire him out."

"It's the puppy." I shrug.

She laughs. "You mean the puppy that is currently curled up at his feet?" She winces. "I'm not going to get in trouble for that, am I? I doubt the dog will be allowed in the rooms once guests start arriving."

"Yeah, Vanessa would have a fit. We're going to have to train the little guy, that's for sure."

"Well, you're running out of time."

"Yeah, I know." I cringe, gripping the edge of the counter and watching her heat the water in the microwave and pull out a teabag.

"You want one?"

"Nah, I'm good." I brush my hand through the air, my heart starting to thrum when her dimples pop into place.

She turns to me, her brown eyes lighting with a smile that calls to me like a siren's song.

"Thanks for being so great with him. You're so kind and patient."

I shrug, brushing off the compliment. "He's an easy kid to like."

"Because he never says anything?" She smirks and shakes her head.

I let out a soft laugh. "Has he always been that quiet?"

"I guess. He speaks when he has to." She quirks her eyebrow. "Sound familiar?"

I'm sure I'm blushing as I tip my head and cross my arms. "I always think it's best to wait until you have something of value to say. The world's already full of enough bullshit."

The microwave beeps and she takes out her mug, cradling it in her hands and gazing up at me. "I always loved that about you." Her eyes start to glass over, and she gives me a watery smile. "I've really missed you, you know? I've missed *us*."

CHAPTER 23
TAMMY

There. I finally said it.

And Baxter looks like a soft breeze could blow him over right about now.

With a quiet tut, I reach for my teabag and start dunking it in the boiling water.

I'm probably venturing into really dangerous territory here, but I can't help myself.

I've been here for two weeks, and Baxter and I have yet to have one decent conversation. It's all surface features and stuff about Kai.

He hasn't asked about what went down with Hudson. He hasn't asked me how I'm really doing or where I'm planning to go in the future.

He's just acted like me being here is the most normal thing in the world.

Which it kind of is, but also totally isn't.

I know I can never get back what we once had, but the

least we can do is remember it. Maybe reminiscing might help fix what's broken between us.

Dropping the hot teabag in the sink, I take a seat on the kitchen stool, leaning my arms against the island. "Do you remember that time we tried to make teabags fly? You saw that clip on YouTube—Bill Nye the Science Guy or something—and you wanted to try it."

There's a heavy beat before he snorts out a laugh and shakes his head. "I burned a permanent mark into your mom's kitchen counter."

"And we told her it was Dad when he was cooking dinner." I wince, fighting a laugh.

"And she banned him from the kitchen."

I start giggling. "He had no idea what she was talking about, but he didn't care. The guy hated cooking anyway."

He snickers and shakes his head. "I remember that time your mom was away and he was in charge of meals. I'd never seen him so stressed."

"Your mom had to come over and rescue him." My laughter gets a little louder as I picture that look on my poor dad's face. Sweat was pouring off his forehead, and he was muttering curses—the kind he told us off for saying. I remember my sister being grounded for a week over the stuff that had been coming out of his mouth that night.

"We got up to some crazy stuff, didn't we?" He moves to sit opposite me, the stool scraping on the ground as he shifts it to fit.

His broad shoulders fill his shirt so perfectly. The fabric strains just a little as he adjusts the stool one more time, then finally takes a seat.

My stomach trembles as I picture what must be beneath that cotton. Layers of taut muscle and raw strength. I saw the promise of it that summer before senior year, but I bet it's even more impressive now.

With a thick swallow, I focus back on my tea and sip the peppermint brew.

Baxter draws pictures with his fingers on the countertop, the silence falling between us soft and comforting.

"I used to love doing science experiments with you. Or magic tricks." His voice is low and husky, and my insides twirl with pleasure when he glances up and gives me one of his lopsided grins. "Do you remember that Halloween when I wanted to be a magician and you were gonna be my assistant?"

I cough up my mouthful of tea, spluttering and laughing as I wipe the drips off my chin and remember. "There was no way I was being an assistant, so I made you wear the red dress, and I got the top hat."

"Yep." He nods, his face turning fire-engine red. "How the hell did you talk me into that?"

"I have no idea, but you were always better at the card tricks than I was." I shake my head, then start to laugh again. "Man, did you look hot in that dress."

He closes his eyes with a deep cringe. "Ugh. Don't. I can't believe I didn't get arrested for that shit."

"Yeah, well, I'm pretty sure 'Officer Pam' wanted to arrest you."

His ears start pulsing red as I wiggle my eyebrows at him.

"She had such a massive crush on you."

"Yeah," he murmurs, his eyes darting to the counter.

"But she gave up pretty quick when she realized you were afraid to talk to girls."

"I wasn't afra—" He tips his head. "Okay, fine, I was petrified. But I wasn't scared to talk to you."

"I didn't count." I shrug. "I was your bestie. It wasn't like that betw—" My words cut off, and the silence that follows is far from comforting. I'm sure we're both remembering the swimming hole right about now, and I can sense Baxter's urgent need to flee.

Before he can bolt, I quickly change the subject.

"One of my favorite memories is actually the *Die Hard* movie marathon. Do you remember that?"

"Of course I do." His shoulders relax, and I let out a breath as he starts quoting lines from the movies.

"The first one's still the best."

"Agreed." He nods. "Although number four's pretty good too."

"With Justin Long, right?"

"Yeah."

"I love that guy." I grin. "I think we spent the next couple weeks playing cops, didn't we?"

"Yeah." He cringes. "And we were like way too old to

be doing that. We must have been like fourteen or fifteen by then."

"I know." I laugh, finishing my tea and grinning at him. "We were kids for probably way longer than was necessary, but that was all part of the fun. I mean, we used to play Simon Says all the time. Remember that teacher we had in junior year, I think it was? Mr. McCaulkin. He was super strict."

"And super boring." Baxter bulges his eyes.

"Which is why I started that game again. Remember? I passed you that note..."

His gaze grows distant as he shakes his head, obviously reliving the scene. "Simon Says make a fart noise."

"And you did. You actually did it." I can hear the glee in my voice as I'm transported back to that classroom and the laugh I could barely contain as Baxter put his hand to his mouth and let out the loudest, wettest fart sound I'd ever heard.

The class erupted, and Mr. McCaulkin spent the next five minutes trying to figure out who made that noise. No one gave Baxter up... and they kept me safe, too, when ten minutes later I was reading his note.

Simon Says: Do the Taken *speech in the Batman voice.*

He knew I'd memorized those epic lines by Liam Neeson, and when Mr. McCaulkin's back was turned, I quickly rushed out the words in the deepest, roughest voice I could.

The girls behind me started tittering, and the guys turned with impressed grins as I got to the end of it before the teacher spun with an angry glare and shouted, "Who keeps disrupting my class!"

"Man, we played that game all year." I grin, loving this reminiscing.

"It definitely turned algebra from the worst class to my favorite that year."

"Oh yeah, it did." I raise my hand, and he gives me a quick high five.

Just like old times.

Just like us.

We keep smiling at each other until I drop my hand, curling my fingers back around that mug.

"We were the best, BB."

"Yeah," he croaks.

"Senior year wasn't the same without you."

His brow buckles in confusion. "I was still there."

I shake my head, my eyes starting to glisten. "No, you weren't."

CHAPTER 24
BAXTER

Shit. I don't want to do this right now.

She's blaming me for not being there for her senior year?

She pulled away from *me*.

She was the one who just wanted to be friends.

But you weren't her friend.

You pulled so far back, you became nothing.

"Bax, that day by the swimming hole..."

Fuck, she's not going there.

"Please, can we not..." I shake my head, rising from the stool with a sharp jerk.

"I didn't know that was going to ruin everything." She keeps talking, ignoring my plea, and I want to bolt from the room like it's on fucking fire. "I kissed you because I was curious, and then... things just went so fast and..." She winces. "When I said I wanted to just be friends, I still meant that, but you took it like the ultimate rejection.

You just stopped talking to me altogether, and I never meant for that to happen! Why did you... do that?" Her voice suddenly drops to a quivering whisper. "Why did you not want to be my friend anymore?"

Resting my hands on my hips, I turn my back to her, not wanting to see her tears. They kill me every time, and I can't speak when she's looking at me like I hurt her.

"I *did* want to be your friend." My voice is rough, as if I'm speaking through a layer of rust. "I was just so humiliated by what happened. I needed space for a minute, but then I got back, and I was prepped to start senior year with you. I was gonna drive you to school, and we were gonna walk though those halls like we always did." Spinning back, I dare to look at her face and tell her the truth. "But you took a ride with *him*. And I knew the second I saw you guys together that what we had... our friendship... it was never gonna be the same again."

She stares at me, blinking, her chin bunching as she obviously struggles to respond.

I stand in the awkward quiet, gripping my hips, then crossing my arms. My socked feet swipe across the hardwood floors, and I can feel them itching to run.

But I stand.

I watch.

I listen.

And then I wish I hadn't.

"You hurt my feelings, Bax." She sniffs, curling her fingers around her mug. "I needed friendship, and you just... stayed so far away."

My chest hurts, my insides writhing as I run a hand through my hair. "That was never my intention. I was just struggling to face you after what happened between us... and then you hooked up with *him*." I can feel my face puckering into a frown. "You said you weren't ready for any of that. You didn't want sex, but... you wanted it with him. There was no space for me anymore. I couldn't be your best bud when you had a boyfriend. It wouldn't have worked."

She starts to nod, her head bobbing up and down in jerking movements as she spins her empty mug on the counter.

After a thick swallow, she shrugs and looks back at me. "For some reason... it felt more terrifying with you."

"What did?" My arms drop to my sides.

"Sex." Her shoulders hitch, her face crumpling with a desperate look for me to understand. "The idea of crossing that line with you... it was scarier."

"Why? I wouldn't have hurt you. I... I wouldn't have done anything you didn't want me to. I would have—"

"I know." She holds up her hand to cut me off. "It wasn't that." Getting up from her seat, she walks around to stand in front of me. She's so tiny sometimes. The top of her head reaches my chin, and it's tempting to pull her against me and perch my short whiskers on her black hair.

Her fingers skim through the air above my arm, like she wants to run her hand against me but can't quite make herself do it.

"When it came to you, I had so much to lose." Her voice is feather soft, and my skin starts to tingle. "And I was worried that if we went that way... if we became romantic... that everything would change between us." Her lips purse as she crosses her arms, taking a step back from me. "Hudson was low risk compared to you." A tear slips free, trailing down her bronze skin, her brown gaze filled with so much sorrow that it's going to break me. "I never meant to lose you."

"You could never lose me," I whisper, cupping her cheek because I have to. Wiping her tear away because it's the only thing that matters right now. "Tammy, I... I've always been yours."

CHAPTER 25
TAMMY

My heart jumps into my throat, lodging in my airway and making it hard to breathe.

It's the sweetest sentiment, but the look on his face right now... it says so much more.

I see it again... just like I did the night I told him I was pregnant.

He wants me.

He's always wanted me.

And not just as a friend.

Was I blind back then? Or just too afraid to see it?

Placing my hand on his chest, I feel his heart thrumming beneath my touch.

A heart that belongs to me?

A heart that's always been mine?

My insides melt with warmth and affection, then start to simmer and heat the same way they did that afternoon at the swimming hole.

The difference is that I know what I'm doing now.

This isn't curiosity anymore. It's something stronger, bigger, more powerful.

More meaningful.

A soft breath wisps out between my lips as I lurch to the tips of my toes and, for the second time in my life... initiate a kiss that will change everything.

I'm so here for it.

This time I'm in. All the way.

The complicated shit in my life can disappear for a second.

I'm not afraid anymore.

Curling my fingers around the back of his neck, I pull Baxter down to meet me.

"Wait, wait, wait..." He jerks back before our lips can connect.

No! My insides wail, and I keep my hand on his neck, not willing to let go and lose this moment.

"You're married," he rasps. "Tammy, I can't go kissing you."

"I'm not." I shake my head, holding up my bare ring finger.

He frowns down at me in confusion, and I swear I see hope lighting his eyes when he takes my finger and rubs his thumb over the spot where my rings usually are. It still feels weird not wearing them all the time, but his soft touch is easing that tension.

My stomach trembles, my lips shaking as I admit, "I mean, technically, I still am, but that's only because I haven't figured out how to make it all official yet, but... I'm planning on asking Hudson for a divorce."

"Really?" His whisper is so soft, that hope like a sunrise dawning across his face. "You're leaving him for good?"

I nod, a tentative smile curling my lips, my voice barely more than a whisper. "I want to be yours."

And to prove it, I lurch for his mouth again.

There's no resistance this time, and his lips crush to mine like he's breaking a hunger strike.

The pressure is perfect—deep and beautiful.

We hold still against each other like we're soaking this in, like if we pull apart, the magic will shatter.

But then he eases back from me, his lips parting, his breath skimming my mouth before he glides his tongue against mine.

I meet him halfway, my soul releasing a satisfied sigh. This kiss is warm and inviting, hot and intoxicating.

Straining up on my toes, I cling to him, wanting to get closer. His hands grip my waist, fisting my sweater and tugging me until I'm fused against him.

My breasts rub his torso, the nipples hardening immediately. The intensity of my desire is overwhelming, and I can't hold back a soft moan, dragging my fingers through his hair as our tongues dance like they were born to tango.

Baxter splays his hand against my back, molding us together, then bends his knees, coming down to my level before lifting me off the ground and planting me on the kitchen counter.

A breath pops out of me, my erratic heart making me puffed and heady.

Baxter pulls away to look at my face, his eyes darting across me like he's trying to memorize every little feature. Like he still can't believe this is actually happening.

I smile with my eyes, my glistening lips barely curving as I brush my thumb down his neck.

He doesn't say anything, just tells me I'm the most beautiful woman in the world. Tells me I'm the only woman in the world without having to speak.

My chest pulses.

My ears start to buzz.

Heat pools between my legs, and I know I have to have him.

I'm pretty sure I'll die if I don't.

Dramatic? Yes.

Real? Hell yes.

It's not just a matter of want. I *need* him. I need to experience Baxter in this way. It's like my body's finally telling me what my brain was too stupid to hear.

All those years of unconscious pining.

All those nights I lay awake thinking about him and trying to convince myself I'd done the right thing.

But I hadn't.

I screwed up.

And I'm going to fix it.

Right here.

Right now.

A soft whimper punches out of me, emotions clogging my throat as I reach for him again, wrapping my legs around his waist and digging my heels into his butt.

The heat between us is searing, our tongues no longer a warm oasis but a scorching volcano.

My voracious hunger turns my kisses messy, and I don't even care.

I suck his lower lip, lick his jawline, nibble his earlobe.

His hands roam my back, his thumb skirting my boob before ducking away again. I want him to squeeze me, massage all my private places. I want him to make me come with his tongue. To push his fingers inside me. To glide his naked body over mine, then bury his cock so deep that I can feel him all the way to my soul.

Fisting his shirt, I tug it out of his jeans, freeing the fabric before scrambling for his belt buckle.

"Wait." Baxter jumps away from me, slapping his hand over the buckle and blinking at me.

He's panting, wide-eyed, and looks like I'm holding a shotgun to his head.

"What?" I breathe, my chest heaving.

Glancing down at his jeans, I can see his straining cock, and my insides weep with desire. My panties are wet with it, and I bite my lip, unable to control my lusty imagination.

"I..." Baxter lets out an awkward huff. "I can't."

CHAPTER 26
BAXTER

She's looking at me like I've lost my mind.

"But I told you Hudson and I are over," she whispers.

I snap my eyes shut. This has nothing to do with Hudson. Fuck! I don't even want to hear his name!

I wish to God I could explain this to her, but there are no words.

None.

There's barely thought.

Actually, there's a shit ton of thought, and it's all nightmares.

She wants to do it with me.

Holy shit, she wants me!

I should be dancing, stripping off my clothes like it's my day job.

But...

She's going to touch my dick, and she'll make me come before I can even get it inside her.

Will my cum hit her in the face again?

Will we be right back at that swimming hole with nothing but an awkward haze shrouding both of us?

I can't go through that again.

I can't...

I just...

"I can't," I whisper, turning my back on her ashen expression and bolting from the room.

CHAPTER 27
TAMMY

I stay on the kitchen counter, running a hand over my lower lip and willing my heart to slow the hell down.

What just happened?

It's like history repeating itself.

Things get awkward, so he pushes me away, then bolts from the room like sleeping with me is the worst.

He wants me.

I can tell he does, so...

"What the hell is his problem?" Jumping off the counter, my feet land with a smack, and I cross my arms, figuring I can play this one of two ways: pretend like nothing just happened between us... or chase him and force whatever he's feeling out of those stubborn lips of his.

I deserve an explanation, don't I?

I know I screwed things up back then, but he can't kiss me like that and then give me the cold shoulder.

"Dammit," I mutter, spinning for the door and rushing through it.

My feet thump on the stairs, and he can probably hear me coming. I'm nearly out of breath by the time I make it to the top floor. I pause outside his bedroom, resting my hand against my stomach and trying to steel my nerves.

Sucking in a breath, I attempt to regulate my heartbeat before knocking and walking in without waiting for a response.

He's standing by his bed in all his shirtless glory—and I can confirm that yes, he's gotten even stronger and sexier since the swimming hole. Holy shit. I drink in his rigid contours, my lips parting at the defined muscle in front of me.

Everything about him is perfectly sculpted, with a smattering of hair across his chest. I want to run my fingers through it, then follow that line of hair from his belly button down to the top of his belt buckle. I want that thing undone and gone.

Geez, I sound like a horny housewife mooning over some poster boy.

But maybe that's exactly what this is right now, because with a body like that, he could grace every freaking month of a firemen's calendar.

"Tammy, I..." His words trail off, but it's enough to snap me out of my lust-filled stupor.

Blinking, I avert my gaze and give myself a chance to think coherently.

"Please, you should... go to your own bed." He points to the door behind me, looking kind of desperate.

Is he trying to be honorable right now? Is that it?

I shake my head. "You can't just walk away from me like that. It's not fair to kiss me that way and then just bail. I know words scare you and talking about your feelings is terrifying, but I don't care right now. You owe me more of explanation than... *I can't.*" I give him a pointed look, and he stares at me like I'm holding a gun to his head. Again. He's got that whole deer-in-headlights thing down pat.

What is he so afraid of?

"Is it the marriage thing? Because I love how honorable you are, but—"

"No, it's got nothing to do with that. I just..." He shakes his head. "I..." He swallows, his eyes gleaming as he opens his mouth, then shuts it again. I can feel his struggle like it's my own, but I'm not letting him off that easy.

"Why can't you, then, Bax? Why?"

"We..." He shakes his head, cringing deeply. "We tried it once before, and it didn't work." Now it's his turn to give me a pointed look. "You don't remember that?"

"Of course I do! It may have been five years ago, but I can still see it—*feel it*—like it was yesterday." My eyes start to burn, my nose tingling as I cross my arms and try to keep myself together. "Five years. Five years of you not really talking to me anymore." My head starts to bob. "And I know that a lot went down. We've established that you were embarrassed, and then I got with Hudson and —" I squeeze my eyes shut, my voice starting to tremble. "But I made a mistake that day by the swimming hole, okay?"

His head jerks back, his expression crumpling with confusion. "*You* made a mistake?"

"Yes!" I flick my hands up. "I chickened out, okay? I wanted you so badly, even after you came early. I wanted to know what it'd feel like to... to have our bodies rubbing together. I wanted to feel you inside me. I wanted to be naked with you." His eyes bulge so wide, I think they might drop out of his head. There's no way in hell any words can come out of him now, so I just keep talking. "I wanted you so much that it scared me. And I freaked out and started worrying that if we did it, maybe you wouldn't look at me the same anymore, and all our silly antics and laughter and play would be gone. Maybe our friendship would be over. And then I was like... well, what if we got together and became all romantic?" I cringe, scraping my fingers through my hair. "But then I started thinking... what if we broke up?" Tears line my lashes as I'm taken right back to everything I went through in that moment. "If we broke up, things would never be the same again, and... and I totally spiraled. That's why I got dressed so fast. That's why I told you I wasn't ready. It wasn't because you... came early. That had nothing to do with it."

He's staring at me like he's in a trance, and I wonder if I'm going to have to keep talking, but then he blinks and rushes out a breath. "I thought you were disgusted by me."

"No." I let out a disbelieving laugh. Like I could ever be disgusted by Baxter Brown. My cheeks heat as my voice drops to a whisper. "I guess it was kind of a compliment that I could turn you on like that."

He rubs a hand down his face. "You got so crazy hot that summer. I'm surprised you didn't catch me drooling every time I looked at you."

My lips twitch, and I desperately try—and fail—to fight my grin...

Especially when he rakes his gaze over me and murmurs, "You're still crazy hot."

I bite my lower lip, fidgeting with the cuffs of my sweater and failing to hide my smile. I can't remember the last time anyone made me feel so beautiful. "Is that why you suddenly bailed in the kitchen? Worried I might make you go off early again?" My tone is light and playful, but the way his expression drops makes me wonder if he heard me wrong or... "What did I say? You know I was only teasing. I'm sure you've got amazing stamina now. I'm sure—"

"Tammy..." He shakes his head, swallowing and looking super uncomfortable. "You're..." He winces and lets out a heavy sigh. "Can you just... go. Please."

What? Why? Why is he doing this?

I want to tell him a thousand times over that I was only kidding. If that would help.

But the look on his face right now is so tortured, and he's turning his back to me again.

Shutting me out like he always does.

My heart sinks, sizzling to ash in my stomach as I quietly spin on my heel and walk out of the room.

Wow, he really is resolved to not want me.

But that can't be right. The way his body responded to mine was a dead giveaway. The man wants me. I can tell.

I pause at the top of the stairs. Maybe I should go back and talk to him again.

He's asked you to leave enough times tonight, Tammy. Just go downstairs, for God's sake!

With a soft huff, I pad back down to the kitchen. I don't know what to do with myself, so I start spraying and wiping down the already clean kitchen counter. Then I notice the smallest mark on the door beneath the sink and decide to wipe down every freaking door in the kitchen.

What the hell else am I going to do?

My chin bunches, those tears I've been fighting threatening to spill free.

I messed up so badly that summer.

And it appears that there's nothing I can do to fix it.

CHAPTER 28
BAXTER

Shit, I'm a douchebag.

No, I'm a fuckwit.

Or maybe I'm just a...

"Coward. You're a coward." Saying the words out loud is like punching myself in the balls.

I plunk onto the edge of my bed, gripping the mattress and swearing under my breath.

"Fuck!" Digging my toes into the rug beneath my bed, I glare at my knees and wrestle with the war going on in my stomach.

Or maybe it's my brain.

Shit, they're both going nuts.

Half of me wants to hide under the covers and never come out.

Another wants to run downstairs and pull Tammy into my arms and promise her that she's the only girl for me. Tell her how much I want to worship her body. Tell her how much I desperately want to be the guy who can make her come... make her feel better than she ever has before.

But what if I can't do that?

I don't know shit.

"Fuck." I squeeze my forehead, my leg starting to bob uncontrollably.

What's she doing right now?

Has she walked out fuming?

She was definitely upset, but was she angry upset or hurt upset?

"Dammit," I softly whine, closing my eyes and hating myself.

If she's hurt upset, I can't live with that.

I have to find out.

Jerking up, I stagger to my door, my legs and brain fighting the whole way down the stairs. I'm about to tap softly on her bedroom door when I hear a thump from the level below.

Holding my breath, I softly descend and soon find her in the kitchen, furiously cleaning kitchen doors and slapping them closed when she's done.

I flinch as another one slams shut, then feel my stomach drop out my asshole when she glances up and sees me.

Her eyes are bright with tears, and my throat starts to ache.

She sniffs, swiping at her cheeks before jerking up straight and throwing the dishrag in the sink.

The silence stretching between us is thick and painful. I need to break it. I need to rip that Band-Aid off and just—

"What?" she clips, spinning to face me.

Her expression is fierce yet achingly vulnerable, and I just have to fucking say it.

My body revolts against the idea, my stomach twisting into a painful knot as my voice box tries to shut down in protest.

But that look on her face...

"I'm a virgin." The words are ripped out of me by some cruel, invisible force. Maybe it's willpower. Maybe it's just plain stupidity.

But the words are out there now, dangling between us, and I just have to stand here while she lets that sink in.

Her lips part, and she blinks at me like she doesn't understand what I just said.

Great. Now I'm gonna have to repeat myself and... *Fuck! Why is this so hard?*

"You're... a virgin?" she squeaks.

I close my eyes so I don't have to look at her. Is being a virgin really that bad? Why do people have to make such a big deal about this?

Frustration simmers inside me, but I start spitting out an explanation in spite of my reluctance. "I was so paranoid after our time together that I didn't want to risk..." I pinch my bottom lip. "I felt safe with you... And then it all fell to shit, and I couldn't put myself through that again. So, I haven't dated anyone. I haven't made out with... anyone. I'm..." I huff and dare myself to look at her.

Her eyes are bugging out big-time. "You haven't even kissed another girl?"

I'm not sure if she believes me, but I nod to try and prove my point. Then I shake my head and whisper, "It's only ever been you, Tammy. You're the only one I ever wanted."

I'm pretty sure that death would be less painful than this.

Getting these words out hurts my throat, my chest, my brain.

I want to bail.

She knows now. Can I just run away, please?

I turn to leave.

"No, wait." Her voice is so desperate, like if I walk out of this room, she's gonna start crying again.

So, I force myself to turn and face her.

She's still looking kind of surprised. Maybe it's taking a minute to absorb the shock of my unexpected news. Then her lips curl into the smallest smile, and she starts walking toward me.

It takes everything in me not to step back, to hold my ground when she squeezes my naked shoulders, then settles her hands on either side of my neck.

"You only wanted me," she whispers, her eyes glimmering with tears despite all my efforts.

"Don't cry," I beg her.

"I..." Her breath catches, and then she lets out this soft laugh before pulling my head down to meet her lips.

Our mouths crush together, her arms wrapping around my neck.

And my body responds the only way it can...

CHAPTER 29
TAMMY

Baxter's strong hands grab my hips, cupping them tightly before pulling me close. His fingers glide around my back, splaying at the base of my spine, before traveling up to cup the back of my head. He tips his head, deepening the kiss like this is nothing new. Like kissing me is old and familiar and what he was born to do.

I give in to every sweep of his tongue, my nipples hardening against his chest. I want to tear my clothes off, just so I can feel his flesh skim across mine.

My breath is ragged as I pull away from him, quickly yanking off my sweater and nightgown. I'm now standing in nothing but my cotton panties, the warm kitchen lights casting an amber glow across my exposed skin.

Baxter gapes at my boobs, his eyes transfixed. I brush my fingers over the hardened nipples, sinking my teeth into my bottom lip before whispering, "Do you want to touch me?"

He nods, a breath punching out of him. The pads of his fingers skim my waist, his knuckle curling around my belly button as he inches his way north. His touch is so soft it tickles, and I can't help a quiet titter.

He immediately stops, jerking away from me.

"What?" I snatch his wrist before he can disappear on me. "It's okay, Bax. It's gonna be okay?"

"What if I come early?"

The poor guy looks terrified.

I shrug and smile. "So what if you do? We've got all night." I can feel my dimples forming as I reassure him. "I'm not scared anymore. I'm not going anywhere. I want this. With you."

He swallows, still looking nervous, but he's not straining against my hold on him anymore.

"I want us to do this. I'm all in." The tip of my tongue skims across my bottom lip. "Are you?"

His sigh is deep and long, a relieved breath rushing out of him as he steps back into my space, wrapping his arm around my waist and lifting me off the floor. My legs automatically curl around his hips as he carries me to the counter and perches me on it again. His hungry lips devour my neck before inching down to the tops of my breasts.

I tip my head back, letting out a soft moan as he trails his fingers up my back. I'm desperate for him to suck my nipples, to take me into his mouth. My body is burning for it, but he's still busy peppering kisses across the tops of my boobs, like he's too scared to take things deeper.

"Bax," I whisper.

He jerks up, out of breath, and pants against my cheek. "I'm not really sure what I'm doing." Leaning back, he cups my face and gives me a pained frown. "I don't know what you want. I don't know how to make you feel good."

Aw, his face right now.

My heart cracks wide open for this man. This sweet, kind man who wants to kiss me just right. Who's terrified of messing this up.

Skimming my fingers down his chest, I brush my thumb over his nipple and smile when an idea hits me.

"Wanna play a game?"

"A game?" He frowns. "What do you mean?"

"Let's play..." I skim my tongue across my top lip. "Let's play Tammy Says."

His confusion morphs into a crooked smile, the right side of his mouth edging up. "Tammy Says?"

"Yeah." I scrape my teeth across my bottom lip. "Tammy says... kiss my lips."

He does as he's told, swiping his tongue deep into my mouth. He seems confident with this and holds my face, claiming my mouth like I'm his alone. His warm, hot presence makes me groan, and I suck the tip of his tongue before finally releasing him.

"Tammy says... lick my neck."

Nibbling his way from my mouth down to my chin, he then tips my head back and turns my neck into a popsicle stick, his delicious tongue stroking me until the fire in my belly is building to an inferno.

With a soft laugh, I murmur, "Stop."

He pulls back, but I catch the back of his head before he can move too far.

My giggle is throaty as I whisper in his ear. "Tammy didn't say. You forget how to play this game, BB?"

With a soft growl, he launches back at my neck, flattening his tongue against my smooth skin and leaving a trail of himself from my collarbone to my ear.

"Tammy says... suck my nipple."

"Which one?" he murmurs against my skin, working his way down my body.

"I don't care. They both want you." My voice is wispy, heat pulsing through me like a heady cocktail.

He smiles against my skin, then starts on the right, sucking my hardened nipple between his lips. It feels so freaking good that I can't help crying out, fisting a handful of his hair and thrusting my chest toward him.

He massages the other breast, brushing his thumb over the nipple, like he's reassuring her that he'll be there in a minute.

I groan when he swirls the tip of his tongue around the areola before moving to the left side of my body. He takes great care with that breast, too, drawing lusty cries out of me, sending liquid fire down between my legs.

"Tammy says take my panties off."

His breath hitches, then whooshes back over my skin before he leans away with a hesitant smile.

"Tammy says *now*, Baxter."

His eyes dart to my legs, spread on either side of his body. His Adam's apple bobs in his throat, his touch feather soft as he lightly trails his fingertips from my knees to the waistband of my underwear.

"Tammy says hurry," I squeak.

His fingers hook into my underwear, tugging the fabric down. I lift my butt off the counter, helping him out, then raise my legs. He pulls them off, his eyes drinking me in with this fascinated awe that makes my heart swell.

As soon as my panties hit the floor, he spreads my legs and stares down at the mound of black curls covering my pussy. He brushes his hand lightly over them, his chest heaving like this is the most exciting thing he's ever done in his life.

"Tammy says touch my pussy," I rasp. It's hard to speak over my thundering heartbeat.

I want to bathe in the look on his face right now, dive into those wonder-filled eyes and soak myself.

Baxter's gaze darts to my face, and I give him an encouraging smile.

"Wh-What am...? How do I...?" He lets out a desperate sigh.

"Just follow your instincts. I'll let you know." My voice is wispier than ever, my pulse so strong, I can feel it thrumming between my ears.

"Does Tammy say?" He arches his eyebrow, a teasing glint in his eyes.

I giggle. "Tammy most definitely says."

"Okay." He tries to smile but can't, his mouth forming an intense look like he's about to disarm a bomb.

It makes me laugh for a second until his hand cups me, his thumb brushing over my clit. I let out a soft gasp.

"Is that good?"

"Yeah, just... there."

"Where?"

Grabbing his thumb, I put it back on my clit. "There."

A soft hum vibrates in his throat as he brushes his thumb over my clit again, making me whimper when he deepens the pressure.

I glance down between my legs, watching the tendons in his hands work. He has beautiful hands, so strong and capable. I whimper again, letting out a high-pitched gasp before biting into my bottom lip. My insides are going crazy, the sensations buzzing through me almost too much to contain.

Tipping my head back with a groan, I lean my hand on the counter and whisper, "Tammy says start kissing my breasts again."

He does as he's told, still working my clit while sucking and nibbling my tits until my mind is half crazed with lust and desire.

I'm on the edge of coming when he acts on instinct, exploring my pussy and finding my dripping opening.

His finger explores the slippery edges before nudging inside me.

I gasp again, leaning back to give him better access.

"Is this okay?" His gaze darts across my face, looking for any signs of displeasure, but that's not possible. I'm so fucking pleasured right now I can't even think straight.

All I manage is a little "Uh-huh."

Licking between my breasts, he works his way back up to my mouth, inching his finger a little deeper inside me at the same time. I'm on the cusp of a full meltdown, and I know exactly what will tip me over the edge.

Part of me wants to hold out, to elongate this thing, but my impatience wins out.

"Tammy says touch my clit again," I cry to the ceiling.

He does as he's told, keeping one finger inside me while using his other hand to draw circles over my clit.

"Ahhhh." A guttural, uncontrolled scream punches out of me, and then I start panting these high-pitched squeaks that should be embarrassing, but they're not, because I just opened my eyes, and Baxter's gaze is bright with affection and awe and...

I lurch forward, gripping his arms and trying to kiss him but failing, because another cry flies out of my mouth as the strongest orgasm I have ever experienced takes me out.

CHAPTER 30
BAXTER

Watching Tammy come is beautiful and amazing. My cock is straining against my jeans, and I'm worried I'm going to blow in a second. The only thing holding off the explosion is my determination to make sure Tammy has the time of her fucking life.

She releases her pincer grip on my forearms and wraps her arms around my shoulders, drawing me close and trying to kiss me. My hand gets squashed between us, my finger still inside her as she shakes and jerks on the counter.

The soft, warm oasis of her pussy is magnificent. I've never felt anything like it. I want my dick to experience that pleasure... if it can.

Come on, body. Help me out.

I can feel the edge of my own orgasm building, and when she whispers against my mouth, "Tammy says come inside me," I jerk back with a worried frown. "You can do it." She smiles at me.

I adore her dimples.

I adore the way her eyes are glowing.

I adore the soft puffs of air popping out of her mouth and hitting my skin.

Easing my finger out of her, I grin as she jerks and flinches, then starts to laugh. "My gosh, my body's going nuts. I need you inside me, Baxter, please."

Yeah, that kind of pressure is so not helping right now.

I don't want to make her feel bad, so I keep the thought to myself, desperately willing my body to behave.

This is all so new and wondrous. I can't even begin to explain how hot watching her come is. How hot her kisses are. How much I love her tits and want to spend the rest of my life playing with them. How her pussy is the sexiest thing on the planet, and I want to explore every inch of it... in all the ways I possibly can.

Her fingers scramble for my belt buckle, and I stand there holding my breath, trying not to let my brain run away on me. Trying to focus and not explode all over her face when she yanks my boxer briefs down and lets my dick spring free.

The air touches it, and then her fingers curl around the shaft.

"I'm gonna lose it," I whisper frantically. The pressure inside me is unbearable.

"It's okay. It's okay." She shifts to the edge of the

bench, spreading her legs wide and fitting my tip between her glistening folds.

"Fuck," I whisper.

"You can do this." She smiles, and I keep my gaze on hers as I push my cock inside her.

Her gasp is sweet, her lips parting, and she lets out this cry that could be either pleasure or pain. I can't tell, and I don't have time to tell, because the second my dick is wrapped in her warm center, I am gone.

The orgasm hits me like a nuke, taking out all my senses so the only thing I'm capable of doing is grabbing her thighs and doing a few jerking thrusts inside her.

My mouth pops open, but no sound comes out.

I'm a trembling mess, like I'm being melted from the inside, my butt cheeks clenching as I cup her ass and go deep. Every muscle in my body is on high alert, strained taut by this mind-blowing sensation pounding through me.

"Fuck," I manage to rasp, my body reeling.

That was... incredible.

And so fucking fast.

I wince as my system slowly comes back online and frown at her. "I'm sorry."

"For what?" She shakes her head and starts to laugh. "That was amazing. That was—"

"So quick."

"Aw, Bax." She sits forward, playing with the hair at the nape of my neck and smiling at me. "That was perfect."

"It was over before I could even…" I shake my head.

"Before you could what? Pleasure yourself?"

"No." I frown. "Pleasure you."

"Oh my gosh." She tips her head back, her boobs jiggling as she lets out a melodic laugh. "Baxter…" Looking me right in the eye, she holds my face and assures me, "You pleasured me. Big-time."

"But you wanted me inside you, and I—"

"Tammy says stop talking."

I clamp my lips together.

Her smile is kind and beautiful as she leans up, squishing her breasts against my chest and kissing me long and slow. When she finally pulls away, she rests her forehead against mine. "I promise you this is the absolute truth… You were amazing. My body is sated right down to my core. I'm not sure if my legs can currently hold my weight. Believe me when I tell you that I have been thoroughly pleasured."

Leaning back, I stare down at her sincere expression and feel my lips twitch with a grin.

"Don't be so hard on yourself. That was your first time, and it was epic for me."

"Me too." I quickly nod.

I'm still inside her, but I can feel myself retreating as my cock softens. For a hopeless second, I lament the fact that I can't stay inside her forever.

"We're gonna do this again." She kisses my shoulder, working her lips up my neck, then whispering in my ear,

"We've got all night, and we are definitely doing this again. And maybe even again." Her fingers send tendrils of pleasure shooting down my spine as she lightly tickles my skin and laughs. "And maybe even again."

CHAPTER 31
TAMMY

The fire crackles as Baxter adds another log to it. I watch the flames jump and dance around the wood, mesmerized by the orange glow, until my eyes track across to the sexiest back in the history of man.

I perch up on my elbow and reach forward, tracing the lines of Baxter's tattooed angel wings. He must have gotten them after high school, and I want to know the story. I want to soak in every detail and reinvent our friendship. I want to make up for all that time we lost.

Will he let me do that?

He glances over his shoulder as if he can sense my perusal.

His smile is gentle and sweet, and my chest seems to expand, like my heart is beating just for him.

"C'mere." I lift the blanket covering me, and his smile grows as he lies down on the floor beside me.

After our tryst in the kitchen, he led me into the

parlor, creating a bed out of cushions and starting up a fire. It's romantic and beautiful, and I'm not sure a bed will ever be better than this.

Sure, the pillows move, and my hip will no doubt end up on the floor by the morning, but I don't care. I'm naked. Baxter's naked. And we're snuggled together under this blanket like we're the only two people in the world.

Baxter lies on his stomach, resting his head beside mine and draping his arm across my waist. I continue drawing lines on his back, my finger tracing the intricate details of each feather.

"When did you get this?"

His nose twitches, and he mumbles against the pillow, "Dad and I both got tattoos on our road trip, after Mom..." His voice trails off.

"My heart broke that day," I whisper.

His eyes dart to mine.

"I wanted so badly to come and see you. I just wanted to sit beside you and hold your hand."

"You were married," he mutters.

I shake my head. "You were my friend. I would have done anything for you."

He sniffs, his lips dipping. "You were married."

Tears sting my eyes, and I have to nod, because he's right. I'd been married a week when it happened. The whole town was rocked. Everyone attended the funeral, and I stood next to Hudson but couldn't take my eyes off Baxter.

I'd never seen his face so ashen. He looked like a lost boy, not even crying while he stood beside his father, who looked just as wrecked. It was impossible to know what to say because there were no words good enough to bring comfort. They just had to grieve.

I rested my hand on my belly. My baby bump wasn't really showing yet, but my pants were tight, and it was only a matter of weeks before I'd be wearing new clothes and accepting the fact that town gossip would be rife. It already was. Who the hell gets married in high school? The people who didn't want to acknowledge the truth thought we were soulmates who couldn't live without each other. They thought it was romantic that Hudson had proposed in front of the entire school. They thought it was sweet that we couldn't wait and tied the knot before graduation. Then there were the people who liked to judge. They whispered around every corner and made me feel like Hester Prynne every time I walked past them. Once I started to show, it would only get worse, but I couldn't think about that.

All I could do was stare at Baxter's ashen face and weep for the wonderful woman who was lost to us all.

"She was an angel," I whisper.

His lips curl up in a smile. "She was."

"Do you remember those cookies she used to make?" I laugh. "Who needs chocolate chips when you can use dried apricots and raisins."

He snorts. "Or kiwifruit. Do you remember that disastrous batch?"

"Your dad was so stoic, trying to make out that they were delicious." My stomach shakes with a giggle. "I mean, I guess they weren't all bad, but..."

"They weren't great, TT." He perches up on his elbow so our noses are basically touching. "But nothing can be worse than that cheese-less vegan pizza thing she tried that one time. You don't put pumpkin and eggplant on a pizza. That's just wrong."

I tip my head back as a loud laugh pops out of me.

Baxter lightly slaps his hand over my mouth. "Shhhh. You don't want to wake Kai. The poor kid will be traumatized if he walks in to find us both naked."

My boobs jiggle, and I keep on laughing.

They draw his eye, and he stares at them with a mix of affection and desire. His hand drops from my mouth, and I let him look, finding his gaze a turn-on. He makes me feel sexy in a way that no one ever has before.

"I want you inside me again," I whisper.

His fingers graze my breast, trailing down the curve before twirling around my nipple. His eyebrows flicker with a frown. "What if it's as quick as last time?"

"Then I'll enjoy it just as much." I lean forward and start nibbling his neck.

His throat vibrates with a groan, and my knuckles whistle down his torso until my fingers are wrapping around his iron cock. He's hard as granite, and my insides immediately melt to liquid.

I'm ready for him with zero foreplay and roll him onto his back.

"Wait, what about protection?" He holds me at arm's length when I try to climb on top of him.

"I'm on the pill." I smirk down at him. "And that didn't seem to bother you last time?"

"Last time my brain was functioning on zero blood flow."

I laugh and stare down at his cock, which is standing to attention, the head beading with anticipation. "It looks like you might be suffering from the same problem now."

He closes his eyes and swallows. "Yeah, I'm feeling pretty incoherent, but…"

"But nothing, Bax." I wait until he opens his eyes before smiling down at him.

Taking his hands, I place them on my boobs. He immediately starts to massage them and tries to sit up so he can kiss them, but I push him back down. My hands look small on his broad shoulders, and I know he's letting me boss him around without any kind of fight. He's strong and more than capable of being in charge, but he just lies there while I straddle him, lining up his cock with my weeping folds and sinking onto him.

He grabs my hips, his fingers digging into my soft flesh as he lets out a guttural moan.

I keep pushing, stretching myself to the point of pain, but the good kind. He's big and all-consuming. He fills me, and I'm not even sure if I can take him all the way in, but I can't stop myself either.

A soft cry punches out of me, my fingers digging into his pecs as I lower myself all the way to the hilt.

"You okay?" He gives me a worried frown.

I snap my eyes shut and nod, biting my bottom lip, unable to speak.

Am I okay?

My body's buzzing with an electrical current that's overpowering. My insides are going nuts, and all I can feel is his large cock taking me to the edge.

"You're big," I whisper.

"Too big? I'm not hurting you, am I?" He goes to move, like the thought is too much.

"Stay," I order him.

"But..."

"It's good, Bax." I rise, then slowly slide back down on him.

He groans as if this is sweet torture. I know exactly what he means.

His thumbs graze my nipples, and he squeezes my breasts again when I start to ride him. It's slow at first, long, languid pumps that soon pick up speed.

His chest starts to heave. "Fuck, Tammy, you feel amazing."

"So do you." I grin, triumph soaring through me as I lean back, changing the angle and loving the new moan that fires out of him.

His hands move back to my hips, then slide down my legs, squeezing my knees before trailing back up to my breasts. I lean forward so he can squeeze them again.

"C'mere." He beckons me forward, catching my rocking boobs and sucking my left nipple into his mouth.

"Ahhhh," I cry out on a sigh and stop moving for a second, lost in how good he feels until my pussy demands friction once more. I break away from him and start to move again, finding a heady speed that makes us both groan.

The sound of our sex fills the room, our gyrating bodies making a symphony that's only us.

Me and Bax.

Baxter and me.

Our coupling is long overdue and feels so right, I can't even wrap my head around it. I don't want to think anyway. I just want to feel.

Scraping my fingers through the hair on his chest, I can't help releasing a series of soft squeaks as the energy inside me builds to explosive.

"Oh shit." Baxter's eyes pop open, his breath coming out in quick pants as he grips my hips to almost painful and starts to jerk inside me. "Ah! Oh fuck! Ah!"

I can feel him come, my insides rejoicing as he thrusts deep and uncontrolled. My smile is so wide it hurts, but then my mouth drops open as his thumb finds my clit and quickly sends me over the edge as well.

It takes all of about two seconds with him still deep inside me, and I feel the orgasm from both inside and out. Between my clit and my G-spot, I am done. The cries punching out of me are recklessly loud.

"Shhhh." Baxter covers my mouth again, and I moan into his palm, my body vibrating as I continue to orgasm on him.

His head tips back with a grunt, like he's feeling my internal spasms and barely able to control his own groans of pleasure.

"Fuck, Tammy," he whispers. "Fuck, you feel so good."

The words stretch out of his mouth—long, lean sounds that I can barely decipher.

But I know what he's saying.

I *feel* what he's saying.

And he couldn't be more right. Being together this way is so fucking good.

CHAPTER 32
BAXTER

I fall asleep with Tammy curled against my side. It's kind of uncomfortable on the floor, but I couldn't move after our last session. The thought of having to climb a staircase was too much. My body was spent, drifting down from a high of mega proportions.

Having TT orgasm straight after me was fucking hot. I've never felt anything like it. Her pussy squeezed and spasmed around my cock. Not only did it feel sensational, but the view was amazing. Watching her ecstasy was the sexiest thing I've ever seen, her perfect tits rocking, her muscles taut with pleasure. Her teeth gently bit my fingers as I tried to quiet her and not wake Kai, and then she sucked my digits into her mouth before leaning over me and kissing me deep and long.

Her tongue is magic fire.

Her delicious nipples brushed against my bare chest,

and I never want us to wear clothes around each other again. Skin on skin is the way God intended it, right?

I curl my arm around her back and nuzzle my nose into her hair, inhaling her sweet scent and feeling like the luckiest guy on the planet. I never knew she wanted me that day. I always assumed that I'd screwed it up, but she had regrets too.

Shit, if we'd managed to overcome it all, would she not have married Hudson?

Hudson.

Fuck.

She's still married to the guy. I mean, only technically. She's getting a divorce, but it's not final yet. I wonder when she'll file that paperwork. I don't even know how that all works. Does she need a lawyer first? Does she have a lawyer? Does she want my help, or is it best to stay right out of it?

I've heard the tail end of a few terse phone conversations, but I never know exactly who she's talking to. I've seen her texting with a deep scowl and assumed she was interacting with him, but she's never said, and I haven't asked.

But maybe I should.

It's probably time I find the courage to talk to her about all this, ask for details I don't want to hear. I need to be there for her in whatever capacity she wants me. So far, we've avoided all mention of Hudson. I've gotten the distinct sense that she doesn't even want to bring him into this place. She's after full escape. I get that, and I'm more than happy to honor it.

But... things have changed tonight, and maybe it's time we have some serious chats about her failed marriage. The thought makes my insides spasm and revolt. I hate those kinds of conversations.

I wish Hudson could get shoved into the past and stay there.

But that's impossible, because he's Kai's father, and even though I've picked up that he works long hours and isn't around much, surely he still cares about his kid, right? Surely he'll want to see his son again?

My stomach starts to ache with worry, and I feel like I'm losing Tammy all over again. It hurts, so I squeeze her a little tighter, brushing my lips across her soft skin. She rouses in the darkness. The fire is down to embers now, and there's only a faint orange glow highlighting our bodies. Our hands start to explore in the shadows, and soon I'm under the blanket, tasting her perfect body, painting pictures with my tongue and reveling in her sleepy moans. She spreads her legs for me, plunging her fingers into my hair and asking for me to kiss her in a sleepy voice that makes me wonder if she thinks she's dreaming.

I'm nervous, wondering exactly how to pleasure her as I tentatively stick out my tongue. Her moans guide me, and I taste every inch of her pussy, trying different angles and seeing how it affects her. She starts panting, fisting my hair to almost painful, especially when I sink my fingers inside her. With my tongue working her clit and my two fingers curling within her, she falls apart, shattering beneath my touch. Her wispy gasps and writhing body make me feel like a king, but it's not until I'm slipping inside her that I'm truly home.

I take things slow, rocking against her and lavishing her sleepy smile. Cruising my hand down her leg, I lift her knee, and she tucks her foot behind my back. I dive a little deeper, kissing her lips and holding her. She's my precious diamond, and I worship her body the way I always wanted to, marveling at how epic this all feels. I could stay in her all night, but my cock doesn't play fair. The orgasm suddenly hits me with an unexpected force. I bury my face in the crook of her neck and pour myself into her, feeling large chunks of my heart go with it.

She's always owned me, but now I'm lost to this woman.

No matter what happens, there can never be another.

Curling to her side, she nestles her luscious ass against my cock, and we fall asleep as one unit, two bodies fused together in perfect harmony.

Until the soft pattering of feet wakes me.

My eyes snap open, and I become instantly aware of the sky paling outside the window. I have no idea what time it is, but I ease away from Tammy's body, tucking the blanket around her to keep her warm and protected.

Scrambling for my jeans, I pull them on and carefully zip the fly before creeping out to the kitchen.

Fezzik is at the back door, scratching to get out. I open

it for him, watching him shoot off the back stairs and race to the closest tree to relieve himself.

"I can't find Mommy." A worried voice makes me spin, and I glance at Kai's scared little face. "She didn't come to bed last night."

I scratch my chest, all too aware that I'm shirtless, then crouch down so I can be eye level with the kid. "She had a sleepover in the parlor last night." I hope my smile is casual enough. "She wanted to fall asleep by the fire, so we built a bed out of cushions."

His shoulders relax, but then he tips his head with a confused little frown. "Did you sleep there too?"

"Um... yep." I nod, panic sizzling through me as I try to come up for a good reason why. "I just wanted to keep her warm."

"She does get cold." Kai nods, like this is reasonable, then turns to go find her.

I grab his arm before he can take off. I doubt she wants to be discovered naked.

"Actually, buddy, she's not awake yet. Why don't you let her have a sleep in?"

"But I'm hungry." His lips turn into a pout.

I grin. "Well, luckily for you, I make some pretty mean pancakes. Wanna help me?"

"Pancakes?" If he was a puppy, his ears would be perking up right now.

I grin. "Yup."

"You got maple syrup?"

"Of course we do."

"And bananas?"

"You know it."

His eyes start dancing with enthusiasm as I tip my head toward the kitchen and lead him into the pantry. We pull out ingredients, and I find a couple aprons. I tie one around his tiny little waist, and we get to work, sifting flour, cracking eggs, and making a big ol' mess.

By the time Tammy shuffles into the kitchen, her hair all mussed, Kai and I are both covered in flour, have batter smeared across our faces, and he's singing some pancake song his mommy taught him.

"You wait for the bubbles, then you flip it o-ver." His little off-key voice is adorable and blends perfectly with Tammy's delighted laughter.

As I spin to drink her in, we share a special smile, and I swear I've never been so happy in my life.

Her eyes start to glisten, like maybe she's thinking the same thing, and I take a mental snapshot of her smile and those perfect dimples.

CHAPTER 33
TAMMY

I sip wine from the bulbous new glasses Rachel purchased this week and try not to laugh at the look on Mikayla's face.

"What is this crap?" She sticks out her tongue and gags.

"Oh, stop it." Rachel lightly slaps her arm. "You have no taste."

"I think it's delicious." Lani licks her lips, then tries another sip. "I really like it and think you should definitely have this on the drinks menu."

"As long as you've got normal stuff too," Mikayla mutters.

Caroline starts to laugh. "For the plebs like us, who can't tell the difference between a five-dollar bottle of wine and some ancient bottle made in France, right?"

Mikayla lifts her glass. "That's right, my friend. That is so right."

Rachel and Lani roll their eyes, then share a look.

"Why did we invite them to this tasting again?" Lani murmurs.

"We didn't! They just showed up and parked it." Rachel looks around the table with a pointed glare that has no real venom to it.

"What else were we going to do?" Caroline blows a red curl off her face. "The guys are at practice, I'm caught up on my assignments for a change, and Jolie wanted to hang out with you guys."

Her cousin gives us a shy smile, and Mikayla leans forward with a conspiratorial whisper. "Is that actually true, or is she just being polite on your behalf?"

Jolie's cheeks turn neon pink as her eyes dart to each of us. "It's true. Being here's always fun."

Rachel's expression softens as she nudges the cheese board closer to the freshman. "How are things going? Is it getting easier?"

She bites her lips together, then nods. "Yeah. I'm writing an article for the school paper. I mean, they may not publish it. It's kind of like an audition."

"What's it about?"

"I'm not sure of my exact angle yet, but I'm interviewing some guys on the basketball team and thought I'd do a feature to highlight their season. Well, the start of their season, anyway."

"They've got a solid team this year. From what I've heard." Mikayla grabs a cracker and dips it into the hummus Rachel made from scratch. "But I think you should focus on the girls' team. They're way better."

"I did think about that, and I'm considering interviewing some of the female athletes as well. Like maybe I could do a story about the similarities and differences, but I know I'll need to be really careful what I write there, because I can't show favoritism."

"True." Lani nods. "As much as I hate to say it, sometimes it's better to play things safe."

"Plus, there are some really hot guys on the team, right? That can't be all bad." Caroline winks at Jolie, who goes bright red again. Her cousin gasps and nudges her with her elbow. "Wait, are you crushing on one of them?"

"No." Jolie shakes her head, so obviously lying.

"Which one? Do I know him? Who is he?"

"It's not..." Jolie shakes her head more vehemently. "No one. They're just cute. That doesn't mean I'm falling for any of them." She grabs the wineglass and takes a big sip, then cringes and puts it back on the table. "Do you have Sprite or... Coke Zero?"

Lani starts laughing as Rachel tries to stifle a groan. Getting up, she runs to the fridge and pulls out a can of Coke Zero, delivering it with a smile. "She's too young to drink anyway, Ray."

"This is a *tasting* while I try to decide which wines to serve and pair with the food I want to offer our guests. No one is going to get drunk!"

An hour later, Rachel is eating her words as Caroline and Mick giggle their way through a game of Truth or Dare. I have no idea how it even started, but somehow I'm caught up in this mess, sitting on the floor in the parlor watching Mikayla spin an empty beer bottle... which lands on me.

Thankfully, I'm sober enough not to suggest dare, because this crazy-ass girl opposite me would come up with something totally humiliating, I'm sure of it.

Instead, I risk "Truth" and instantly wish I hadn't.

Her eyes light with glee, and she asks the question that has obviously been on everyone's mind.

"What's the deal with you and Baxter?"

"What do you mean?" I swallow.

"Oh, don't act all coy. Ever since we got back last weekend, something has changed between you two."

"We've all noticed it." Rachel gives me a kind, hopeful smile. "Are you two...?" She wiggles her eyebrows, and now *I'm* the one turning fire-engine red.

"I knew it!" Caroline points at me, then high-fives Mikayla. "I told you. Didn't I tell you? They're totally doing it."

It's impossible not to choke out a laugh as I try and fail to deny it.

Sensing the inevitable, I quickly give up and admit, "Yeah, we hooked up the weekend you guys were all away."

"Woo! My girl!" Caroline holds up her hand, and I lightly slap it, feeling giddy giggles rumble in my stomach, followed swiftly by a heavy dose of guilt. I've been fighting it ever since the latest phone call with my mother, who has no idea about Baxter—I do value my life, after all—but she gave me another lecture on the importance of family stability and what Kai needs. How will this work? If Baxter and I become a permanent thing, what am I supposed to say to Kai? Or Hudson? Should Baxter and I even *become* a permanent thing, or is this just us getting some unfinished business out of my system?

I can feel myself starting to spiral and then notice all eyes are still intently on me.

So, I force a smile and tell them what they most likely want to hear.

"Being with Baxter is pretty amazing." *Truth.* "He's always been the sweetest guy and..." *Another truth.*

I shake my head, wondering why I feel so compelled to share. "We were best friends growing up... but then we grew apart. Being with him again is so familiar and fun and comfortable and... taking things to this next level is..." I let out a soft laugh, biting my lips, my skin burning. "It's incredible." *And yet another truth.*

But it's also super complicated, which is a truth you can't just keep ignoring, Tammy.

"Yay." Rachel distracts me, holding her hand over her heart. "I'm so happy for you guys. Baxter is such a closed book, but he once admitted to Lani and me that there was a girl in high school who he'd always loved. And then you show up here, and I've been desperate for you to finally make his wish come true."

My smile grows even wider.

It's been doing that a lot lately, and their joy for me only spurs me on, pushing me deeper into this love bubble... this make-believe place where everything outside of it stays away so I can keep living a faux reality surrounded by fun people who are so easy to like and a man who is quickly consuming my heart and soul.

I want to stay here and forget about my old life.

But I know that's not going to be possible.

Sooner or later, I'm going to have to face Hudson and the practical realities of my future. I can't keep saying I'll divorce him and then not actually do anything about it.

This isn't some fairy tale where Prince Baxter can whisk me away to his magical kingdom. There are papers to draw up, a lawyer to hire—I'm still not sure how I'm going to afford that—and I can't keep pretending that my marriage will evaporate all on its own.

Plus, there's Kai to think about. I have to put his needs above all else.

As much as I hate to agree with my mother, Kai does deserve a stable home, good schools. Can I give that to him without Hudson?

Does Baxter even want to take that on?

He probably would, but...

Thinking about all this stuff gives me a headache.

I guess I just want to delay the inevitable for as long as I can.

I'm not ready to go popping bubbles.

CHAPTER 34
BAXTER

As soon as Casey invited Kai to one of the Cougar practices, the little kid was begging to go. We're technically not allowed in here, but of course Casey pulled a few strings, and Asher helped him sweet-talk the coaches into letting us watch one practice. So here we are, sitting in the stands and watching my friends speed across the ice. Kai's snuggled up on my knee for a better view, and because the kid's so skinny that staying warm in the arena is nearly impossible for him.

I tuck my arm a little tighter around him, loving the way he cheers and keeps glancing up at me with a huge grin. His eyes are like *"Did you see that?"*

"They're pretty fast, right, buddy?"

He nods, his gaze glued to the rink.

The practice finishes up with a short game, and Kai flinches every time someone gets checked, then laughs as they tussle for the puck.

When Ethan flicks his stick and the puck goes firing into the goal, Kai lifts his hands in a cheer. Nothing comes out of his mouth, of course, but I can tell he's excited.

"Think you might want to play hockey one day?" I murmur.

He whips around to look at me. "Like that?" He points at the rink.

I nod.

His thoughtful little face is adorable, and I wait him out while he slowly thinks about it.

"Do you think I can?" His voice is so soft, I nearly miss it.

I lean my head a little closer. "Kai, I think you can do whatever you want. With a little hard work and determination, anything is possible."

It's like I'm handing him a gold star. His face lights with the sweetest smile, and I'm pretty sure I just made his day.

His back straightens with a proud grin, his chin rising just a little, and I'm pretty sure I'm falling hard for this lil' dude. I'm already in love with his mother, so it makes sense, right? But I never thought I could love a kid so much as well, especially one that isn't mine.

But this quiet, sweet boy on my lap is turning my heart to putty.

Assistant Coach Fisher blows the whistle, ending the practice and shouting at everyone to hit the showers. He's one of the younger coaches, just started this year, and seems to be pretty capable. He's strict and no-bullshit. I watched him working with the defensemen this session, and he seemed pretty switched on and decisive. Hopefully, he'll be a good asset to the team.

Casey skates to the edge and beckons us down. "Come on, kid, I'll give you a spin on the ice."

Kai's eyes pop wide, and he turns to check with me.

My heart pinches with affection, and I nod, letting him off my knee so he can walk down the stairs.

He gets to the edge of the rink, and Casey picks him up, nestling him on his hip and skating around the sides. Kai squeals and clings tight as Casey builds up speed, laughing at Kai's reaction.

"Pierce! Get that kid off the ice!" Fisher shouts at him.

"Just one more lap, Coach." Casey raises his arm and flies around the rink for a final round, ice spraying off his skates when he comes to an abrupt stop next to me.

Kai's laughing, his eyes sparkling like he's never had so much fun in his life.

"Did you like that?" Casey ignores Coach Fisher's fuming and grins at Kai.

The little guy bobs his head, then wraps his arms around Casey's neck in a hug that must be his form of thank you.

Casey grins at me over his shoulder, patting his back before handing him over to me. I grab him, throwing him over my shoulder and scoring a bunch of new squeals as I spin him around, then walk him out of the arena.

Like Casey, I ignore Coach Fisher's glares. The guy

must only be a year or two older than me, so I don't find it that intimidating, although the good boy in me does hustle to get out the doors. It was a privilege to even come to this practice, and the only reason I got in is because the head coach likes me. He's always loyal to his players—past and present.

"Can we go again?" Kai asks me when I tip him back, resting him on my hip and walking him to the car.

"Not sure we'll be allowed. That was a special treat. But…" I bounce him on my hip. "You can come to my practices anytime you want. I'm sure your mom won't mind."

Kai nods thoughtfully.

"You know…" I stop by the car and hand him the keys so he can press the button to unlock it. "Once your skating gets better, maybe you can join my Mini Mite team."

"Really?" His eyes bulge wide, his small mouth popping open.

"Yeah, totally. If you're into that idea, maybe we can go skating tomorrow, get your practice up."

He nods, then swallows like he's a little nervous.

I smile at him, placing him on the ground so he can climb into the car on his own. He buckles his booster seat, and I check that it's secure before sliding behind the wheel. I catch his eye in the rearview mirror. "You're gonna be a great skater, Kai. It's all about confidence and time on the ice. As you get better, your confidence grows, and then you can do even more. You're gonna be awesome."

He grins at me, then bites his bottom lip, looking out the window and humming to himself as we drive back to Ponderosa.

I've never felt more like a dad in my life. And shit, it's a great feeling.

Too bad he's not my kid.

I glance in the rearview mirror again, the thought sitting like an ugly weight in my chest.

He's not mine.

But, oh man, I wish he was.

CHAPTER 35
TAMMY

By the time the boys get home, the game of Truth or Dare is over—thank goodness. Although, it was kind of fun to learn that Lani's goal when she was six was to become the first female POTUS, and Rachel used to write love letters to her eighth-grade teacher and hide them under her bed.

"What? He was the first male teacher I'd ever had. He was so dreamy."

Caroline's big truth came out, and we all fell over in hysterics when she told us how she once bought her parents "special" brownies from a guy on the street.

"I was like sixteen, and I had no idea why he was selling these cakes. I didn't even know what 'special' brownies were, and they smelled delicious. He said it was a secret, magical recipe. It was Dad's birthday, so..." She shook her head and snorted. "He got so high."

Jolie giggled. "Was that the night he did that really weird sermon at the youth event?"

Caroline snorted and started nodding.

"He was talking total smack, and we had no idea what was up with him."

"Then we sang him 'Happy Birthday,' and he started dancing on the stage!"

Jolie gasped while Caroline's mouth opened with one of those silent laughs that was so strong she couldn't even make a sound.

She flopped against her cousin, who was close to hysterics as well, and then we all couldn't stop giggling.

After that, Mikayla, who was well tipsy on wine tasters by this stage, snorted hot sauce up her nose. Tears were pouring out her eyes, and her nose didn't stop running for like fifteen minutes. The funniest part of it all was that she'd dared *herself* to do this. So, yeah, maybe she was drunker than I thought.

Thankfully, she's currently in the shower and hopefully sobering up so my sweet little four-year-old doesn't have to see her totally hammered.

Caroline and Jolie have left now. I think they're meeting up with Casey and some of the other guys at Offside. Lani and Ray are in the kitchen finalizing their thoughts on wine, which doesn't really interest me.

I skip down the stairs, pushing up my sleeves as Kai and Baxter walk in. My little boy comes racing over to me, and I catch him in my arms, lifting him high and swinging him around.

"How's my boy?"

"I want to be a hockey star!" he shouts. His loud enthusiasm surprises me, and I can't help laughing as I share a quick look with Baxter.

"Do you now?"

"Yeah, I want to be like Casey and go fast and get goals like Ethan."

"Or you could be a goalie like Baxter. Saving the day all the time."

I love the way Baxter's cheeks splash with color whenever someone gives him a compliment.

Kai tips his head in thoughtful consideration, then wrinkles his nose and wriggles out of my arms. "No, I want to score the goals and go fast!" He takes off, running for the kitchen, and I turn to Baxter, my eyebrows rising high.

"Okay, who is that kid, and what have you done with my son?"

He gives me a shy smile. "He loved being there today. You should have seen his face."

I'm instantly disappointed that I didn't join them. Not that I'd been invited. Kai was clear it was a boys' trip, and it was so freaking adorable, I couldn't argue with him.

"Maybe we should take him to a game sometime."

"I'd love that." Baxter's eyes start to dance as he glances around us, checking the coast is clear before pulling me into his arms and lightly kissing my lips.

I chase his mouth when he pulls away from me, giggling and palming the back of his head, forcing him to deepen the kiss and give me some more of his delectable sugar.

He obliges, and my insides simmer with desire.

We haven't shared another night since the weekend. With the house full and Kai sleeping in the same room as me, it's a little awkward. But the girls all know now, so maybe it's okay for me to sneak up to Baxter's room tonight.

I pull away from him, ready to tell him about my afternoon when my phone starts ringing. Tugging it out of my back pocket, I glance at the screen and deflate.

Baxter frowns, looking at the screen too.

"Oh," he murmurs. "I guess you better get that."

"Do I have to?" I mutter.

"He's Kai's father, so... yeah, you have to." His voice is flat as he lets me go and walks away without a backward glance.

With a heavy sigh, I slide my thumb across the screen and shuffle into the parlor for a little privacy.

"Hi, Hudson."

"You're divorcing me now? What the fuck, Tamara? Were you even going to talk to me about this?"

I grit my teeth. "I take it you've been speaking to my mother."

"Actually, *my* mom told me."

"Of course she did." I roll my eyes. Our parents are way too close, sitting in the background trying to organize our lives for us. It doesn't matter that we've moved away from Gladstone and are grown-ass adults now. They still want to control everything.

"You can't do this."

"Actually, I can."

"You said you wanted space, and I've given you that. You can't just cut me off, ignore me, and then decide you want a divorce without giving me any say in the matter. This is ridiculous." I clench my teeth again, gripping the phone as he lets out a huff, then lowers his voice. "It's time for you to come home. I don't know where you've been, but it's obviously given you no perspective. You've had plenty of time to process what you saw, and now we need to be mature adults and work through this."

Frowning at my reflection in the window, I open my mouth to deny him, but he just keeps going.

"I need to know where you are."

I shake my head.

"You need to tell me where my son is." His tone gets harsh and snappy.

I blink in surprise. "He's with me. Safe and happy. You can talk to him right now if you like."

"I called to talk to you!" he barks. "Tell me where you are. Right now."

"I—" Biting my lips together, I force air through my nose, willing myself not to start yelling into the phone and alerting everyone in this villa of the heinous phone call I'm enduring. "I don't want to tell you where I am, but if you'd like to talk to Kai, I can pass him the phone."

"It is my right as his father to know his physical location. You are essentially kidnapping him if you don't tell me that."

"What?" I squeak. "You're accusing me of kidnapping my own child?"

"He's my kid too!"

"Really? Because you know, we've been away for three weeks now, and not once have you texted to ask how he's doing or called to talk with him. Every communication I've had with you has been about us, not him." I tut. "Where is this even coming from, anyway? You work such long hours, he barely knows who you are. It's not like you ever play with him or—"

"He's my kid, and I miss him. I want to see him. I want to see *you*." He sounds so desperate that it makes my heart stutter.

I snap my eyes shut.

"Don't make me take you to court over this, Tamara."

The sudden threat and his icy change in tone makes my heart go from a stutter to a dull thud. My breath catches, my brain pulsing with a sickening beat that makes me want to throw up.

"You can't just divorce me and walk away with my kid. I have rights too. He's my son, and I'm not just handing over custody without a fight. You know I'll demolish you. Why would you risk losing him?"

My insides run cold. What the hell is he doing? Why is he saying this stuff? Where is—

I go still, a dull ache spreading through my system like a virus when it hits me. Hudson's parents. His mother is a force to be reckoned with, and as soon as my mother mentioned the D-word to her, she would have gone into battle mode. She's probably demanding Hudson step up and start getting tough with me.

I can just hear her voice in my head. "Stop pandering to her need for space and rattle her cage, Hudson! Kai's your son, and you will fight for him. Do whatever it takes!"

"You don't have to do this." I wish my voice was coming out stronger, but it's getting shaky as I rest my head against the cold glass and try not to cry.

"Don't think for a second that I'll just back down and let you do this to us. What do you think a judge is going to say when he hears you just took off with our kid and refused to tell me where you were?"

"What do you think they'll say when they find out I left because you cheated on me?"

"That has nothing to do with parenthood. Now stop denying me access to my son!"

"I'm not denying you access," I argue, feeling sick to my core. "I can go and get him right now. You guys can talk."

"You know he's allergic to talking on a phone. He'll just stand there saying nothing."

"But he could hear your voice."

"Tell me where you are. I need to know *where* you are for my own peace of mind. You've got my kid. I deserve to know his location."

With a heavy sigh, I murmur, "We're in Nolan. It's a small town in Colorado."

"Why'd you go there?"

My insides pinch so tight it actually hurts. I fist my sweater and agonize for a moment over what to say.

If I mention Baxter, will he freak out?

It's none of his business anyway... is it?

"Tammy? You still there? Why Nolan?"

"Because it's a safe, happy place," I blurt. "We're staying in a beautiful old villa that's about to be opened up as an exclusive bed-and-breakfast. It's peaceful here. And Kai's doing really well." I suck in a breath, then say what I know I'm supposed to say even though I really don't feel like it. "Now, if you want to see him, let's set a time and I'll bring him to you."

His stony silence settles into my bones, and I shudder when he finally breaks it in a gruff voice. "I'll check my schedule and get back to you. But stop ignoring my messages. I'm his parent too. I... I miss you guys. I want you to come home."

I shake my head, and it's like he can sense me doing it.

His sigh is heavy. "I made one mistake, Tam. Are you going to hold that against me forever? We're a family."

Closing my eyes, I ward off the tears.

A family?

Are we really?

When a wave of raucous laughter reaches me from the kitchen, I have to wonder. How is it possible to feel more at home with someone I haven't seen in years and a bunch of strangers I've only just met?

How is it that speaking to my husband fills me with zero warmth, yet one smile from Baxter can make me feel like I'm glowing?

Family. This old villa filled with hockey players and their girlfriends... that's family.

CHAPTER 36
BAXTER

"Kai." Tammy's voice is shaking as she steps into the kitchen with a forced smile and holds out her phone. "Your dad wants to talk to you."

Kai jumps off the stool, brushing cookie crumbs off his mouth before taking the phone. He doesn't say anything, just holds it against his ear and listens.

I try to catch Tammy's eye, but she won't look at me. She crouches down beside her son and holds his hand, giving him an encouraging smile.

"Say hi, back. Remember? He can't see your face, so you have to use your voice."

Kai nods but still doesn't talk.

Tammy closes her eyes, dipping her head for a moment. I can feel her pain and frustration from across the room. This situation sucks for her. I can only imagine what Hudson said on the phone—was he mean? Demanding? Or gentle and cajoling?

The guy could sell anything to anyone. Seriously. He'd always been cheesy and persuasive. I used to convince myself that the only way Tammy got with him was because he cast a spell on her and she was swept away by his effervescent charm.

But did she really love him?

My insides twist. I don't want to think about that right now. Tammy and I had the best weekend. She cares about me.

But does she love you?

Or are you just a fling to satiate some long-lost need that wasn't met back at that swimming hole?

With a thick swallow, I turn my back, grateful when I hear the front door open and the guys come in with all their gear. I dart out of the kitchen to help them, only just catching Kai's voice behind me.

"Good... Because a dog lives here. He's barking."

I'm sure Hudson is telling him how cool puppies are and offering to buy him one if he comes back home.

Shit! Is Hudson going to convince Tammy to change her mind about the divorce? Is he going to woo Kai back and make him beg Mommy to take him home?

I'm going to lose them.

I can already feel it coming.

Walking out into the entryway, I watch Casey pick up an excited Fezzik and greet him. Lani appears behind me, and Asher's face lights up. He pulls her into a hug, murmuring something against her cheek.

She starts to laugh. "Just wait until I tell you about my afternoon."

A fresh envy that I've never felt before scorches me.

I want what they've got.

I want to walk in the door and have a woman greet me and offer to tell me about her day.

You did, just before.

Yeah, and then her husband called. And even when he's officially her ex, he's still going to call... because he's Kai's father.

A bitter acid fills my stomach as I walk up the stairs and decide to hide away in my room until dinner. In fact, who needs dinner? Maybe I'll just spend the evening up here. That way I don't have to pretend that I'm fine and nothing is bothering me. Shit, I wish I had the excuse of studying. I used that all the time at Hockey House, hiding away in my room so I didn't have to deal.

I've always been that way. But after Mom died, it got so much worse. She was taken so suddenly that I didn't even know what to do with the pain inside me. Watching Tammy marry Hudson the week before didn't help, and I was sucked into this vortex of despair.

Hiding away is just easier, you know? It takes so much energy to put on a show.

Shutting the door behind me, I flop onto my bed like a starfish, staring at the ceiling I painted over the summer and once again lamenting the past.

It's dark by the time there's a soft knock at my door.

I'm writing in my journal and am tempted to stay quiet, but after a soft huff, I murmur, "Come in."

Tammy's face appears, her smile gentle and sad. "Hey. You okay?"

"Yeah." I nod, placing the pen between the pages and setting it on my nightstand.

"You were really quiet at dinner."

I shrug, kind of wishing I hadn't gone down after all. Manners forced me to the dining room, so I ate and listened while Casey told stories that made Kai laugh. The kid seriously adores the guy. Rachel ended up telling everyone about Mikayla's hot sauce incident, and I swear the smile on Ethan's face was glowing. He loves how crazy his lil' mouse is. Lani talked about school, and Asher talked about business with Rachel. Conversation flowed all around me, and I sat watching it all like I usually do, trying my best not to look at Tammy, because every time I did, it hurt.

And now she's standing in my doorway.

I beckon her in, because I can't help myself.

She looks soft and vulnerable tonight—her eyes bigger than usual, glinting with a tumultuous look that makes me want to wrap her in a hug.

"You okay?" I ask once the door's shut.

"Yeah, I just settled Kai and thought I'd come up and check on you before going to bed." She tugs on the sleeve of her Tweety Bird pajamas, and I adore her.

I crave her.

I so desperately want to rewrite history.

Her short little toes curl into the carpet as she studies me. I try to keep my expression neutral, but she's always been too good at reading me.

"Hudson's phone call really threw you, huh?"

Clenching my jaw, I look down at my knees and shrug. "Seemed to throw you too. I'm guessing he wants you back."

She lets out a sigh, her lips trembling as she stares at the carpet. "I'm guessing his parents are putting pressure on him to want me back."

I glance up then, checking her eyes for tears, but she just sniffs and shakes her head. "If he cheated on me, then I mustn't have been enough, right? Why isn't he just telling his parents that we're over? Why is he fighting for me?"

It's tempting to tell her it's because Hudson is a complete tool, but I probably shouldn't go insulting the guy to her face.

"Maybe he realizes what a catch you are and that he made a really stupid mistake."

Her expression bunches into a frown. "Are you standing up for him?"

"No." I shake my head vehemently. "I'm just..." I keep shaking my head, then let out a heavy sigh. "I don't know what the fuck I'm saying. See, this is why it's better not to talk."

Her lips twitch, her dimple winking at me as she tips her head and shuffles closer. Running the back of her knuckles down my face, she then draws her thumb across my bottom lip. "I'd be quite happy not to talk right now."

My hands automatically land on her hips. "Tammy."

"I just want... to be with you. I don't want to think. I just want..." Her lips part, and then she's smiling down at me again. "I just want to play a game."

"A game?" My face flickers with a frown as she finds a perch on my lap, straddling my legs and smelling like heaven and feeling like the world's strongest narcotic. When her arms wrap around me and her tits squish against my chest, I immediately harden in response.

Her lips brush against my ear as she whispers, "Let's play Baxter Says."

CHAPTER 37
BAXTER

My throat goes instantly thick and gummy the second her words hit me. They whistle into my ear like a siren's song, and I'm powerless against them.

I do try.

I lean back, look at her face. I take in her little nod and the gleam in her eyes.

And then my mouth starts working with a force I have no control over.

"Baxter says kiss me," I croak.

She lurches for my mouth, holding my face and kissing me deep, sucking my tongue between her lips while I fist her pajamas and resist the urge to tear them off her body.

Her lips continue to massacre and delight me, peppering my jawline before sucking my earlobe then nipping my neck.

"What's next, Bax? Tell me what you want," she breathes against my skin.

"Um... Baxter says take your clothes off."

She leans back, grinning at me and sliding off my knee. When I said it, I thought she might just undress like a normal person, but she's giving me a little dance, seductively taking off cartoon pajamas like a professional stripper.

Holy shit.

My cock is straining against my pants, begging for release.

I try to ignore the sensation, drinking in her lithe body and soft curves as she sways before me. Her hips are full and beautiful. I want to grab them again, run my fingers around those perfect ass cheeks, and hold her against me.

"C'mere." I beckon her with my finger once she's fully naked.

"Uh-uh." She shakes her head with a soft giggle. "Baxter didn't say."

My lips twitch, and I growl, "Baxter says get your ass over here."

She laughs. "Oooo. I like this Baxter." She wiggles her eyebrows, sashaying over to me. "What else does he want me to do?"

It's hard to breathe when she's this sexy. It's hard to speak. To think. All I can do is touch her, palming her ass and pulling her between my legs.

She lets out a soft squeak, which turns into a groan

when I suck her nipple into my mouth. My tongue lavishes her until her legs are practically buckling. Holding her up, I work my way to her other breast, not wanting it to feel left out.

Gripping my shoulders, she whimpers, murmuring, "I want you naked too."

"Baxter says undress me."

She obeys instantly, tugging on my shirt and whipping it off, throwing it over her shoulder, then dropping to her knees between my thighs. The sound of my belt unbuckling and my zipper coming down has never been sweeter.

Lifting my hips, I help her tug my pants and boxers off. She throws them aside but stays on her knees, staring at my cock like it's beautiful or fascinating.

Her tongue darts out, wetting her lips before looking up at me with those big brown eyes.

She's waiting for another command. She wants this game to continue.

I know what I want to ask. I'm curious. I've never felt it before.

But what if she doesn't want to?

"Say it," she whispers before looking at my hard cock like she's hungry for it.

"Uh…" I clear my throat. "Baxter says… suck my cock?" I wince, feeling crass.

But she just licks her lips, wrapping her fingers around the shaft and kissing the tip. I flinch because it feels like nothing I've experienced before, and when her mouth wraps around my head and she sucks me in, I swear I've entered a different universe.

"Oh shit." I fist the duvet, barely able to breathe as she sucks me off.

It's fucking fantastic, the sensation enough to make me want to blow. But I fight it. Closing my eyes, I tip my head back and drown in this awesomeness.

Fuck, fuck, fuck. If this kills me, I'll die the happiest human on the planet, I swear.

She stops sucking, obviously catching her breath, then licks my shaft like a popsicle before taking me into her mouth again.

Her fingers lightly cup my balls, setting off different pleasure sensors which make my heart take off. My chest is heaving as I cradle the back of her hair, lightly threading my fingers into her thick locks.

Shit, I'm gonna come.

I'm gonna blow right in her mouth.

I don't want that.

"Stop," I rasp.

She keeps going.

"Baxter says stop." My voice rises with urgency.

She pulls away, looking up at me with her glossy lips. "What? What does Baxter want now?"

My lips curl into a tender smile as I brush my thumb across her cheek. "Baxter wants to bury his cock in your perfect pussy."

CHAPTER 38
TAMMY

Holy shit. If that's not the sexiest thing I have ever heard.

I'm so wet from going down on this guy and his glorious dick that I'm practically dripping.

It takes no effort at all to rise to my feet and ask him, "How do you want me?"

The thought obviously hadn't occurred to him, so I crawl onto his bed with a playful giggle and give him a seductive look over my shoulder.

"Uh…"

"It's okay." I smile at his nervous expression. "This is gonna feel awesome."

Brushing his hand over my butt cheeks, he tentatively gets on the bed, kneeling behind me.

His face takes on that wonder-filled expression, like I'm a rare beauty he's discovering all over again. The pads of his fingers trail my back like he's trying to memorize each curve and crevice.

It stills me. Humbles me in ways I've never experienced.

My body is this wondrous mystery to him, and he's obviously loving unearthing all my secrets, peeling back new layers and discovering me in different ways.

Pulling my cheeks apart, he studies me like I'm a scientific discovery. It's a little unnerving, but I can't complain when he leans forward and licks my opening. His tongue plunges into me, and I cry out at the overwhelming pleasure. His fingers skim my clit, searching for that perfect spot that sends me over the edge.

Snatching the pillow, I bunch it, biting into it as he destroys me with his perfect tongue and fingers.

My legs are quivering as the orgasm rockets through me—an earthquake of epic proportions. My lusty screams are muffled by the pillow as the shock waves travel to the tips of my toes, but he keeps going, keeps touching me until I turn my head and beg for mercy.

"Stop, stop. I need you inside me. Please. Now." The words are coming out in whimpers, and the relief that powers through me as he thrusts into my body is breathtaking.

Rising up on my hands, I move my hips back, taking more of him while he moans and grabs my ass.

"This is..." His voice gets lost to a grunt as he thrusts into me again.

"I know," I squeak, about to beg for more, when he delivers with another powerful thrust that electrifies my body.

272

He's deep and filling me whole.

I can feel him throughout my entire body and drop to my elbows, changing the angle. He groans, his fingers skimming down my legs and grabbing my feet. He pulls them up against his thighs and continues to pump into me. His rhythm is heady and addictive. I match it, taking in all of him with every thrust, until things turn a little wild and uncontrolled.

He's about to come. I can feel—

"Wait," he whispers, slowing the pace, dropping my feet and leaning over me.

"Baxter says c'mere." Cradling my beasts, he pulls me up so my back is resting against his sweaty torso.

The fire that was about to consume me settles for a moment as he draws out this erotic session on his bed. His lips nibble my shoulder, and I turn my head so I can kiss him. His tongue slides against mine—intimate and beautiful. Fisting the back of his hair, he rocks inside me while our tongues dance.

I start to lose my breath, having to pull away so I can pant and moan. That fire is building again, heat pouring through me as I drop back down to my elbows, fisting the pillow and groaning into it.

He grabs my ass again, his speed picking up while that fire builds and builds, flames licking every point in my body before consuming me like an inferno.

"Baxter." I cry out his name when he starts to jerk, punching out short noises of pleasure as he thrusts and gasps to a messy finish that's pure abandon.

Burying himself deep, he explodes inside me, and I feel every second of it, another orgasm ripping through me so we're coming in unison. Breaths punch out of us, and his heart is no doubt hammering just as fast as mine.

My knees can't hold me anymore, and I start to flop. He catches me around the waist, lowering us together so he can stay inside me.

Resting his weight on his elbows, he pants into my ear, not saying anything. But the gentle kisses he caresses my cheek with are words enough.

I smile beneath his soft lips and wish for time to stand still.

CHAPTER 39
BAXTER

Tammy nestles her head against my chest as I run light patterns over her naked back. That was fucking amazing. I'm tempted to ask if she wants to play Baxter Says again. Or we could play Tammy Says. I don't care. I'll happily follow her lead, just as long as I get to be naked with her and worship her body in every way I can.

"I guess I should head back down to Kai."

"You don't have to," I whisper. "Stay with me. He can find us in the morning."

"I don't want to confuse him." Her voice is soft, and I don't understand why the words sting so much.

"We could just explain it to him," I try to argue as she sits up and goes to leave my bed.

She glances over her shoulder. "Explain what? How? What am I supposed to say to him?"

"Uh…" I shake my head and shrug. "I don't know.

Maybe that you and Daddy are getting a divorce because he did something terrible."

Her expression buckles. "I can't tell Kai his father cheated on me."

"Why not? He did."

She looks at me like I'm stupid. "Kai's too young to understand the concept of cheating in that way. I'm not exposing him to that. He's four."

"You're going to have to tell him one day."

"Do I?" She slides off my bed. "Can't I just not say anything?"

Sitting up, I shake my head at her, frustrated that she's putting her pajamas back on—covering up her sexy nakedness and leaving me. "Won't he eventually be curious as to why you guys don't live with Daddy anymore?"

She runs a hand through her hair, closing her eyes and avoiding my gaze.

"Tammy." I soften my voice. "Why don't you just tell him that you really like living here and that you're gonna stay?"

She goes still, a breath punching out of her before she turns to face me. "I'm staying?"

"Well, yeah. Aren't you? I mean, I know you said this was just a vacation while you figured everything out, but it's pretty clear, isn't it?"

With a thick swallow, she straightens her Tweety Bird pajama shirt and stares at the floor... and I get the distinct impression that she's not telling me something.

"You are still divorcing him, right? That's what you said. We hooked up because you're no longer in a relationship. Right?"

She's not saying anything, so I decide to be helpful and map it out for her.

"Hudson's a dirtbag cheat who doesn't deserve you. He never really did anyway. The only reason you guys got married was because you were pregnant."

Her eyes snap to mine, and my heart starts to shrivel.

"Right? You wouldn't have married him otherwise... right?" My voice sounds tiny and dies completely when she shrugs.

"I don't know," she murmurs, her face bunching. "I just don't feel like I can tell Kai that, okay?" Snatching her pajamas bottoms off the floor, she wrestles herself into them, the fabric twisting in her haste and slowing her down. "It's so complicated, you know?"

"It doesn't have to be," I mutter, my insides writhing. I'm hating every second of this conversation. "Just tell Kai that you're with me now and that you guys can live here."

"How?" She flings her arms wide. "This place is about to become a bed-and-breakfast."

"So?"

"I doubt the owners are gonna want me raising a child around their guests."

"They won't mind."

"Really? Have you checked? I'm sure Vanessa would have something to say about it." She gives me a pointed look, and all I can do is dart my eyes away from her. "And

277

what about Kai? He gets nervous around strangers. This environment will unsettle him."

"So, we move someplace else."

"We're moving in together now?" She blinks at me in surprise.

I match her expression with a confused frown. What is she not getting here? Why is she acting like this?

Unless...

Oh fuck.

I clench my jaw and stare at the rumpled duvet cover, willing my heart not to die on the spot.

She doesn't love me.

This *is* just a fling for her. She's not serious about wanting to set up a life with me. I'm just... I don't know what the fuck I am.

But I'm definitely not Kai's father. And I'm obviously not Tammy's boyfriend either.

Sex must mean something different to her.

I thought we were making love, but she's not on the same page as me.

So, I do the only thing I can.

I go quiet.

CHAPTER 40
TAMMY

The expression on Baxter's face is glacial. I can feel him retreating into himself, and part of me wants to fight for him to come back, but I'm too exhausted to try.

I don't know how we can go from epic sex to a disagreement, but it's happening.

I can't even remember exactly what I said to make him shut down like this.

Maybe I'm just kind of reeling that he's wanting to move in with me—form some kind of family unit. I wasn't expecting that. I get that I'm his high school crush. I get that he's only ever wanted me. And that is so freaking sweet and endearing, but we've barely spoken for five years, and now he's wanting to set up a life with me?

I'm not the girl I was from high school.

He doesn't know what he's proposing. Taking on a kid who's not even his? Taking on what could be a brutal custody battle? If Hudson gets even a whiff of Baxter, he'll no doubt use it against me, making this whole process a million times harder.

And even if we do survive all of that, how is Baxter going to support me and Kai? I don't even know if he gets paid to work here. And I'm guessing he makes minimal money as a hockey coach. Kai and I can't live off that.

And even if I do get a job and we somehow scrape together enough to live off, what if things go wrong? What if Baxter decides stepfatherhood isn't for him, and then Kai has to go through losing another parent all over again?

Why the hell are you spiraling right now, Tammy?

Stop being so fucking practical!

You should be stripping off your clothes and getting back against his warm, solid body. What the fuck are you doing?

An apology is wedged in my throat—soft words that might have him opening up to me again.

But for some reason, they won't come out.

I should explain what I'm feeling—tell him each and every one of my fears. Tell him about Hudson's threat and my primal need to protect my son above all else.

But... Baxter won't even look at me right now. It's happening again. I say something he doesn't want to hear, so he silently pushes me away.

Why isn't he begging me to stay? Fighting for me? Telling me I'm wrong?

Disappointment wars against my practical logic.

What will getting back into his bed really achieve? More confusion.

Kai can't wake up to find us naked together. How will I even explain that to him? We're lucky we didn't get busted on the weekend and that he so easily bought Baxter's sleepover story.

But sleepovers are an occasional thing, which means I need to get back to my son.

I open my mouth to say good night, but Baxter won't even glance my way when I move. His eyes are fixed on the wall, and the stony expression on his face is killing me.

So I slip out of the room and head downstairs.

Kai's blissfully unaware of my turmoil as I slide into the bed. His soft, sleepy sounds can usually lull me to sleep as well, but I can't switch off. Tears make my eyes ache, and I sniffle into my pillow. It's cold and lonely without Baxter, and part of me wishes I had the courage to invite him into my life this way.

But how are we supposed to make it work?

Ponderosa is a dream. A break from reality. But it's not a long-term solution. It's time for me to stop running away and ignoring the problem. I need to figure out a plan for my life, and the question has to start with "What's best for Kai?"

A soft knock at the door wakes me. I have no idea what time it is, but there's light behind the curtains, and Kai is sitting up in bed, flicking through a stack of picture books.

Rachel's head pops through the door, and she cringes at me.

"What?" I sit up, my head groggy after such a restless sleep.

"You've got a visitor," she softly tells me. I can sense by her tone and the pained look on her face that it's a visitor I don't want to see.

For a second, I worry that it's my mother. But how'd she find out where I was?

Ugh. Hudson probably called and told on me.

Anger bubbles as I try to steel myself for whatever awaits me.

"I'll be there in a minute," I grit out.

"Okay." Rachel disappears, and I turn to look at Kai.

"Hey, Mommy." His sweet smile does my heart in, and I touch his face.

"Morning, kiddo." I kiss him and force myself out of bed.

I'm shaking as I pull on some sweats and a hoodie that's still stained from the last time Kai and I made chocolate cake. We had a bit of a cocoa powder incident. Our laughter skips through my memory, and I smile down at my son, knowing that whatever choices I make going forward have to be for his benefits. That's the role of the mother, right? Children first.

What does he need?

Sucking in a breath, I turn for the door and hear him jumping off the bed. When we step into the hallway, he grabs my hand, and we walk down the stairs together.

My stomach drops the second Hudson comes into view. Part of me is relieved it's not my mother, a small part of me skitters at the sight of him—he'll always be handsome—and the last part of me seizes up in mild panic. Shit. This is the moment I've been trying to avoid, but it's here now, and there's nothing I can do but face it.

"Hey, family." Hudson smiles up at us, as if nothing has even been wrong. As if I didn't ask him to call and arrange a time with me first.

Anger splashes through me, another emotion to throw into this Molotov cocktail I'm trying to deal with.

I gave him too much information yesterday. Why didn't I just say Nolan? Why'd I talk about this being a bed-and-breakfast? In my attempt to cajole him, I spilled way too much and now he's here and—

"My two best people." Hudson's voice rings with that upbeat quality I first fell in love with. He was always so enthusiastic about life, so charismatic. Then we moved to the city and he became a stressed-out workaholic trying to provide for his family. We had to grow up way too fast.

Kai squeezes my hand, leaning against my leg as he peers down at his father. "Hi, Daddy."

Hudson grins. "I got you a present." He holds up a large wrapped box, and Kai lets out a delighted gasp, nearly tripping down the stairs trying to get to it.

Hudson is always buying him stuff.

I guess it's a way to make up for when he's not around. Working late nights in town or going to sales conferences on the weekends means he doesn't get to spend much quality time with Kai. Whenever he's away, he always brings back gifts, and he's gone extra big this time around.

"What is it?" Kai takes the box.

"Open it and see." Hudson musses his hair, then kisses his forehead and glances up at me. His smile is broad and proud—*Look at me being dad of the year. Aren't I doing great?*

I can't smile back. Instead, I stay on the stairwell, gripping the railing and watching my son's delight as he unwraps a remote-controlled car. "Wow!" He gives his dad a shy smile, then turns to me and beams.

"That's very cool." I nod.

"Why don't you go outside and play with it?" Hudson points at the door, and for some reason, my hackles go up. Once again, Kai gets dismissed.

"You can play in here," I tell him. "It's a little cold outside. Why don't you set it up and drive it around the entryway?"

"Or a different room," Hudson suggests with a bright smile. I frown down at him, and he meets my glare with a pointed look. "We need to talk."

I know we do, but that doesn't mean I want to.

With a soft sigh, I walk down the rest of the stairs and tip my head toward the parlor.

Kai's too busy unboxing his new toy to really notice the tension, and I try to keep my voice low as I walk to the parlor window and stare out of it.

"What do you want?" I murmur.

Hudson huffs, scraping his hand through his hair. "Gimme a break, Tam. I drove through the night to get here, okay? The least you can do is listen."

He drove through the night. For me. I wish I could ignore that fact, but I can't, because it's kind of huge.

It says a lot.

And that probably means I should listen.

Closing my eyes, I rest my head against the window and wish I could disappear. I get why Baxter shuts down sometimes. It's safer that way, right? You can just block out the world and pretend the bad stuff doesn't exist.

If only it'd take away the problems at the same time.

But life is not that simple. And unlike Baxter, I don't have the luxury of just turning my back on the things I don't want to deal with.

Hudson's here.

And it's time to face this.

Gritting my teeth, I force myself to stand tall, open my eyes, and look at the man I married.

CHAPTER 41
BAXTER

I barely slept last night and feel like shit this morning. Even putting on clothes feels like an effort. I need to keep myself busy today. I'll finish painting those bedrooms on the third floor, take Fezzik for an extra-long walk, and thank God for hockey practice this afternoon. I can make myself scarce and avoid having to have any uncomfortable conversations with Tammy.

Real mature, man.

I ignore the irritating voice in my head, shutting it up with a soft growl.

"Baxter?" Kai's hesitant voice makes me spin.

"Hey, buddy." I force a smile as he holds up a car and remote.

"Daddy bought it for me."

My insides crawl, but I try to hide it as I crouch down. "Oh yeah? Looks pretty cool."

"Wanna play?" Those big eyes of his have some kind

of magical power, because I nod and take the car from him, placing it on the floor and helping him with the remote.

"Those two." I point to the toggles. "Yep, and go left." I wince when the car whips right and smashes into the doorframe. "Try the other left."

He misses my joke and goes the other way, grinning when the car shoots into the hallway.

Chasing after it, he guides the car down to the end and then struggles to turn it around again. It keeps bumping into the walls.

"Here, can I help?" I take the remote when he hands it to me and show him how to do a three-point turn. "When did your dad give you this? I haven't seen you playing with it before."

"Just now," Kai says casually, oblivious to the fact that the world is crashing down around us. I can practically see the walls crumbling, can feel the floorboards shifting beneath me.

"Your dad's here? Now?"

Kai nods, still more focused on his controller and car than me.

"He's downstairs?"

"Uh-huh." Kai glances my way. "He's talking to Mommy."

I can't breathe.

Holy fuck, I can't breathe.

"Do you... um... has he come to take you home?"

Kai shrugs, and I try to read his face, wondering if this bothers him. Probably not as much as it's bothering me!

"Do you want to go with him?" I ask softly.

He pauses, looking thoughtful as he stares at the car, frozen in the middle of the hallway. His voice is quiet when he finally says, "I want to be with Mommy."

Me too.

My lips feel like lead weights as I try to form a smile. "Good call, man."

He nods and gives me a closed-mouth smile. For a second, I think he looks sad, but then he goes back to focusing on his car.

A boulder has lodged in my throat, making it hard to swallow, and there's a bass drum playing in my head.

He's here.

Hudson's here.

Downstairs.

Talking to my Tammy.

Not your Tammy, his.

No, she's divorcing him. She said she was leaving him for good.

Bile surges in my stomach, and I jerk to my feet, struggling to keep my tone even. "Wanna go downstairs?"

"Okay." Kai runs and grabs his car. "I'm hungry. Can you make me pancakes again?"

"I'm sure we can do that," I croak, my chest spasming when he captures my hand on the top step. I hold it as we walk down to the bottom floor, my head spinning when I hear Hudson's voice in the parlor.

It takes me back to high school and that desolate feeling that washed through me every time I saw him talking to Tammy. He used a special voice for her. It was soft and hypnotic somehow. And the way she used to look at him...

She drank him in like he was everything.

"You're my wife. I love you." His tone is soft and beguiling.

But his words are sulfuric acid. I want to throw up.

"Come on, Tam. I'm sorry, okay? I'm *so* sorry."

"I know." Her voice sounds broken and weary.

"Please, you can't just walk away from us. Are you seriously willing to turn your back on the life we've been building together? We love each other. We love our son."

Tammy doesn't say anything, and that's all I need to hear. My doubts from last night are amplified to the point of deafening me.

Fuck, I can't hear this shit.

Walking through to the kitchen, I force polite conversation with Rachel, who seems overly excited by the prospect of making Kai pancakes. Fezzik scratches on the back door and I let him in, picking him up and petting him, drawing what comfort I can. He licks my chin, but even his excited tail isn't making me feel better.

I'm losing Tammy all over again.

But somehow, this time feels worse.

CHAPTER 42
TAMMY

I'm so confused right now I can't even think straight.

Hudson is looking so remorseful. He's in agony over losing me and Kai. I can see it, hear it in his voice. Am I being a heartless bitch if I turn my back on that?

He's the father of my kid, and he's desperate to make it work.

He wants me back, and he's willing to fight for me.

Dropping to his knees, Hudson clasps my hands, tears lining his lashes when he notices I'm not wearing my rings anymore. "Please," he chokes out, "I'd do anything to take back what I did. I don't know what came over me. You were away, and I was lonely, and I just let her in, you know? I didn't mean for it to go that far, but we got caught up in a moment."

I close my eyes, not wanting to hear the details.

I don't know who she is or how she's related to Hudson. I don't know if he's making it sound like a onetime thing when it might have been going on every time Kai and I visited my parents.

Maybe I should be asking those questions, though. *Is she a work colleague? Are you going to see her again? Cheat on me again?*

But if I ask that stuff, is that indicating that I want to try and resolve these issues with him? Am I going back to my marriage?

I said I wanted a divorce. I was so clear on that... and now I'm standing here struggling to know what to do.

The bubble Baxter and I lived in last weekend. I want that. When the rest of the world disappears and it's just the two of us remembering old times and playing games.

But that's not practical, is it?

I'm not a child anymore. Now I *have* a child who is relying on me to look after him and provide for him and give him the best life.

I can't live in my past, reminiscing and playing pretend.

I try to force myself to take the emotion out of this and think logically.

"I'll take care of you. I'll do better," Hudson is saying.

He's still on his knees, tears streaming down his pale cheeks. I wipe them away without thinking, and he leans in, kissing my palm and smiling up at me.

It's so obvious he still loves me.

Even though he screwed up, he's desperate to make amends.

And maybe that would be the easier option, you know?

Kai and I could go back to a place we know. My little man will start preschool where he's already enrolled. I won't have to worry about finances or trying to find a job.

It's all so practically convenient.

Yet it hurts in ways I can't explain.

But what's best for Kai?

"I just want a chance to make things right." Hudson sniffs. "I swear, I'll make changes for us. I'll be home earlier. I'll do better. I'll be around more. I love you. I don't want to lose you."

Staring down at him, I can't ignore the fact that I loved him once. He swept me off my feet. I married him, didn't I?

I could have refused.

Really? Could you have?

Closing my eyes against the questions, I bite my bottom lip, my mind flooding with Baxter.

I need to talk to him.

I want his help to figure this out. Maybe he can tell me what to do.

He'll just beg you to stay, the same way Hudson is begging you to go.

You have to make this choice, Tammy. Only you.

"I just don't know what to do," I whisper.

Hudson's expression crumples, and he rises to his feet, holding my shoulders and leaning his head down to rest against mine.

"Why is this so hard for you? I'm asking you to choose between forgiving me and divorcing me. I'm telling you I won't let this happen again. Our marriage will be stronger than it's ever been. Why wouldn't you choose that over a life of being single and having to share custody... or lose custody of Kai."

I step back, shrugging him off me. "You say you love me, yet you threaten to take my son away?"

He sighs, dipping his chin. "Of course I wouldn't take him from you. You're a good mother. I just... It would make life a million times harder, Tam. I don't want to be a single father, and I know you don't want to be a single mother. Come on, be sensible about this. Do you really want to put Kai through all that?"

He's right.

Divorce is complex and horrible. Maybe that's why I've been hesitating to find a lawyer and get the process started. Because it's freaking terrifying.

And I don't want to put Kai through it.

I hate the idea of him having to take sides or choose. The whole back-and-forth thing. It'd be a nightmare. And if I did live in Nolan, that's a huge commute. Everything would just be so difficult if I stayed here.

And it'll be easier if you go.

The thought hurts my heart. It's an overwhelming, physical pain, and I press my hand against it, trying to understand it, yet maybe not wanting to know.

Baxter.

The name whistles through me like a broken prayer.

If I do this for Kai, I'll be forfeiting my chance with Baxter.

And part of me knew that, right? Which is why I walked away from his bed last night. But now that the reality is so much closer, it hurts that much worse.

My head starts to spin as heartache, desperation, and pain swirl through me.

I don't want to make this choice.

I wish none of this was happening to me!

It makes me want to scream and fist my hair, crumple to the floor and start slapping my hand on the ground.

But then Kai comes running into the parlor, beaming at me.

"Rachel made pancakes! You want one?"

Hudson flinches at the interruption and spins to give him a tight smile. "Not right now, kiddo."

I shake my head as well, and Kai frowns, turning back for the kitchen, his momentary enthusiasm instantly smothered by the tension in the room.

He shuffles away, and I cross my arms, my insides vibrating.

Hudson's staring at me, his face still so handsome. Women have always thought it, and I used to feel so privileged that he chose me above everyone else.

And now he's choosing me again.

Begging for me this time.

Promising to make up for his past mistakes.

He's fighting for our marriage... do I owe him the same?

CHAPTER 43
BAXTER

Kai creeps back into the kitchen, looking just a touch sad as he climbs back onto the stool.

"What's up?" I muss his hair, forcing myself to eat Ray's pancakes, even though I don't feel like it.

"Mommy and Daddy don't want any."

"Yeah, well... like I said, they're talking right now."

I tried to stop him running through before, but he wouldn't listen. Sweet Kai, so oblivious to how awkward it would be for Hudson to see me.

I don't even know if he's aware that Tammy and Kai have been staying with me. Has she mentioned my name or kept me out of the picture?

If I was just a respite while she processed what Hudson did, it'd probably be easier if my name never came up in conversation.

A bitterness twists through me as I try to relive, and analyze, the look on her face when she held up her bare ring finger and told me she was divorcing Hudson. Did she mean it at the time? Or was she just lying to me? Maybe she was lying to herself.

My heart is heavy, my chest aching.

The kitchen door swings open and Tammy walks through it, looking pale and wrecked.

I stand up, wanting to go to her, wrap her in my arms, and comfort her.

But it's not my comfort she seeks, right?

She looks at me, her eyes teeming with sadness.

Shit.

She's about to tell me something I don't want to hear.

She's gonna break my heart, and I can't...

"I can't do this," I murmur.

"Baxter, please. Can we just talk for—"

"No." I shake my head, backing away from her. "I can't hear you say goodbye."

Rachel's gone still by the stove, her large green eyes staring at me while I walk for the door.

"Baxter," Tammy whimpers.

I stop in the archway to the mudroom, gripping the frame and looking over my shoulder. "It's okay." I try for a brave smile. "I know you're going back to him. I can tell by the look on your face."

She goes to shake her head, but she'll be lying to the whole room if she does that.

It's not just about her and me.

It's about Kai.

And even though I could be his stepdad, I'm not his flesh and blood.

She knows it.

I know it.

The easiest choice is that she returns to her marriage. She still loves Hudson. Who wouldn't, right? He's the big catch.

Clenching my jaw, I sniff and force myself to say it. "It's probably the right thing to do anyway. Can't go breaking up a family."

Her chin bunches.

"It's always been him anyway. I get it. We're friends…" My jaw shakes as I try for a smile. "High school buds."

Fuck, my heart is being ripped out of my chest right now.

Rachel lets out a trembling breath, and I can see her fighting tears.

Tammy can't speak, and I'm not gonna last much longer.

"Baxter? Where are you going?" Kai's little voice is like another knife blade in my back, but I hide all my pain, walking back over to him and holding out my fist.

He bumps my big knuckles with his little ones.

"I've got to go do some jobs."

"Can I come?"

"No, buddy, you're going home with Mommy and Daddy now."

"Oh." Kai looks to his mother for confirmation. He

doesn't really get the gravity of all this, but I'm sure he's picking up the emotion in the room.

Tammy's lips wobble as she stares at her son.

"But thank you so much for staying. It's been the best vacation with you."

"I had fun." Kai's voice is soft and wispy, maple syrup dripping off his fork as he holds it in the air and looks at me. "Can I come back sometime?"

"Of course. You're welcome anytime." My voice breaks, and I clear my throat. "And you keep in touch, okay? You call me whenever you want. Your mom's got my number." I sniff and lean my arms on the counter. "And when you become a professional hockey player, you send me some tickets. I'll come to your games." I wink, and Kai grins.

Shit, losing Tammy my senior year was a piece of cake compared to this.

"Look after Mommy for me, okay?"

"I will." He smiles, and I bolt out the door before he tries to hug me.

Before I have to look at anyone else.

Before they see the tears blurring my vision.

CHAPTER 44
TAMMY

I stay in the kitchen, swaying on my feet as I listen to Baxter in the mudroom. He shoves his big feet into those boots he loves so much, and I hear Fezzik yapping excitedly. The door opens, then slams shut. I flinch, Fezzik's happy bark fading into the distance as Baxter walks away from me.

Again.

Why does it hurt so freaking much?

Haven't I chosen Hudson?

Haven't I done the right thing for my family?

Anger flares through me, a white-hot emotion I wasn't expecting.

But it burns bright as I think about Baxter, no doubt shoving his hands into his pockets and hunching his shoulders as he leaves me to piece my marriage back together.

Why didn't he fight for me?

He never has, and he never will.

I might be the only girl he's ever wanted, but once again he's let Hudson sweep into our lives and take me away.

Maybe that's how it's meant to be, you know?

Maybe I do want a man who will drive through the night to win me back.

I try to bolster myself with that fact as I clear my throat and put on a bright smile for Kai.

"Once you've finished your breakfast, we're gonna pack up our stuff and follow Daddy home, okay?"

Kai's lips purse for a second, but then he nods. "Okay, Mommy."

"Good boy." I kiss the top of his head and avoid Rachel's heartbroken gaze as I slip out of the room.

As soon as I'm out of sight, I rest my back against the wall and fight an onslaught of gut-wrenching sobs. My body jerks with them as I struggle to keep my composure.

"Tam?" Hudson appears in the hallway.

His expression folds as he takes in my wrecked face, and then he's against me in a heartbeat, pulling me to his chest and holding me.

"I've got you," he whispers. "It's okay. We're gonna get through this."

I let me him hold me because I'm too distraught to do anything else. He has no idea why I'm so broken, and it's probably best that he never does.

"Shhhh, it's okay, baby." His soft voice comforts me,

and I end up clinging to him, crying against his shoulder as his arms envelop me.

He's not turning his back and walking out the door.

He came for me. He drove through the night for me.

And that has to count for something.

So, I'll go back to my marriage, I guess.

I'll go back, and I'll make it work because it's the right thing to do.

Because my heart can't handle the pain of having Baxter push me out of his life yet again.

CHAPTER 45
BAXTER

I stayed away from the house for as long as I could.

I walked so far that Fezzik ran out of steam and I had to carry him most of the way back. Poor little guy. It was selfish of me to go so far, but I couldn't stand the thought of watching Tammy and Kai drive away.

By the time I get back to the house, Lani and Asher are there, along with Liam, who obviously came back to comfort a distraught Rachel. Why is she so destroyed? It's not like her heart just drove off down the highway.

The second she sees me, her eyes start to glisten, and she bunches a tissue into her eyes.

"They're gone. They left about half an hour ago."

I nod, not saying anything as I get myself a glass of water.

"She was pretty upset. Trying to hold it together for Kai, but... you could tell she was wrecked."

Clenching my jaw, I grip the sink and fight the urge to smash my glass on the floor.

"How could you let her go so easily?" Lani's voice is soft, but there's a measure of heat underlying her tone.

I snap my eyes toward her and notice Asher rise a little higher in his chair, putting a protective arm around her shoulders.

I glare at him, too, unable to find any words to make this better.

How could I let her go?

Because I love her, and I want what's best for her!

Hudson is Kai's father.

He'll give her security, which is obviously what she wants.

All I can offer is... fuck, I don't even know what I can offer. It's not like I've got a high-paying job or a nice car.

I can't fucking give her anything!

You'd give her your whole heart, and you'd never cheat on her. Ever!

Yeah, well, I'm sure Hudson said he wasn't going to do that again either. That fucker better keep his word. He better step up and be the best fucking husband on the planet.

She was happy with him once.

She can be happy with him again.

And that's all I want for Tammy—her happiness.

It doesn't matter how I feel.

My friends are all still staring at me, expecting some kind of answer. There's probably not enough that I can say to satisfy them, so I settle for a gruff "She made her choice, and I wasn't going to stand in her way."

"But... you love her."

"And she loves him." I give them a pointed look before stalking out of the room and running upstairs.

It takes me all of two seconds to decide to pack a bag and hit the road.

That's what I do when life gets to be too much.

And right now... it's way too fucking much.

I call to find a replacement coach for my Mini Mites, giving lame excuses about my dad needing me, then saying quick goodbyes to my friends, ignoring their confused frowns and myriad questions.

"Are you coming back?" Rachel chases me outside, while Liam scoops up Fezzik and tries to hold him still.

Throwing my bag in the back, I glance over my shoulder and give her a half-hearted nod. "Probably. I'll keep you posted."

"Please don't run away."

"I'm not," I grit out. "I'm gonna go see my dad."

"Just for a visit, though, right?" Lani steps onto the porch, crossing her arms with a stern frown. "You'd better get your ass back here when you're done."

A faint smile curls my lips before I slip into the car and start the engine. It roars to life, and I shoot out of the driveway, keeping my eyes on the road ahead and not letting myself look back.

CHAPTER 46
TAMMY

Kai and I followed Hudson all the way home. It was an awful trip. Once Kai finally realized we were actually leaving and he couldn't say goodbye to Fezzik or Casey, he lost it. He begged to stay, then started crying about not being able to go skating.

"He said he'd take me again. I'm going to be a hockey star! I need to skate!"

I tried to calm him, quietly panicking that he'd mention Baxter's name in front of Hudson, but by some miracle, that didn't happen. In the end, Hudson stepped in and promised to take him to the ice rink once we got back to Chesterfield. This calmed him a little, but as soon as we were alone in my car and we hit the road, Kai's tears started up all over again. He blubbered three names on repeat—Fezzik, Casey, Baxter—and cried himself to sleep.

We stopped twice on the way back. Kai didn't say a word during lunch or dinner. He sat there quietly nibbling his food while I tried to make polite conversation with my husband. He seemed happy and relaxed, his smile growing a mile wide when he noticed I was wearing my rings again. He took my hand, brushing his thumb over the diamond he bought me last year to replace the tiny speck he'd given me in high school. He gazed at me across the table, obviously hoping for some kind of gushy smile, but I couldn't look him in the eye. He'd have to be completely blind not to notice how tense I was, but he acted as if everything was cool and we were a happy family heading home from a road trip.

Happy family.

Shit. I need to get that into my head, right? If I want to avoid some ugly custody battle and give Kai the best chance of a smooth, stress-less upbringing, then I'm going to have to find my happy somehow.

As we drive back into Chesterfield and hit the familiar suburban streets, I honestly don't know how I'm going to do it. But then I glance into the rearview mirror and spot my son's sweet face, and I know I have to try.

Kai is still asleep when I pull into our driveway. It's nearly one in the morning, and I feel physically sick as I unload my son and carry him up to bed. I'm exhausted after the eleven-and-a-half-hour drive. I can only imagine how spent Hudson must be, but he seems to be running on adrenaline as he leads us inside, being the ever-attentive husband and father, paving the way so I can easily walk Kai to his room.

Settling him under the covers, I brush his hair back and kiss his forehead, inhaling his sweet scent and reminding myself why I'm doing this. He needs stability. He thrives on routine. Raising him here is a better choice, right?

It's like I'm working overtime to convince myself of that.

Rubbing my arms, I try to ward off the chill seeping through me as I walk to my bedroom.

My veins are running with pure ice as I step back into the familiar room with the king-sized bed and the waffle duvet I picked out. Everything in this house was carefully chosen by me. The furniture all matches, the large pillows on the bed, the comforter draped across the armchair. This house has my stamp all over it.

"You cold, honey?" Hudson asks from his side of the bed. He's taking off his watch and unbuttoning his cuffs.

I shrug, my throat feeling rusty when I try to speak. "Just tired."

"Why don't you jump in the shower to warm up, and then you can get some rest. I'll keep an ear out for Kai in case he wakes."

I stare across the room at him and finally nod. I'm feeling robotic and lifeless.

Shouldn't I be happier?

I've made the best decision for my son, so you'd think

I'd feel some sense of relief, but as I step into my bathroom, I'm frozen all over again. All I can do is stare at the shower and picture my naked husband in there, his ass cheeks squished against the glass as he took some nameless woman against the wall.

My throat burns as I snatch a towel off the railing and walk out of our en suite.

"Where are you going?" Hudson calls to my back.

I pause at the door and mutter, "I can't shower in there. I'm going to use Kai's bathroom."

Not bothering to look back, I walk into the main bathroom and take my sweet time in the shower. Exhaustion is tugging at me from every angle, but I stay beneath that hot spray, the glass steaming up around me as I rest my head on the wall and weep beneath the water. I don't even wash myself; I just soak until I'm completely empty.

I do a useless job of drying myself, missing a huge section on my back and forgetting all about my hair. Droplets run down my body, catching in the towel I've wrapped tightly around me. When I pad back into the master bedroom and see Hudson reading off his iPad in bed, my stomach starts roiling all over again.

He glances up at me, smiling like he always does.

It's all so familiar, yet it somehow feels wrong. I'm a stranger in my own home.

Hudson's still looking at me while I hover in the doorway, stuck once again. Frozen and numb as I try to get my brain to work properly.

"I put toothpaste on your toothbrush for you." The side of his mouth tips up.

It's been something we've been doing for each other ever since we got married. Because I'm always going to bed before him, I prepare his toothbrush and it sits by the sink until he sneaks in the door after work and gets ready for bed.

I'm usually up and reading, waiting for him to get home, and the role reversal is throwing me.

When I still don't move, he lets out another heavy sigh. "I'm sorry I tainted the shower for you. We're gonna get through this, and you can use your en suite again. I promise."

My throat hurts when I swallow.

"I'm gonna find us a counselor tomorrow, and we can—"

"I'm sleeping in the guest room." I grab a fresh pair of pajamas out of my dresser.

"How's that going to look for Kai when he wakes up? Won't that just confuse him?"

I close my eyes, gripping the edge of the dresser.

"Do you want to explain what's been going on? As far as I'm aware, he just thinks you two have been away on vacation, right? You didn't tell him anything else, did you? He knows we're still together. That his Mommy and Daddy love each other. Right?"

I don't know how to respond to that.

But I guess that's what Kai needs to hear for his own

security. Every kid wants to know their parents love each other, right? That they're staying together.

So, with a slow nod, I turn to face the man I married. I try for a smile, but my lips are too heavy. All I can do is stare at that bed and whisper, "I don't want you touching me."

My words hurt him, but the thought of him trying to spoon me... or anything else... is too much.

He nods, shuffling farther over to his side of the bed. "I won't."

A twitch jerks my spine when I finally shuffle to the bed. I took way too long brushing and flossing and putting my pajamas on in the bathroom so he couldn't see me naked. This all feels so weird. He's my *husband*, and I'm acting like I'm hopping into bed with a perfect stranger. I stay right along my edge, grateful we own a king.

"So..." He flicks his iPad off and looks at me. "One question I've been meaning to ask..."

I tense.

"How did you get to stay at the bed-and-breakfast? It doesn't open for a couple weeks yet. Did you just show up and beg or...?"

Clenching my jaw, I think about telling him that I fled to Baxter, but I'm exhausted, and I don't have it in me to deal with that conversation right now, so I shake my head and avoid the lie with an honest excuse. "I'm really tired. Can we talk later?"

Flicking off my lamp, I snuggle beneath the blankets, feeling anything but cozy.

"Yeah, of course." He follows my lead and settles down for the night.

I keep my back to him, hugging my edge of the bed and wishing for a moment that Kai didn't exist. How different would my life be if I never got pregnant?

Would Hudson and I have stayed together?

I honestly don't know. I loved him then... I probably still love him a little now, but being with Baxter changed something within me.

If I hadn't gotten pregnant, I probably would have gone to college. I would have pursued a career. I'd been thinking about teaching... maybe preschool or kindergarten.

Who knows how life would have panned out if I'd gotten out of Gladstone as a young woman?

Maybe Hudson and I would have broken up and met other people.

Maybe Baxter and I would have found each other again.

My heart writhes in my chest every time his name whistles through my mind.

I close my eyes, fighting off another wave of tears.

But if I had never gotten pregnant, Kai wouldn't exist.

And he's the most precious thing to me.

Whatever decisions I make while he's in my care have to be for his sake.

And he deserves a stable family. I won't put him through some messy divorce. It's not fair to him.

Somehow, I have to forgive Hudson and find some level of contentment with him.

Somehow, I have to put Baxter out of my mind and turn the time we just spent together into a precious memory that I can hold and cherish on those nights I'm feeling especially lonely.

CHAPTER 47
BAXTER

Dad was surprised to see me when I showed up on his doorstep, but his smile faded when he took in my expression. He stepped back to let me in. Without Mom around, the house is always painfully quiet. I usually relish quiet, but not within the walls that used to ring with Mom's laughter.

I don't know how Dad stands to live here without her.

I don't know why I came back.

The need to get out of Ponderosa was overwhelming, and I flicked into autopilot, hauling ass home, then realized the second I walked in the door that it can't be home without her.

And now Ponderosa is going to reek of that same feeling. Because Tammy was there for nearly a whole month, and having her around was perfect. Until, yet again, Hudson came along to ruin everything.

I glare at the flames flickering in the fireplace. I've

been home for a couple days now and have barely left the house. I did go and help Dad on his latest building project yesterday, but only because it's just outside town—an old farmhouse that is getting major renovations done. It felt good to work and lose myself in nails and sawdust. On the way back to the house, I slumped low in my seat as we drove down Main Street. The idea of bumping into anyone from Gladstone makes my skin crawl. Anyone but Tammy.

"Shit," I mutter under my breath, closing my eyes and tipping my head back. The couch cradles my head as I clench my jaw.

"You gonna tell me exactly what happened?" Dad murmurs.

I've told him bits and pieces. Little snippets keep dropping out of my mouth when my guard is down.

"I've told you already," I mutter.

Dad sighs. "All you've said is that Tammy showed up crying, you took her and Kai in... obviously fell pretty hard all over again..."

My head pops up. "I never said that."

Dad gives me a side-eye before sipping his beer and then finishing, "Hudson shows up and drags her away. Is that about right?"

"He didn't drag her, she left. She chose to go."

"And you didn't stop her." His shoulder hitches.

My frown gets deeper. I can feel my eyebrows bunching tight. "What was I supposed to do? He's her husband. The father of her kid."

"Did she know how you felt before she walked out that door?"

I close my eyes and nod. "We shared some pretty personal conversations, and..." I shake my head.

I can hear him shuffling in his armchair and creep my eyes open to see that he's facing me now, studying my expression with a surprised look. "You slept with her, didn't you?"

Running my tongue over my top teeth, I refuse to answer his question, but my silence no doubt speaks volumes.

"Wow." Dad settles back in his chair, facing the fire again. "And then you just let her go."

"What?" I jerk forward. "She *chose* to go."

"Did you tell her not to leave you? Did you tell her you love her?"

I open my mouth to try and ward off some of the stinging guilt and remorse riding through me, but no words come out.

Instead, I slump back against the couch with a hard thump.

Dad looks at me again. I can sense his gaze and refuse to meet it.

"I told her she was the only one for me," I finally murmur. "Told her I'd been saving myself for her."

With his beer halfway to his mouth, he pauses, his lips curling up at the edges. "Good for you, son."

"Yeah, right," I scoff. "Saving myself for a woman I

was never supposed to have in the first place. She's married!"

"Well, she shouldn't be married to that jerkoff," Dad mutters.

I snap my head to gape at him.

"Oh, come on." He winces. "Your mom and I knew you two were always meant to be together. If Tammy hadn't gotten pregnant, I'm sure she would have broken up with Hudson eventually, and you would have been there waiting for her." Dad's eyes glisten for a moment, his lips curling into a barely there smile. "Mom would be so happy to know you two finally figured it out."

"We didn't figure anything out." I hunch forward, resting my elbows on my knees and squeezing my forehead. "You don't know that she wouldn't have married him anyway. She was pretty in love with the guy. And she still must be, because she left with him after one conversation. He fucking cheated on her, and she forgave him and followed him home!"

"Did she tell you why?"

"What do you mean?" I snap.

"Well, did she say, 'I'm forgiving him because I'll always love him and want to make my marriage work'?"

"No." I glare at the flickering flames in the fireplace and mumble, "I don't know."

"What do you mean, you don't know?"

"It's not like we talked about it!" I throw my hands out wide. "She came through, and I knew what she was going to say, so I told her I couldn't say goodbye and left."

Dad frowns at me like I'm an idiot. "That's it?"

"I said goodbye to Kai." My throat constricts. "And then I..." I shrug before deflating on a heavy sigh. "I told her it was probably the right thing to do."

There's a horrible, thick pause that makes me want to dry retch before Dad makes it a million times worse.

"You told the woman you have been in love with since you were a child that it was probably best that she went back to the arrogant prick who was cheating on her?"

I refuse to answer that question because I feel like total shit right now.

"You didn't tell her that you love her and that you'd never do something like that to her?"

"Marriage is a sacred vow," I mutter.

"Which he broke!"

"He said it was just a onetime thing, and he was really sorry."

"Bullshit!" Dad barks. "It's Hudson Clark we're talking about here. Don't sit there and tell me he could ever love Tamara Tan the way you do. That he could ever take care of her the way you would."

I clench my jaw and grit out, "He's rich, and they have a kid together, and he can give her—"

"I don't give a flying fuck how much money that guy makes." Dad shoots out of his chair. "True love is a rare and beautiful thing. I would give anything to have your mother back... even just for a day." His voice breaks and he squeezes his mouth, obviously struggling to pull his emotions in check. I've never seen my dad this impassioned before, and all I can do is gape at him. "You got a second chance to finally win that girl over… and then you just let her walk out the door."

Bile surges up my throat and I clamp my teeth together, staring at the floor.

The silence permeating the room is the worst it's been since I got here, and I'm gonna drown in it if I don't move.

Jerking off the couch, I face my father and try for one last justification. "He's her husband, and she loves him. I couldn't stop her."

Dad shakes his head, his disappointed expression quietly calling me out on my bullshit before I stalk from the room and thump my way upstairs.

Acting like a petulant teen, I slam my door shut to let him know how pissed I am before snatching my pillow off the bed and hurling it at the wall. It hits my framed photo of Mom, which topples to the floor. Bending down with a curse, I pick it up, brushing off the dust, relieved that the glass didn't crack.

Caressing my thumb over her pretty smile, I slump onto the floor and rest against my dresser. Mom and Dad had the best marriage. I always wanted one just like it. Mom told me once that she married her best friend, and that's why they hardly ever fought and were so happy together.

"Marriage is the easiest thing in the world when you marry the right person." Her smile was so sincere, and I knew she meant it.

I think I'd been about twelve, and that's when I knew I had to marry Tammy Tan one day.

But I lost my chance.

Because I couldn't get over my humiliation at the swimming hole.

Because I didn't try to fight for her when Hudson came along.

Because I let her walk out that door three days ago.

"Fuck." I hit my head against the dresser and wince, rubbing the sore spot, then opening my eyes and spying a dusty box beneath my bed.

Crawling toward it, I wrestle it out of hiding and flip the lid. I can't remember what's in here, but the second I spot the worn leather journal on the top, I know exactly what I'm looking at.

A deep loneliness swamps me as I unearth the book and all the pictures and memorabilia beneath it.

I always loved to write—something no one but my mom knew about me.

That's why she bought me the journal. I'd sit up in bed at night, scribbling my thoughts and dreams. Writing love poems to Tammy in secret.

The pads of my fingers travel lightly over the pages and photographs I'd glued into the book. Mostly Tammy and me, the odd one of my mom and dad.

My eyes catch on a poem I wrote for Tammy in my freshman year of high school.

. . .

It's your smile that gets me, like an arrow through the heart.
    Cupid knew what he was doing, right from the very start.

The first day I saw you, it took my breath away.
    And as I've grown to know you, I have loved you more each day.

I wish that I could tell you how you make me feel.
    But what if you reject me? The pain would be so real.

And so I'll be the best friend that I can possibly be.
    And wish upon each falling star that one day you might see.

That I could love you better than anyone else could do.
    And hopefully one day I'll hear you say, "I love you too."

I let out a sad laugh, cringing over how cheesy it is. Rachel would no doubt think it was adorable. A fourteen-year-old boy, scribbling words like that about his best friend. My hockey bros would never let me live this down, which is why they will never, ever see this journal.

But a small part of me wishes I'd shown Tammy.

Maybe if I'd given her this poem in high school, she wouldn't have married Hudson.

"But she loves him," I mutter darkly. Why else would she have been so willing to forgive him and go back?

Dropping the journal back in the box, I slap it closed and shove it back under my bed.

My fourteen-year-old self was delusional. Wishing upon falling stars. What the fuck?

Dreams like that don't come true.

Reality is harsh and filled with unexpected pregnancies and fatal car accidents and the only girl you've ever loved walking back into your life for a fleeting moment, stealing your heart all over again, and then leaving you gasping for air.

Part of me wishes I'd never had the second chance in the first place.

But then I wouldn't trade it for the world.

I got to love Tammy the way I always wanted. I got to show her a piece of my soul.

Shit, I'm always going to love her.

There is no other girl.

There was no other goal.

She's always been it for me.

And I just let her walk away.

CHAPTER 48
TAMMY

"I don't suppose you've heard from Baxter?" I ask, my insides roiling as I wait for a response. I shouldn't even be asking, but I can't help myself. The number of times I've pulled out my phone and stared at his contact details.

But I haven't had the courage to call him.

I shouldn't.

He's my friend, but... for those fleeting few days, he was so much more. My heart hurts every time I think about it.

Rachel clears her throat. "He's texted a few times, but..." Her voice is soft through the phone, and I press it closer to my ear, wishing I was sitting in the kitchen at Ponderosa and helping her prepare food while we chatted. She always made me feel so comfortable and at ease.

I want to be back there with a desperate pull that's overwhelming.

But I made the right choice for my son.

Right?

Kai and I are trying to settle back into our normal routine. I took him to an indoor playground yesterday— the big one he loves so much—and watched him have fun on the slides and in the ball pit. I even made myself jump in with him, pretending to be a sea monster and crawling through the plastic balls with growls while he giggled and shouted at his imaginary crew. "Don't let the sea monster sink our ship!"

It was a sweet moment of reprieve. Kai's laughter is the best sound in the world.

It's taking a lot of energy to be the playful mother I used to be, but I have to keep doing it—hiding my pain for the sake of my son.

Tomorrow, I'm supposed to be meeting up with another mom from the Skip-A-Doo music class Kai and I attend on Fridays. We're going to the library together so Kai can get out some new picture books. It'll be great. I have to make it be great, because Kai needs my smiles. He needs to know that everything is okay.

I also need to go shopping and get his Halloween costume organized. Our street will be doing a special trick-or-treat like we always do, and Hudson's promised to be home in time for it.

He's promised a lot of things this week. He's been trying to step up in every way he can, and yet it still doesn't feel like enough.

"I'm not sure how long Baxter will stay with his dad. According to Liam, he only goes for short visits because he doesn't love his hometown or something. We don't know all the details. Baxter's always been a closed-off guy." Rachel's voice is sad, and I wonder how badly she's missing him.

It can't be as much as I do.

The last two nights, huddling against the side of my bed so no part of my body can touch Hudson's, I've ached for Baxter in ways I can't even describe.

We had one full night together, and it's ruined me for life. Falling asleep with his arms around me, cocooned by his body... I'm never going to experience that again, and it breaks my heart.

Why hadn't I seen him sooner?

Why had he let me go so easily?

Why hadn't—

The front door clicks open, and I flinch. "Ray, I gotta go."

"Okay." I can see her smiling in my mind as she tells me to keep in touch... and give Kai a kiss from her.

"And a bear hug from Casey!" he shouts in the background, and I can't help a watery laugh.

"Will do." I end the call as Hudson and Kai walk into the kitchen.

"Who were you talking to?" Hudson places the grocery bags on the counter, and I immediately crouch down to hug Kai so I don't have to look at my husband... or answer his question.

"Hey, Mommy." Kai nestles his head against my shoulder.

"You have fun shopping?"

"Yep." He nods, then darts his eyes to Hudson before looking at me. "Daddy let me buy three candies."

"Oh, really? Just before dinner." I can't help an annoyed little huff. "Promise me you'll still eat your vegetables."

Kai gives me an impish grin, and I'm about to ask if he wants to help me start preparing our evening meal, but Hudson speaks before I can. "Kai, go play in your room."

"But—"

"Now. You can open the new Legos I bought you."

"You said you'd help me build it." He takes the box from Hudson and stares down at the cargo train he'll be constructing.

"Get started without me. I'm just gonna talk to Mommy first."

"Okay." Kai sighs and shuffles out of the room, hugging the box to his chest.

I gaze after him, tension coiling my stomach. Something's off with Hudson. Spending time alone with Kai has always frazzled him, and maybe he's irritated at having to do grocery shopping and then build Legos. It hurts my heart a little, although it is good to see him spending time with his son. That's why I came back, because I'm trying not to rip this family apart. I should be happy that Kai's father is putting in so much effort. It'd just mean more if he actually enjoyed it. I'd like him to *want* to do it, rather than just do it because he has to... or he's trying to prove something to me.

A shaky sigh rushes out of me, and I make myself turn, forcing a smile at Hudson before starting to unpack the groceries.

He leans against the counter, watching me with a terse frown. I don't know what he's waiting for, until I hear Kai's footsteps stop upstairs. He's in his room now and far enough away not to hear Hudson mutter a curse and snap, "When the fuck were you going to tell me you were staying with Baxter Brown?"

I freeze by the fridge, gripping the handle and trying to sound unfazed by his venom.

"When the fuck were you going to tell me you were cheating on me?"

"Oh, don't throw this back in my face," he spits. I spin in time to see him point a finger at me. "Why didn't you tell me he was there?"

I cross my arms. "Why should I?"

"Because!" His hands fly up before slapping back down on the counter. "The guy was in love with you in high school. Anyone with working eyeballs could see it! And you just run to him the first time we have any trouble?"

My heart starts thrumming, and it makes my voice shake. "He was my best friend."

"Yeah, a pretty shitty one! The number of times you cried over the fact that he was pulling away from you..." Hudson rolls his eyes.

The cool air from the fridge swirls across my back,

but I leave the door open, too stunned by the look of disgust on his face. "You knew he was in love with me?"

"Of course I did. That's why I had to work so hard to keep you away from him. I didn't want him ruining what we had! And then you just take off with *my son*—who can't seem to shut up about the guy—and go and move in with him?"

The fridge starts beeping and I slap the door closed, the bottles rattling in protest. "I didn't know where else to go. It's not like I could head back to Gladstone, or should I say Judgment Central. They would have just sent me right back here to you."

"As they should! I'm your husband!"

"Who cheated on me!" I scream. "You were doing it in our shower!" My chest heaves as I try to control the burst of anger exploding inside me. I point up the stairs, my finger shaking when I realize Kai probably heard me.

I need to lower my voice and get control. I don't want to scare him, but this blinding rage coursing through me right now is hard to counter. My eyes burn as I suck in a few short breaths and grit out, "If I hadn't caught you, would you ever have mentioned it?"

His nostrils flare as he runs his hand through his hair and looks away from me.

"I thought so." My voice is bitter.

"I wouldn't have wanted to hurt you."

"Right." My voice snaps off the *T*, stalking back to the counter so I can unpack the rest of the groceries.

"We need counseling," he mutters. "You can't hold this against me forever."

"Which means you can't get pissy that I ran to a friend when I was in need. Someone I trust. Someone who I knew would take me in no questions asked."

Hudson's mouth curves into a malignant frown. "You tell him about us?"

"About what you did?" My eyebrows rise. "Yeah, I told him."

The anger pulsing off my husband right now is like a shock wave, and I step away from him. I'm not scared, I just don't want to be near him when he's like this.

But I don't want him near Kai either.

"Maybe you should go for a drive or something. I'll get dinner ready, and then when you get back, we'll both be calm enough to have a pleasant meal. For Kai."

Hudson grips the back his neck, still not looking at me. "Did you sleep with him?"

My blood runs cold.

"Did you sleep with Baxter to get back at me?"

I swallow and am relieved to be able to answer him honestly. "No, I did not sleep with him to get back at you."

He snorts and shakes his head, thankfully snatching the keys and storming out the front door. It slams shut, and I flinch at the shattering sound.

My insides are splintered glass as I rest my hands on the counter and try to still my thundering heart.

I definitely misled Hudson with my answer, but I can't bring myself to tell him the truth either. That malignant look on his face warned me that he probably wouldn't be able to handle the news. How do I look him in the eye and tell him I slept with Baxter because he told me I was the only girl he'd ever wanted? He practically told me he loved me without actually saying it, and I had to be with him. I had to make up for that afternoon at the swimming hole... and then I wanted him over and over again because he made me feel things I never had before.

Then he told me to go back to my marriage and walked out the door.

My legs buckle and I slump against the counter, my heart fracturing in new places.

"Why, Bax?" I whimper and try to tell myself that if it weren't for Kai, I'd still be in Nolan.

But would I?

Baxter told me to go back with Hudson.

He told me it was the right thing to do!

He let me go so easily. Does that mean he doesn't really love me?

I don't want to answer that question.

I snap my eyes shut, shaking my head and gritting my teeth. The point is, Kai *does* exist, and I can't put my sweet little boy through some heinous custody battle and endless back-and-forth between his parents. It's not fair.

I just have to get over myself. Somehow, I have to forgive Hudson and learn to love him again.

Did you ever really love him?

Of course I did. I wouldn't have slept with him if I hadn't loved him.

I'm just not sure I love him anymore.

I'm not sure that the starry-eyed virgin I was in my senior year of high school is the woman I am now.

I'm not sure if what Hudson and I had then is strong enough to last the distance.

But it must.

Because I have a son who I love more than anything. A son who deserves a stable, happy home.

Slashing the tears off my face, I straighten as I hear Kai coming down the stairs. He creeps into the kitchen, his eyes big as he looks around.

"Where's Daddy?"

"He had to go out for a little drive, but he'll be back in time for dinner." I put on a bright voice, though I doubt I'm doing a very good job of hiding my emotion. I'm sure my face is blotchy.

Snatching a tissue out of the box, I quickly blow my nose, then wash my hands.

"Want to help me make dinner?"

He nods, pulling his stool around the counter so he can reach.

"Sorry Daddy couldn't help you with those Legos."

"That's okay. I didn't think he'd come anyway."

I still, my hand frozen on the carrots I'm about to peel. "You didn't?"

Kai shrugs.

And that cold sadness I'm trying so hard to fight decides to settle into the marrow of my bones.

CHAPTER 49
BAXTER

The sky is overcast, the chilly wind whistling down my collar and catching the ends of my hair. I pull my beanie down a little lower and hunch my shoulders, tramping over the wet grass and fallen leaves until I reach Mom's gravesite.

Crouching down, I brush the dead leaves away, cleaning up her plot and tracing the letters of her name engraved on the headstone.

"Hey, Mom," I whisper, my soul heavy and sore as I find a perch on the grass. My ass will get wet, but I don't even care. "It's been a while." I hook my elbows onto the top of my knees and stare at her inscription. "Dad's good. He asked me to say hi. We've been hanging out at the house a lot, just... you know." I shrug. She does. Dad's convinced she's watching over us, and I like to believe that, too, so she would have heard every conversation and seen every quiet evening watching hockey on TV and not talking at all.

I work my jaw to the side, wondering why I'm even here if I'm just gonna sit and say nothing. I'm so fucking good at that.

I can bleed ink straight from my heart to a page, but do you think I can say anything aloud?

It's a curse. The words get all jumbled in my throat, and I can't get them out... or I say the wrong thing.

And then the woman I love walks away from me thinking I wanted her to go.

My fingers are trembling as I rub my forehead.

"Dad thinks you'd be stoked that I finally hooked up with TT. You always loved her. And I think you knew how much I loved her too."

"I did." I can see Mom's smile and hear the way she'd answer me.

It brings comfort and despair in equal measure.

"I feel like such a coward sometimes, you know? Like I look back, and I have so many regrets. Why couldn't I tell her how I felt? Why couldn't I tell her to forget Hudson and be with me instead?"

Silence.

It's long and thick and hollow.

Clenching my jaw, I sniff and force myself to talk some more. "I think maybe I was scared that if I tried, she'd tell me she didn't want me, and I just... I couldn't handle that, you know? So I convinced myself that she was happy with Hudson, that she loved him more than she could ever love me." Now my jaw's shaking, the words sounding raspy as I force them from my mouth. "But after spending that time with her in Nolan... the way we were together... what if I was wrong? What if she could love me as much as I love her?"

The breeze picks up and I snap my eyes shut, stiffening my body against the chill.

"But is it right to break up a marriage? To pull apart a happy home?"

He cheated on her. Were they really that happy?

"He made one mistake." I scratch my chin.

Why the fuck am I standing up for this guy?

I frown, glaring at the ground.

You'd never cheat on her. Not ever. You know you wouldn't.

My eyes dart to the gravestone again, and I think about how happy my parents always seemed to be. They were so honest with each other. They laughed together all the time. They told each other every embarrassing secret they had. I'm sure they did, because they knew they wouldn't be judged for it.

My house was a judgment-free zone. It was like this little safety bubble in the middle of Gladstone. That's why Tammy loved coming over so much. She could be herself...

She could just exist, and that was always enough.

"I wish I could tell her that," I whisper to Mom. "Tell her that she's enough just the way she is. That she wouldn't have to change one little thing for me." I purse my lips, emotion rising in me so thick and strong, I feel like I'm on the verge of splintering... or drowning in an ocean of tears.

Yes, that's melodramatic, but... it kind of feels true.

I'm drowning in my own misery.

"I love her." I sniff, battling the burn of tears in my eyes and nose. "I should have told her. I shouldn't have said that going back to him was for the best. Marriage is supposed to be this sacred vow. I know it is. And yeah, people say you have to work at it. That it's a lifelong commitment. But does that rule still apply when it never should have happened in the first place?"

The breeze tickles my neck and I rub at the spot, pulling my collar up.

"Why did she marry him, Mom? Was it just because she was pregnant? Or did she want it? Did she want him to be her husband?" I shake my head, remembering Hudson's big proposal on the field. He'd hooked up the marching band to play her this song at the end of the pep rally. The girls in the stands all swooned as he surprised Tammy and got down on one knee. The place erupted with cheers, and all I could do was stand there as my heart shattered into tiny little pieces. She smiled down at him, bit her bottom lip, and then nodded like she meant it.

I thought she loved him the way I loved her.

But what if I was wrong?

What if...?

"What if I *was wrong*?" I stand, brushing off the back of my pants and heading for my car. I'm running by the time I reach it, crashing into the driver's door before wrenching it open.

I don't know what the fuck has come over me, but there's this urgent insistence pulsing through my veins as I grab my phone and start googling. It doesn't take me long to track down Tammy's old high school girlfriends. One of them still lives in Gladstone, and I call Grace before I can change my mind.

"Hello?"

"Uh... hi." I clear my throat.

"Who is this?"

"It's, um..."

Silence. I can't seem to fill it, and things are quickly getting awkward.

Grace lets out an impatient little huff, and I blurt my name before she can hang up on me.

"Baxter? As in Baxter Brown?"

"Yeah." I nod, then hold my breath.

"Wow. Are you in town or something?"

"Yep. Visiting my dad."

"Cool." Her voice picks up, her usually friendly tone returning in an instant. "So, why are you calling me? I haven't seen you since graduation. I'm really sorry about your mom, by the way."

"Yeah, I..." Glancing into the cemetery, I take in the light fall of rain and nod. "Thanks. I just, uh..." Biting my bottom lip, I try to think how to make this call worth the effort.

Start with the truth.

"I was just... calling about Tammy. You still see her?"

The silence that follows my question makes me squirm before she finally says, with a smile in her voice, "Yeah, we catch up whenever she comes to town. I saw her a few weeks ago, with Kai."

"Cool." I nod, then realize when she doesn't offer anything else that I probably need to ask another question. Shit! Why is conversation so fucking hard? "Yeah, I just... uh, I was thinking about her. Remembering, you know... high school." I wince.

"High school. Good times." Grace is smiling again, I can hear it... but then she goes quiet, waiting for me to get to the fucking point!

"Is she happily married?" My voice breaks as I blurt out the question. "I mean... did she want to get married? Is she... are they happy?"

There's a pregnant pause that hurts every one of my senses before Grace lets out a soft laugh. "You're still in love with her, aren't you?"

I release a sigh, my chest deflating as I close my eyes and croak, "Always and forever."

"Kind of wish you'd told her back then."

My heart stutters with surprise, and my eyes ping open. "You do?"

"Well, yeah. You were the sweetest and... her best friend. It always made me so sad that you guys drifted apart. You were each other's favorite. And then... you were nothing."

"It kills me," I rasp. "Do you think she would have gotten married if I'd... told her how I felt?"

"Um... well, maybe." Grace lets out a sad sigh. "Truth is... their parents made them. They really didn't have a choice. There was no way in hell Tamara Tan was gonna have a baby out of wedlock. You know how strict and old-fashioned her parents are. They came down *hard*. And Hudson's parents weren't any better. They would have done anything to save face, which is why they pushed for such a fast wedding. We were all smart enough to figure it out when she started showing so soon, but before then..." She lets out a laugh that sounds more cynical than anything else. "We were all young, dumb romantics who could only imagine the perfect fairy tale, right? They were the golden couple."

"But were they? Really?"

"They sure seemed like it... back then."

"You don't think so anymore, though, do you?"

Grace sighs. "I don't know what I think, to be honest. Tammy just... She's lost her spark. You can tell she loves being a mother, but whenever conversation turns to Hudson, she just gets this brave smile on her face."

My eyebrows flicker. "And how long has it been like that?"

"I don't know. Ever since they moved to the city... or maybe since Kai was born? I just don't think marriage has been as easy as she'd hoped. I think, maybe if she hadn't gotten pregnant and she'd gone off to college... maybe she and Hudson would have drifted apart naturally. Eighteen is stupidly young to get married, right? You don't even really know who you are. And she never got a chance to find out." Grace sounds sadder and sadder the more she keeps talking. "It just breaks my heart that it all panned out the way it did. She never even had a chance, you know? And now she's locked in."

"She doesn't have to be locked in, though, does she?"

"Baxter, come on." Grace lets out a pitiful laugh. "She's Tamara *Tan*. Her parents will never forgive her if she divorces her husband. And can you imagine the meltdown the Clarks will have? Good God, that would be thermonuclear. There's no way those four parents are going to let their children break up."

"But Tammy and Hudson are adults now. They can do whatever they like." Anger simmers through me as I spit out the words.

Grace scoffs. "Bax, the Tans and the Clarks are not like your parents. They're *Gladstone* parents. They're controlling and manipulative, and they will peck away at Tammy until there is nothing left. No matter how old she gets, they're always gonna be up in her grill making her feel bad about her life choices. Could *you* honestly live with that?"

"What, so she just has to settle for a life of purgatory? That's not fair!"

"Tell that to the Tans," she huffs. "Look, I don't know why you're suddenly asking all of this stuff, and I probably shouldn't have told you that Tammy seems sad. I don't want you to worry. I know how much you care about her."

"Grace, she's my girl. She always has been. She always will be. I need to know she's happy."

There's a long, drawn-out silence. It's filled with sadness and lost hope.

"Oh, Bax," Grace finally whispers, her voice wobbling. "I wish you'd told her that when it wasn't too late."

"I have told her that," I whisper, forgetting she can hear me.

"When?"

"Last week, when she was staying with me in Nolan. I told her... and she still went back to him."

"She left Hudson?" Her voice picks up. "How? Why? When?"

"A few weeks back. Must have been just after her visit to Gladstone. She found out he was cheating on her."

Grace gasps. "Oh my gosh, that's huge! She must be so relieved. She's got the perfect excuse to leave him now!"

"She went back to him, Grace." My voice sounds as dead as I feel.

"But why would she—" She gasps again. "Kai. Hudson must be threatening to take Kai from her or something. She'd do anything for her boy. She'd give up everything for him. That's got to be it. She knows that if she tries to divorce Hudson, the Clarks will make her life hell, and her parents will be no help either. You should hear them going on about how wealthy Hudson is and what a good life he's giving their daughter. They never got that marriage was supposed to be about love, too, because their marriage is so freaking duty-bound." She lets out a disgusted huff. "She's probably making this huge sacrifice so that Kai isn't put through a custody battle or forced to choose between his parents. She's doing all this to protect him." Her voice quakes, and I wonder if she's about to start crying. Grace always was a softy. "Baxter, I don't know what you can do, but... maybe this might help you understand why she's gone back to him. She probably feels like she's got no choice."

CHAPTER 50
TAMMY

Kai was so exhausted after a busy playdate that I had no choice but to put him to bed for an afternoon nap. He doesn't usually sleep in the afternoon anymore, but he was lethally grumpy, no doubt spent after an entire morning of interacting with other little people. He's an introvert at heart, and I must remember that shorter play-dates work better for him.

We could have avoided the meltdown while buckling him into the car if I'd just left an hour earlier.

Wiping down the kitchen counter, I ring out the cloth, then drape it over the edge of the sink to dry. I've got some laundry to fold while he's sleeping, and maybe I should get a head start on dinner prep. Anything has to be better than last night's frosty meal. The food was hot, but the atmosphere was glacial. Hudson barely spoke, and I had to work overtime, forcing conversation for the sake of Kai.

I guess I'm not used to having Hudson around at mealtimes. He usually works until after eight or goes out for "business meetings"—a.k.a. drinks at the bar with clients. Kai is always settled for the night when he gets home. More often than not, he's already eaten, so he'll walk in the door, pulling off his tie and settling on the couch for some TV time and a glass of bourbon.

That worked for us for so long, because it meant we didn't need to interact too much.

But now he's putting in all this effort, and it's making things so much harder.

Thankfully, he's at work right now, and half of me is hoping he'll text to say he's going to be late.

My stomach pinches at the thought of that message popping up on my screen.

Is he ever really working late?

Or is he meeting up with some blonde with big, pinchable boobs?

I snap my eyes shut, not even wanting to think about it. Or consider the fact that I'm *hoping* my husband will get home late. What kind of wife does that make me? What kind of couple does that make us?

The phone starts ringing, and I'm almost relieved for the interruption, until I hear Mrs. Clark's voice down the line.

"Ah, Tamara. Glad to hear you answering the phone, dear. Hudson told me you were back." Her tone could not be more unimpressed if she tried.

"Hi, Lydia. What can I do for you?"

"Can't a mother-in-law simply call to say hello?"

Yes, she absolutely can, but you never actually do.

I force out a laugh, hoping it sounds cheerful enough.

"Is Kai there?"

"He's sleeping."

"Oh really? An afternoon nap? Isn't he a little old for that?"

My insides simmer, but I work hard to keep my voice light and unaffected. "He was exhausted after a very busy morning. He doesn't usually nap, but on the odd day, things catch up with him."

"I see. Have you been keeping him up too late at night, then?"

"No." I grit my teeth. "His bedtime is pretty routine."

"Even when you were on an extended vacation with him? I know how a lack of routine can really throw a child. Hudson was always such a great sleeper because I made sure I didn't throw him off course too often."

I clear my throat, desperate to get out of this conversation. "So, did I tell you I found a cute little costume for Halloween? Kai's going as a hockey player. He was so insistent, I couldn't talk him into anything else." Is my laughter bright enough? I feel like my heart is being squeezed to a pulp. When Kai asked to go as Casey Pierce, I nearly started bawling in the Walmart costume aisle. "But I managed to find him a jersey that fit, then bought him a little stick and helmet. He looks adorable all dressed up. I'll send you a photo tomorrow night."

"A hockey player. Well, that's new. You'd think he'd want to go as a guitarist like his dad used to be."

"Maybe next year," I rasp, doing whatever it takes to appease this woman and get her off the phone.

"Well, I should hope so. It seems more appropriate that he'd want to emulate his father."

"He's only ever seen his father in a business suit." My voice is flat. "Hudson never plays the guitar anymore."

"Well, that's a shame. You must make sure he does. That'll be good for Kai."

"I'm sure it would, but Hudson works long hours and doesn't have much time. When he is home, he…" *Doesn't want to play with his son.*

The words fall through my body like bricks, wounding and bruising me on their descent.

Clenching my jaw, I try to will the tears away.

What the fuck am I doing?

Why am I still here?

Why did Hudson even want us back?

"Yes, well, I know Hudson wants to do everything in his power to ensure you two are well taken care of. He's a hardworking, good-hearted man. He's sacrificed so much for you two."

I can't help a soft scoff.

I don't mean to release it and instantly regret it when I do.

"Excuse me?" Lydia's stone-cold question makes my insides shudder.

Clearing my throat, I try to brush it off. "I'm sorry. What were you saying?"

"You just scoffed. Do you not think your husband is a good, kind man who works hard for you?"

"I think he works very hard," I manage.

I think he works hard so he doesn't have to come home and deal with his family.

"He would do anything for his family, Tamara. He would fight any battle he had to. He loves you too much to just let you walk away."

The words *fight any battle* ring in my ears, the underlying threat impossible to miss. I clutch the phone, swaying on my feet and having to lean my hip against the counter for support.

"It would be foolish of you to leave him again. You are his wife, and you promised to love him until the day you die. I sat there and watched you share your vows, young lady."

Anger bursts through me in a fiery spray, stealing all common sense along with it. "Did you hear him say his vows too?"

"What?"

"You know, the part about being faithful."

"He has always been faithful to you."

"No, Lydia. He hasn't."

The truth is ugly and sits between us for an awkward beat that's painful.

"Okay, fine. But it was one small mistake," she sputters. "A tiny lapse in judgment, which he is very sorry for.

And he wanted to make amends immediately, but you wouldn't let him. You just took off with his son and ignored him."

I squeeze my eyes shut, my head bobbing erratically. "Have you ever walked in on your husband fucking someone else?" My tone gets sharp and snappy, and my usual shock at saying something so bold to my mother-in-law is nowhere to be found.

Lydia gasps, no doubt clutching her pearl necklace as I bark at her.

"It's not pleasant. So rather than berating me for walking out the door, you should be praising me for having the courage to walk back through it!" I hang up before she can respond, my chest heaving as I try to bring my senses back online.

Oh shit, what have I done?

And why does the word *courage* keep hitting me over the head? Why did it taste like acid in my mouth?

Was walking back through that door really so courageous?

Because right now... it doesn't feel like it.

Right now, it feels like I took the easy out. I've given up on the things I truly want the most. For what? A loveless marriage? Because I'm scared of a custody battle?

Resting my hands on the counter, I stare at the expensive granite and shake my head. Who gives a shit how expensive my kitchen is? How nice my house is?

Is this really my life now? Endless days of living in

this fancy house with a husband I don't even want to be around?

I'm doing this for Kai, but... what will become of me if I stay?

"I don't know if I can do this anymore," I whisper, tears flooding my eyes. "I don't think I can." My voice catches as my stomach jerks with a sob. "I don't think I can."

CHAPTER 51
BAXTER

After my phone call with Grace, I didn't know what to do with myself. We both mumbled our goodbyes, hung up, and then I sat there, drenched in disquiet and wondering what the hell I was supposed to do with myself.

On autopilot, I headed back to the house, then felt compelled to stop and grab some groceries for dinner. Dad has been waiting on my mopey ass, and I need to start showing a little appreciation. Mom's butter chicken recipe was always a winner, so I quickly shoot into the grocery store and get the ingredients. Hopefully I haven't forgotten anything. As I wander back to the truck, I glance up and spot two faces I haven't seen in a long while. Two faces I actively avoid every time I come into town. And opposite them sits Mrs. Clark.

I'm not sure she recognizes me as I stride by the coffee shop, but the other lady sure does.

Mrs. Tan's mouth drops open, her eyes flashing at me when I come to a stop by the table.

Why the hell are you stopping? The question pulses through my brain, but not loud enough to make me move along.

Mr. Tan sits up a little straighter, frowning at me until a light bulb clicks and he whispers, "Baxter Brown? What are you doing here?"

"I'm visiting my dad."

"Haven't seen you around."

My smile is hard and unfriendly as I stare down at him. "We're not exactly the friendliest neighbors, now are we? Since my mom passed, I'm guessing you have nothing to do with my dad, amiright?"

He grunts and focuses back on his coffee while I study Mrs. Tan's face. She looks older, streaks of gray in her black hair, her eyes tired like she'd been up at night worrying. I can only imagine who she's obsessing over.

Probably the same person I can't stop thinking about.

But maybe in a different way.

Definitely in a different way.

Grace's comments about controlling, manipulative parents got my back up. Did they really force her to marry Hudson? Did Tammy put up a fight or just go along with them?

Shit, why'd I tell her to leave the night she told me she was pregnant? I should have offered to be there for her, but I was too hurt and jealous to do anything but act like a total douchebag. And then I did the same fucking thing last week when Hudson showed up.

What the hell is wrong with me!

"Well, if you'll excuse us." Mrs. Clark gives me a polite smile. "We're just in the middle of something important."

"Of course," I mumble, stepping off the curb and turning my back.

Until I hear...

"Now, I don't know what she told you, but it only happened once, and Hudson wouldn't have even behaved like that in the first place unless something was already broken. I raised my son right and—"

"You hold on just a minute there, Lydia," Mrs. Tan interrupts her. "My girl wouldn't do anything to provoke that kind of behavior. Now, you should be thanking me that I insisted she go back to him. Marriage is a sacred vow, and she will not be walking away from it under any circumstances. But you need to bring your boy into line."

I spin in time to see Mrs. Clark's cheeks flare red. "Well, you need to tell your daughter not to run away with his son again, taking off to God knows where and not telling him a thing. She damn near kidnapped that child, and poor Hudson was beside himself."

"Poor Hudson." Mr. Tan scoffs and shakes his head.

"Stay out of this, Jon," Mrs. Clark snaps, and I fucking lose it.

"You stay out of it!" I shout, striding up to the table. My loud voice makes them all start, and Mrs. Clark actually leans back as I tower over them. "Who the hell do you think you are discussing your adult children this way? You don't control them anymore. They're old enough to make their own decisions."

"Young man—" Mrs. Tan tries to warn me off, but I barrel right over top of her.

"How dare you force your daughter to marry Hudson in the first place?"

Mrs. Clark blusters. "Excuse me! There was no forcing anyone."

"You tell yourself whatever helps you sleep at night," I spit, then shake my head at them all. "Do you have any idea how much you've held them back?" My voice breaks. "Tammy deserves love and loyalty and a man who is going to listen to her and make her laugh and smile and feel good about herself. She deserves to live free from any kind of pressure and judgment, but she can't do that with you guys breathing down her neck and scheming behind her back. Don't sit there telling me you didn't order those two to get married when you found out she was pregnant. And don't sit there telling me that you're not still pulling their strings!"

Mr. Tan darts a look at his wife, whose black curls are jiggling as she shakes with obvious rage. I no longer give a fuck. If she wants to hate me, she can go right ahead. I don't need to try and impress her anymore, because Tammy's an adult who can do whatever the fuck she wants, dammit!

"If she wants to leave Hudson, then she has every

right. If she wants to stay, then that's her prerogative too. But whatever she decides, it's *her* choice to make, and she does not need some bullshit custody battle threats." I throw my glare on Mrs. Clark while Tammy's mother lets out a horrified gasp.

"Lydia, you didn't."

"Kai is his son! Of course he's going to fight for custody."

"That's why they must stay together," Mrs. Tan clips at her husband. "Tamara's not strong enough to handle something like that."

Slapping my hands on the table, I get right in that woman's face and tell it to her straight. "Tammy is strong enough to handle anything. And I am going to support whatever she decides."

"You stay out of it," Mr. Tan barks. "You don't go near my daughter. You've only ever been trouble for her."

I pop up straight, frowning down at him. "I'm not the one who got her pregnant and forced her into a life that doesn't make her happy, Mr. Tan."

"Like you could ever offer her half of what Hudson has given her."

The comment stings, but I hold my ground, gripping those grocery bags like my life depends on it.

"I know you've always been after my girl, but you're not good enough for her."

"I'm plenty good enough," I argue, surprised the words are popping out of my mouth so easily. "And if she wants me, I'd have her in a heartbeat, and I would love her with everything I've got. And it would be her choice to be with me, not something imposed on her by over-bearing parents who only care about appearances and the judgment of everyone else in this narrow-minded town!" I'm bellowing now and getting looks from across the street and out storefront windows.

I don't give a rat's ass.

Let all of them look.

Let all of them fucking know.

"I love Tamara Tan! I always will! And she deserves better than an unfaithful husband and a marriage that is broken because it was forced on her when she was a terri-fied kid!"

With their faces flushed and mouths agape, I walk away from the stunned table and slam into my truck.

The engine feels a million times louder than normal as I rev it and squeal away from the curb.

I've gone and done it now.

The gossip tree is going to be shaking something fierce.

I give it less than an hour before everyone in Glad-stone knows about my outburst.

It won't take long for Tammy to find out either, and I can only imagine the reports she's going to get.

Fuck!

I don't want her finding out that way.

Speeding home, I pull into the driveway and park around the back of the house. Dad's still at work, so I stay in the truck, huffing and grunting as I pull up Tammy's email address on my phone. I could text or call her, but I don't want Hudson spotting something on the screen and making things more difficult for her. If he's home when this comes through...

An email notification could pop up, too, dumbass.

My brain starts muttering at me, but I ignore its warning and type with my big, clumsy thumbs...

Hey TT,

You're probably going to hear about this soon enough, but I just went off on your parents right in the middle of town. Maybe not my finest moment, but fuck me, it feels awesome too. I'm sorry if it makes your life harder, but I just wanted them to know that it wasn't their place to manipulate your life the way they have been.

You're a grown woman. A mother. You're strong and tenacious, and you deserve every good thing.

If you want to stay with Hudson because you love him, then do it. Fight for him. Fight for your marriage. Make it work.

. . .

But if this relationship is killing your soul... then do something about it.

You're strong enough to leave him, Tammy.

You're strong enough to face all the ugliness that might come in the aftermath. I know it won't be easy, but you can do it.

And if you want me to, I'll stand by your side all the way.

Even if it's just as a friend.

Whatever.

I'm here for you.

And I love you.

Even if you never love me back in the same way, I'm gonna keep loving you until the day I die.

I want you to be happy.

I want you to be free to make your own choices without worrying what everyone's going to think of you.

Screw them.

Follow your heart.

Live your dreams.

You deserve it.

You are worthy of every good thing, and I want that for you.

I feel like I'm rambling now, but I hope you can hear my heart. Find what makes you happiest and go after that thing.

I should have done that. After the swimming hole, I should have gotten over my damn self and told you how I felt. But I chickened out, and then Hudson caught your attention. Even then, I should have kept myself in your life. And I never should have pushed you out the door when you told me you were pregnant.

I'm sorry for being a jealous jerk. I'm sorry for not being the friend you needed.

But I'm here now, and I'll never push you away from me again.

I promise.

I'm yours forever, TT.

B x

.   .   .

Do I add more *x*'s and some *o*'s? I don't know.

With my thumb hovering over the Send button, I hold my breath, close my eyes, and push that little dart icon before I change my mind.

The rain starts pattering on my windshield as the email whooshes to her inbox. I stare at those droplets, running down the glass like tears, and wonder if I'll ever get a reply.

CHAPTER 52
TAMMY

Hudson texted me to say he'd be home late because a last-minute meeting came up. I paced the floor, wondering if that was the truth.

Is he really in a meeting?

Ugh, am I ever going to be able to trust him again?

Give yourself a break. He cheated on you!

I nod, gripping my arms and trying to lean into that fact, yet unable to ignore the question that's been nagging me.

Why'd he cheat?

If our marriage was so awesome and happy and wonderful... why'd he need to cheat?

The truth is simple...

Our marriage wasn't any of the things it should be.

I'd just been too afraid to admit it to myself, to him... to anyone.

I didn't want to think about what it might mean to

leave him. How difficult it would be for Kai. How terrifying it would be to step out into the big, bad world alone.

But now that I've done it for a short time...

Now that I'm back...

I can't keep denying this truth.

If I stay, I'm gonna die.

I'm going to shrivel into a soulless robot. And what kind of mother will I be for Kai?

He deserves my joy, doesn't he?

He deserves a mother who is energized by life and love and hope.

I can't be those things if I stay. The amount of effort it's taking me to play "happy mommy" is only getting greater. It'll wane, and then what will he be left with?

My throat swells, acid burning my windpipe as I try to swallow and come to terms with this.

When I drove away in shock after I caught Hudson and that woman, I hadn't really thought all of this through.

But I've had all afternoon and evening to mull this over.

And now I can face it with logic.

I just wish logic didn't feel so damn scary.

The garage door starts to whir, and I tense, staring at the internal door like a deer in headlights. Even when it pops open and Hudson appears looking end-of-the-day tired, I can't move.

"Sorry I'm late," he's muttering. "Had to go for drinks with a client after my meeting and then..." He gives me a confused frown, dumping his keys in the bowl on the counter. "Why are you looking at me like that?"

I can feel the color draining from my face.

Is this it?

Is this really happening?

But what about Kai?

I start to panic, terror ripping through me at the idea of an impending court case. Does Kai want to leave? What if he begs to stay with Daddy? What if—

"Tam." Hudson clicks his fingers in my face.

I flinch, snapping out of it.

I can smell the alcohol on his breath as he leans down and lightly kisses my cheek. I go stiff, then quickly shift away from him, stepping into the kitchen.

"Seriously, what is wrong with you?" He glances around. "Is Kai in bed?"

"Yeah, I settled him about an hour ago," I mumble, irritated that he doesn't know his son's routine.

It might be irrational. It's not like he's around to know it.

The thought burns bright in my mind, and I end up slapping the fridge closed after opening it.

Hudson pulls off his tie with a weary groan. "Okay, what? What have I done now?"

"Nothing." I shake my head, then frown. "Why would you ask that?"

"Because you look pissed... or something. Do you not believe that I was with a client? Because I was. Had to sit through the guy's long-ass tirade on some political shit while smiling like I wanted to be there. I wasn't off with some woman, okay? You've got to trust me, Tam. I told you I wouldn't cheat on you again, and I meant it."

I bite my lips together and cross my arms, staring at the floor and willing myself to say it.

Just say it!

"I don't think I can do this."

"Do what?"

My eyes sting with tears as I look back at his face. "Stay."

His lips pinch into a hard line. Resting his hands on his hips, he mutters under his breath. "It's been less than week. You've barely tried!"

"I don't want to try." My voice is so soft in contrast to his barking, and I wish I could be stronger.

"Is this because of Baxter?" he growls. "I knew that guy was going to ruin everything."

"This has nothing to do with Baxter." And part of me knows I need that to be true. I can't leave Hudson just to be with Baxter. I need to leave him for me. I need to walk out that door knowing I'm risking single motherhood for the rest of my life. There's no guarantee Baxter will want me back. He told me to go. He walked away.

But you're the only girl he's ever wanted! He's always been yours.

I snap my eyes shut against his sweet face when he said those words to me. I can't think about that right now. This decision has to be made because... "We never should have gotten married."

I open my eyes in time to see Hudson clench his jaw and look away from me.

My stomach starts to hurt. "I'm sorry, but you know I'm right. If I hadn't gotten pregnant—"

"I would have asked you after college."

"How do you know? Neither of us went to college. We lost our chance of growing up and figuring out who we wanted to be. We were thrust into adulthood with zero say in the matter. Your parents found you your job with your uncle. They helped finance this house. Everything has been decided for us."

"You could have said no when I proposed."

"In front of the whole school? Are you kidding me?" I shoot him an incredulous look. "There was no way our parents would have accepted anything other than our marriage. And for a fleeting second, I thought it just might work. I thought I could settle and be the wife you needed me to be. But then..." I tip my head with a hopeless frown.

"Then what!" He starts pacing.

I let out a sad sigh. "The closer we got to Kai's birth, the tenser you became. And then after he was born..." I shook my head. "You didn't want to be a father at nineteen. It's okay to admit that."

His face bunches into a deep scowl.

"And working your ass off all the time, just to avoid having to be a parent, is wearing you down. And it's wearing me down. We need to stop playing pretend."

"I'm not pretending," he snaps.

"Hudson," I whisper. "You cheated on me. And—" I hold up my finger to stop him from interrupting. "You wouldn't have done that if things between us were great and wonderful... and the way they should be. You were looking for an out. Whether it's conscious or not... you want an out."

He's shaking his head but not verbally disagreeing with me.

Maybe deep down he knows he'd be lying if he tried.

I'm right. I can feel it in my core as my courage builds and I say the things we both need to hear.

"It's okay to fail at a marriage that was forced onto us. We shouldn't feel guilty about that."

"You're my wife," he murmurs. "That's supposed to be a lifelong thing."

"Yeah." I nod. "It is. But not when it's killing you."

His eyes flash with something I can't decipher. I don't know if he's livid or hurt or disappointed—maybe all three.

Sucking in a ragged breath, he rests his hand on the counter and mutters, "You really going to leave me?"

"I think I should. For both our sakes."

He works his jaw to the side, nodding and staring at the wall before finally saying, "Fine. Do what you want. But I'm keeping Kai."

"What?" The word is more of a squeak than anything. He can't be serious. "You... you don't even want him!"

"He's mine."

"That's not the point!" I start to yell. "He's mine too.

And I'm the one who's raising him! He barely sees you! You work all the time. Who's supposed to look after him?"

"I'll get a nanny."

My eyes bulge, my head jerking back in horror. "My son is *not* being raised by a nanny when he has a perfectly good mother who will give him everything he needs and more. You are *not* taking my son away from me."

"And you're not taking him away from me!" he thunders back. "Which means you have to stay!"

My shoulders deflate as I stare at him with a pitying frown. "You're seriously blackmailing me to stay?"

His nostrils flare.

"Why? Why would you want to be married to someone who doesn't even want to be here?"

My words hurt him, and I hate myself for it, but this needs to be said.

"Please," I whisper. "Be reasonable."

With a stiff shake of his head, he snatches his tie off the kitchen counter and stalks out of the room.

I'm too numb to move.

This can't be the end of our conversation.

But do you think I have the energy to keep it going right now?

I guess a small part of me was hoping I could pack my bags and walk out the door tonight. Maybe I still could, but I can't imagine Hudson letting me take Kai without a fight. I won't put my son through that trauma.

My freedom is going to have to wait.

Looks like I'll be fighting for my kid before I can finally leave this house.

I just pray I have the strength to withstand what's coming my way.

CHAPTER 53
BAXTER

It's time to head home. After my outburst on Main Street yesterday, Gladstone is abuzz with gossip of the troublesome Brown kid. I feel kind of bad for Dad as I pack my stuff.

He hands me the box I had hidden under my bed. I don't know why I want to take it with me. It's not like I could look through it before, but I'm shoving it in the back of my truck anyway.

Dad buries his hands in his pockets while he watches me, and I can feel his sad gaze on my back.

With a heavy sigh, I close the trunk and turn to face him. "I'm really sorry if you're gonna get heat over this."

He shrugs. "Don't worry about it. I learned a long time ago not to take any notice."

I wince, studying his lined face. He's gotten so much older since Mom died.

"Why do you stay?" I whisper. "How can you stand it?"

His laughter is soft and humorless, but then he looks up at the house and his eyes get all misty. "She's here, Bax. All the best memories I have of her are within those walls. And I can't leave her."

My heart hurts for him, and I push off the truck, walking toward him and lightly taking his shoulders. I don't remember when I got taller than him, but somehow our positions suddenly feel so different.

"You've still got so much life left to live. And those memories will go with you no matter where you are. I mean…" I run my tongue over my teeth and force myself to say, "Maybe it's time to let go. Move on."

His gaze is bright as he grasps my elbows and murmurs, "I could say the same thing to you."

I let him go, stepping back and crossing my arms.

"When you love her… you love her, you know? I don't want to let go." He shrugs. "She's the only woman I've ever been with. The only one I've ever loved. And I'm okay with that." His smile grows genuine, his eyes warm with affection. "So, I'm staying."

I let out a wry laugh and shake my head. "And I'll keep coming back to visit."

He grins and pulls me in for a hug. We slap each other on the back a few times, and he promises to come to Nolan next time.

"I'll make sure you get one of the nicest rooms in the house." I wink, and Dad lifts his hand with a broad smile.

"I'm gonna hold you to that, son."

Getting behind the wheel, I start the engine and idle for a minute, not quite ready to pull away.

Confusion flickers across Dad's face as he steps up to the truck. I lower the window, and he leans his hands against the frame.

"Did I do the right thing?" I murmur.

"That email you wrote sounded real good to me." He nods. "The ball's in her court now."

"What if she doesn't take it?"

Dad's smile is sad as he pats me on the shoulder. "Have a little faith, son. These things have a way of working out. I don't think God brought her back into your life for no good reason." With a stiff nod, he steps away from my car, and I pull out of the driveway, wondering if he's right.

Mom was always such a big believer in the divine. She always talked about how God was watching out for us and had our backs.

"He wants to make our dreams come true. And He will... if we just get out of the way and let Him." She'd wink, and I'd believe her.

Until the day she was snatched away so suddenly.

With the love of my life marrying some other guy and then Mom being taken, I lost all faith in some supernatural power.

But maybe it's always been there, just waiting for me to wake up... open up... again.

I suck in a shaky breath as I leave Gladstone in my

rearview mirror.

It's time to head back to Nolan and slip into the life I've established for myself. My Mini Mites need me, and I kinda love being the handyman at Ponderosa. As I reflect on my time since graduation, I realize how content I really have been. I love my hockey family... but it wasn't until Tammy and Kai walked through that door that I really came alive again.

Damn, I miss them with an ache that's overpowering.

But I sent my email.

And now I've just got to... "Have some faith," I murmur, willing my heart to believe it.

My phone starts buzzing with texts.

It's Ethan, checking up on me.

I smile and decide to be a good boy and call rather than doing the whole texting/driving thing.

"Hey, man." Ethan's voice is upbeat.

"Put him on speaker," Mick chirps in the background.

Ethan does as he's told, and soon a chorus of greetings is reaching me.

I grin. "Hey guys."

"Where you at, brother?" Casey asks me.

"I'm just heading home. Should be there by Friday. You guys gonna be around, or do you have an away game?"

"Home game this weekend," Liam calls. "You should come."

"Yeah, I will, man. For sure." My voice sounds

brighter. I can hear it, and it makes me smile to realize how much I've been subconsciously missing my friends.

"So... uh... how are you doing?"

Trust Lani to cut through the bullshit and get straight to the point.

I sigh and struggle to know what to say.

"Baxter?" Rachel's voice sounds farther away but then gets closer. "You still there?"

"Yeah, just trying to figure out how to answer Lani's question."

"You don't have to, man," Asher assures me, and then I hear a soft "Ow. Well, he doesn't."

"You're not helping," Lani argues. "He needs to learn to talk about his feelings. Don't give him an easy out."

"Says the woman who is allergic to conversations like this."

"I am getting way better, okay? And you know how I've gotten better?" Her voice gets sharp and snappy. "Because assholes like you make me talk about my feelings!"

Asher chuckles, his voice getting low and husky. "I only do it 'cuz I love you, boo."

"Exactly. And we all love Baxter, so talk, big man. What are you feeling right now?"

I laugh. "Amusement at listening to you two fight over how great you are for each other."

Mick snorts. "He's got you there. You two are ridiculous. Seriously, you guys can argue over an agreement."

"Takes one to know one." I can picture Lani's eyes

bulging. "You and Ethan are the worst! You're constantly bickering."

"Yeah, but in that cute, fun, playful, couple goals kind of way."

Ethan laughs. "It's just so impossibly hard not to tease her when she's such a cute lil' mouse."

"Would you stop booping me on the nose!"

I hear a raucous laugh and then a clatter. I can only assume that Mick has somehow launched herself at Ethan, and they are no doubt wrestling on the floor or something.

Rachel starts laughing. "You guys! Baxter!"

"Oh yeah," Ethan calls from farther away. "We're here for you, man." Mick lets out a squeal, and he keeps talking like he's not tickle-torturing her or whatever he's doing. "How you holding up?"

"I'm okay."

I'm about to wait out their play fight, but then Lani's in my ear again. "Have you heard from Tammy?"

"No." I shake my head.

"She keeps calling to check in on you," Rachel tells me.

My stomach pinches with... what? Hope?

"I think she's really worried about you."

"Yeah, well, I'm worried about her too. She shouldn't have gone back to that douche nugget."

"Preach it!" Casey shouts.

"So, what are you going to do about it, then?" Lani asks.

"Well, I... sent her an email. Telling her what I think and how I feel and..."

"You told her how you feel?" Rachel's voice is bright with enthusiasm. "Yay you!"

"Thanks, yeah..." I chuckle. "I guess I just have to wait to hear back from her."

"You should go get her," Ethan interjects.

"I can't just rock up on her doorstep."

"Why not?" Mick asks.

"Well, because... she's married."

"To the wrong guy."

"Yeah, but... it's her choice what she wants to do. I've told her I'll be there for her no matter what she decides. If she wants to stay with him, then I can't go breaking up a happy home."

"As long as it's happy, I get that..." Lani sighs. "But Bax... do you really think she's happy?"

"No." I check my mirrors, then change lanes. "Although I don't know if that's me just wishing she wasn't so she could have a good excuse to leave and be with me. But—"

"No buts," Liam cuts me off. "You didn't see it because you were too busy being in the moment, but I'm telling you, man. You two have that thing."

"What thing?"

"That soulmate thing. That perfect vibe. I say you go get your girl."

I grip the wheel, an adrenaline surge pumping through me at the very idea of that.

"What if he shows up and she's like 'No, thanks.' Won't that be more painful?" Caroline asks. "I mean, the romantic in me is saying go for it, Bax. Seriously, I want nothing more than for you to be happy. I just... I hate the idea of you getting more hurt over this, you know?"

"Yeah, I hear ya." I nod. "I appreciate that. Thanks."

"If he shows up and she says no, then he comes home, but at least he has closure." Liam's head must be turned toward Caroline or something, because his words aren't as clear, but I can still hear them.

They ring through me, and it's kind of nice to know that if my life falls to total shit, then at least I still have these guys.

"Hey, man, at the end of the day, the choice is yours. We'll support whatever you decide," Asher assures me.

"I know."

"But you should go get your girl." He laughs. "I know it's probably terrifying, but it's not like you're showing up there to steal her away. If she says no, you come home."

"And what about Kai?" I murmur. "Gotta factor him into this mess. What if he wants to stay with his dad?"

"He's gonna want to be with his mother," Rachel says. "I can assure you. Those two are tight, and by the sound of things, his dad's not around much anyway."

"I just hate the idea of him having to deal with a broken home."

"Kids do it all the time, and it doesn't mess all of them up," Caroline tells me. "As adults, you can keep it amicable and make it work for his benefit. You're all mature enough to do that, right?"

"Not sure Hudson is," I mutter.

"Well, you'll just have to make him see reason."

"I think he's threatening some hideous custody battle if she tries to leave him."

"Well, lucky for her, my dad's lawyers have kick-ass connections," Asher tells me. "We'll find her the best divorce lawyer in the country."

"It's true," Lani agrees. "The lawyers they organized for me were freaking amazing with the whole Harvey thing. It hasn't even gone to trial thanks to them. Harvey's doing his time, and I—and every other girl he's hurt— can rest easy."

I'm so relieved it worked out that way for her.

"Just rest assured that we have contacts, and if Hudson decides to be a total asswipe, then Tammy's going to get the support she needs to battle this out."

"Yeah." I nod.

"And if it helps, you go ahead and tell her that."

There's a long pause, and I don't know how to fill it. I can picture them all around the table, exchanging worried frowns. I get it. This situation sucks. Turning up at her door might be romantic and all, but there's a whole shit ton of ugly we'll have to wade through in order to be together.

If she wants me.

"Hey, Bax?" Ethan's voice is deep and sincere.

"Yeah, man."

"Sometimes the greatest pain comes before the biggest blessings, you know?"

"Wow," Mick whispers. "Baby, that's deep."

"I know it's not on the same scale or anything, but the shit we went through before we finally got together fucking sucked. But then I got to be with you, and... it was all worth it."

"Aw." Mick's voice gets all mushy, and I think they're kissing now.

"Yeah, okay. You two, your bedroom's upstairs," Lani mutters. "Seriously, why do they always make us watch this?"

"Because they have zero idea that there are other people in the room right now." Asher's tone is dry, and Rachel starts giggling.

I shake my head with a grin and hang up, which I'm sure nobody even notices.

Staring at the long road ahead, I navigate the highway back to Nolan, wondering the whole time if my friends are right.

Should I just show up at Tammy's door?

Shit, I don't even know where she lives.

But I could find out easily enough, right?

I could find out... and then I could change the course of our lives for good.

It'll either be my chance to get her back... or let her go.

CHAPTER 54
TAMMY

I pass Hudson in the living room on my way upstairs. He's sitting on the couch in the darkness, cradling his precious bottle of bourbon and staring at the flickering images on the TV screen. His face lights in flashes and bursts of color, and I stop to stare at him for a moment.

He doesn't flinch, just keeps his eyes on that screen like he's numb to my presence.

Yeah, I've really pissed the guy off.

I've hurt him.

My throat burns as I ascend the stairs, second-guessing myself like I always do.

Should I have just kept my mouth shut? Suffered in silence?

No! He deserves your honesty.

You deserve your freedom.

His accusations about Baxter haunt me as I pad up the stairs, but when I reach the top, I've managed to convince myself that he's not the reason I'm leaving. He might be the catalyst for my action... but not the reason.

He simply showed me what I've been missing out on.

And that spark has ignited a flame within me.

I never should have left him. I should have stayed in Nolan and fought from there. I should have ordered him to stay in that kitchen and talk to me. To stand by me and fight for me.

But I thought I was doing the right thing.

I felt duty-bound as a wife and mother.

Clenching my fists, I resist the urge to grab my phone from the charging station in my room and call Baxter. I just want to hear his voice. Hear him tell me that I'm his girl and he wants me back. I want him to say that I'm now doing the right thing for all the right reasons. I want his husky timbre in my ear, filling my soul with hope and promise.

But I can't do that just yet.

Until I officially leave Hudson, it wouldn't be right to get involved with Baxter. I know I let myself go in Nolan and had convinced myself it wasn't cheating because I'd decided to divorce Hudson.

But this time seems different somehow.

When I was in Nolan, I was divorcing Hudson because I didn't want to face him or have to resolve anything.

But now I'm leaving him for good because I know we were never meant to get married in the first place.

When I walk out the door next, it'll be official. I'm

making my intentions perfectly clear. There will be no going back. I'm resolved.

And because of that, when Baxter and I get back together (*please let him still want me!*), then there'll be nothing to taint our new relationship.

A thrill skips through me.

New relationship.

With Baxter.

I bite my bottom lip, fighting a giddy smile and reminding myself that I have a long way to go before that can be my reality. Dammit. Part of me just wants to run to him now, but I'm wise enough to do things in the correct order and avoid any unnecessary drama for Kai.

Bless my sweet boy. I just want to give him the best life possible.

Creeping up to his doorway, I push the door open a little wider and peer into his room, using the glow from his night-light to spot him and—

Wait.

Where is he?

Forgetting about quiet, I bustle into the room and double-check his thrown-back covers, searching the darkness for him.

"Kai? Where you are, kiddo?"

Frowning, I head to the bathroom, but it's dark and quiet. I check my en suite, too, and my bed, then race around the upstairs rooms and check every single one, including the storage closet.

He's in none of them.

My breath catches in my throat as I sprint down the stairs, panic steadily growing inside me as I check the den, the laundry, the kitchen, and finally burst into the living room.

"Where is he?"

"What?" Hudson snaps at me, his eyebrows dipping into a sharp V.

"What have you done with Kai?"

His expression morphs again to one of utter confusion. "What the hell are you talking about?"

"He's not in his bed. He's not in any of the rooms upstairs. What the fuck have you done with my son!" I end up screaming, hysteria flirting with the edges of my brain as I try and fail to find some semblance of calm. "I swear, Hudson, if you—"

"I haven't done anything with him!" He slams the bottle down on the coffee table, his movements a touch wobbly. I guess that's what happens when you don't even bother drinking spirits out of a glass. The bottle hits the coaster and tips to the side, spilling amber liquid along the wood. It drips onto the plush rug beneath, and neither of us moves to clean it. Hudson snatches the bottle, taking another swig before placing it on the carpet.

He glares back at me, and we sound like a couple of bulls ready to charge.

"Where is he?" My voice starts to shake.

"I. Don't. Know."

"Well, you better help me find him," I snap. "He's only

four years old, and who knows what he's done or where he's gone." Tears start to burn, then spill down my cheeks. "What if he heard us fighting and got scared? Maybe he ran away or—"

"I'm sure he's fine."

"Don't try to placate me with bullshit!" I storm to the entrance and shove my shoes on, grabbing a jacket and then hunting for a flashlight. "Get off your ass and help me find him."

He stands up with a weary sigh, and I'm struck by my first pull of actual hatred for the man I married. He's not even worried that his child is missing! Fucking monster!

I yell a series of obscenities at him as he slowly shuffles away from the couch and ambles toward me.

"You say you want to fight for him. You threatened to take me to court, and you're not even concerned that he's gone!"

"Because you're overreacting!" he spits. "He's probably somewhere in this house. Where are his favorite hiding spots?"

I brush past him with an angry growl and thump my way back upstairs, hissing over my shoulder, "You know, if you were actually home more often, you'd probably know the answer to that question."

His stare is dry and unimpressed, and I can't help a scornful scoff as I run back upstairs and start my second round of frantic hunting.

CHAPTER 55
BAXTER

It's late by the time I finally check into a motel. I've put some decent miles between myself and Gladstone, and I need some rest before I finally decide what to do about Tammy. I should wait until she's read my email. As I slump onto my bed and check my inbox, I start to worry that she's seen it but is just refusing to reply.

"Shit," I mutter, leaning my head back and closing my eyes.

Is showing up the right thing do to?

Will my knocking on her door be exactly what she needs or her worst nightmare?

I want to respect her choices, but...

Pulling up her name on the screen, I stare at her number, tempted to call it. I want to hear her voice, check that she's okay.

But what if Hudson's in the room?

What if my contact makes things more difficult for her?

Has she told him we slept together?

Has she—

My breath catches as the phone in my hand starts to ring. I stare at Tammy's number scrolling across my screen and sit up, willing my heart to calm the fuck down so it doesn't show in my voice when I answer this call.

"Hey," I manage to rasp, then cringe that I wasn't more friendly.

"Baxter?" Kai's sweet voice is soft and kind of wobbly.

"Hey, buddy." I instantly grin, my tone growing cheerful... until I check the clock and wonder what he's still doing up. "How's it going?"

Kai sniffs in response, and I'm suddenly aware that he's crying.

I soften my voice as concern swirls through me like a tornado.

"Kai? You okay? Where's Mommy?"

"She's downstairs yelling with Daddy."

Jerking up straight, I jump off the bed and start to pace. Anger fires through me at the thought of Hudson going off on her. Why? What's he pissed about?

But Kai said she was yelling, too, and shit, I hate that he has to hear that.

"Sorry, buddy. That's not very nice." It's an effort to keep my voice light and genial. "They're not hurting each other, are they?"

I will kill him if he causes her any kind of harm.

I want to maim him anyway for fucking cheating on her, then having the audacity to raise his voice around her.

What the fuck!

That shithead should be on his knees groveling, repenting, begging for her forgiveness.

"I don't think so. I can't see them, but Mommy's crying, and I haven't heard her like that before."

"Is it scary?"

"Yes." His voice is barely a whisper, and my chest starts to hurt in new and fresh ways.

"So, where are you hiding?"

"In the closet, behind Mommy's coats."

"That's a good spot."

"It's quieter here," he whispers.

"Yeah. If I was in your house, I'd probably hide there too. Do you think there'd be room for me?"

There's a little pause, and then he lets out a confused laugh. "You're too big."

"I can squish down pretty little if I have to."

"No, you can't."

"Hey, I'm a goalie, dude. I'm super flexible."

Kai lets out another soft laugh, and I start to feel better. Keeping him calm and distracting him is one small thing I can do.

"Does Mommy know you have her phone?"

"No. I took it off the charger."

"Okay."

"I'm supposed to be in bed."

"I'm sure she won't be mad if she catches you. She'll understand."

Kai goes quiet again, and I wait him out, not wanting to be the one to end the call. I'm still kind of touched that he called me and wonder why he chose my number when his mom's phone is probably filled with better options.

"Baxter?"

"Yeah, I'm still here."

"Do you want me?" The question is soft and surprising.

I'm not exactly sure what he means, but I respond the only way I can. "Of course. You're my little buddy."

"Really?"

"Yeah, for sure. I love hanging out with you. When you're not around, I don't have anyone to help me paint or watch me coach hockey. I don't get to teach you how to skate anymore, and that makes me real sad. I miss you."

He sucks in a breath and starts to cry. "I miss you too."

"Kai! Where are you!" Tammy's voice is laced with panic, but all I can hear are Kai's heart-wrenching tears.

And then the line goes dead.

My knees give out as I listen to the dial tone, and I slump onto the floor, a helpless wreck.

CHAPTER 56
TAMMY

I hear his tears before I see him.

Rushing into the walk-in closet, I flick on the lights, the hangers screeching against the railing as I push my coats aside in a rush.

"Hey." I drop to my knees beside him, taking in his tear-streaked face and heaving chest. He's doing these little hiccupping sobs as he clutches my phone. "What's up, kiddo? Why are you hiding in here? Why have you got my phone?"

Oh God, I hope he wasn't calling the police or something.

"Who'd you call, baby?"

"I want to go home," he wails, a fresh wave of sobs taking him out as he wraps his arms around my neck and crawls onto my lap.

I rub his back, desperate to comfort him and find out what the hell is going on.

"You are home, sweetie."

"No!" he whines. "I want to go back to Nolan! I miss Fezzik and I want to play hockey and I need a Casey hug and I want to paint with Baxter." His words are infused with sobbing tears, making it hard to understand everything he's saying, but I get the gist, and it feels like a wrecking ball through my back.

Leaning away from him, I hold his face, brushing tears away with my thumbs and trying to smile at him. Who knows what the hell my lips are doing. They feel wobbly and out of control... much like my voice does.

"You miss them, huh?"

Kai nods. "It was fun there. And the noise was happy. Happy yelling. Not angry... sad... scary yelling." He's hiccupping between each word, his chest shuddering as fresh tears pop out of his eyes.

I can't deny my own, and they trail down my cheeks as I try to apologize. "I'm sorry that I scared you. I was talking with Daddy, and I got mad. I didn't mean to frighten you." I kiss his forehead and hug him close. "And I really would love to take you back to Nolan, but there's some stuff we have to work out first."

"What stuff?"

"You know... um..." My voice shakes. "When you'll see Daddy, and when you'll see me, and—"

"I have to be with you." Kai jerks back. "You're my mommy. You have to look after me."

"I'm going to, kiddo," I assure him, forcing a smile I'm

far from feeling. "I'm not gonna leave you. You're my favorite."

My words calm him a little, but he's still tense when I pull him back to my chest.

He's going to want to know what stuff I'm talking about, and he's too young to understand court mandates and lawyers and custody battles.

I hate that I'm going to have to put him through this, and I'm close to bending. To giving in and sentencing myself to a loveless marriage.

But I can't do that.

Somehow, Hudson and I need to find a way through this... for all our sakes.

Rocking Kai against me, I hold him close until he goes soft and pliable in my arms. He always falls asleep so quickly, this one, and I can't help a smile as I cradle him against me and stand.

Walking back out into the master bedroom, I'm intent on settling my son back to bed but stop short when I spot Hudson.

He's sitting on the bed, the bourbon bottle resting on his knees, his eyes glassy as he glares at me. "He wants to go home, huh?"

I bite my lips together, lightly resting my cheek on Kai's head. "We'll keep explaining how this all works to him. He's young and confused and scared by our yelling. We need to really work on keeping things light and friendly around him, okay? We can't scare him like this again."

Hudson's lips purse, and he sniffs, resting his hand on his knee.

"How many guys were you staying with, Tammy?" His voice is bitter. "Sounds like you had quite the harem going on there."

I hope my look is scathing enough as I tip my head and glare at him. "The house was full of people. Baxter lives with a bunch of wonderful friends, and they were very kind to Kai."

"Especially Baxter?" he spits.

"Yeah." I nod, boldly meeting his glare head-on. "Baxter's amazing with him. He's amazing with me and..." I let out a soft sigh, licking my lips and looking away from Hudson. "I know this hurts you, and I'm sorry about that. But I love him. I think I always loved him; I just didn't see it until it was too late." My voice catches when I glance back at him.

Hudson's expression gets a shade darker, his mouth set in a thin line as he absorbs that information. Shit, maybe I shouldn't have told him.

Am I just making things harder for myself?

He sniffs and scoffs, looking away from me. "I always knew he was my biggest threat."

"What?" I whisper.

"Get out." He tips his head toward the door.

I stay where I am, my eyes bulging in surprise.

"Both of you. I want you gone," he snaps. "You don't want to be here with me? Then go. I don't want you." He swigs the bourbon, wiping the back of his mouth and growling when he notices that I still haven't moved.

"Hudson."

"Go!" He stands, pointing at the door behind me. "Get out!"

Kai groans in his sleep, and I shift him to rest his head on my shoulder. His legs dangle by my sides as I gape at his father.

"I don't understand what—"

"I wanted to fight for you. I wanted to try and keep this family together, but I see that it's pointless now. So just go. Get out of my life."

"But Kai's your son. He—"

"He means nothing without you." His voice is curt and rough and... he is so going to regret saying that one day.

The words burn, slapping me in the heart. He doesn't want his own son. He doesn't...

I stumble back, shaking my head and feeling sick as he barks me out of the house.

"Just go! Go be with your new man and forget about me! I don't need you anymore. I can have any woman I want!"

Hudson's shouting wakes Kai, and he starts to cry.

"It's okay." I rub his back, running into his room and grabbing a few essentials while Hudson continues his drunken rant.

"Fuck you, Tammy! I don't need you!"

"What's happening, Mommy?" Kai wails.

"Grab your blanket and Mr. Beans," I tell him.

"Where are we going?"

I stare down at his cute little face and whisper, "Home."

CHAPTER 57
BAXTER

Kai's phone call was more than unsettling. After finally getting my ass up off the floor, I've spent over an hour trying to find out where Tammy lives. It wasn't like I could call and ask her parents, who will no doubt eternally hate me after the way I embarrassed them on Main Street. And it was too late to call Grace and get an address. I probably should have just waited until the morning, but I felt compelled to hunt, so I kept searching until I found a Hudson and Tamara Clark living in Chesterfield, Missouri. It feels right. Chesterfield is only two hours southeast of Gladstone. I write down the address and am tempted to get in my car and start driving. But it's past midnight, and I can't show up in the early hours of the morning, knocking on their door, and I don't want to sit in my truck like some creeper, waiting for sunrise.

I need sleep.

I need to show up calm and in control.

Just a friendly check-in. That's how I'll sell it.

Tammy and I are buddies from high school. It doesn't need to be more than that. I can get a read on the situation and figure out what the hell I'm supposed to say to her then. Maybe I can find out if she's read my email or not.

Hopefully my gut will know what to say when I knock on her door.

I frown at my phone screen, brushing my thumb over the house I'm pretty sure is hers. Doubts start to fire through me again. Will showing up make everything a million times harder for her?

Maybe I shouldn't just turn up unannounced.

Maybe I should call first.

But what if he's in the room when she wants to answer the phone?

What if he's there when you knock on the door?

"Shit. None of that should matter. It's a friendly check-in." I try to convince myself out loud, but I know I'm lying.

It's not a friendly check-in. I'm going there to try and convince Tammy to leave her husband. Does that make me the scum of the earth or her knight in shining armor? I don't fucking know!

"I don't know." I shake my head, hating the complexity of this situation.

With a sigh, I stare out across my motel room and

figure I shouldn't be making any decisions when I'm this damn tired.

So, after a long, hot shower, I fall into bed and drift off into a fitful doze...

"Baxter?" Kai calls my name as if he's looking for me. I search my surroundings, but it's dark, and I'm struggling to find him.

Heading for the light, I stumble down a hallway and walk into a living room I don't recognize.

"Kai? Where you, buddy?" I call out his name, searching behind the couch and the curtains.

It's like a game of hide-and-seek... but not a fun one.

Someone is groaning behind me, and I spin, seeking out the sound. It's not a painful groan, more like sex, and I walk into the kitchen and find Hudson with his pants around his ankles. His ass cheeks are clenching as he buries himself deep in a woman. I can't see her face. It's pressed against the counter while Hudson goes for it. She's moaning like she's enjoying it, and my stomach bottoms out.

I don't want to see this.

Tammy and Hudson doing it in the kitchen while Kai is playing hide-and-seek makes me sick. What the fuck!

I'm ready to bolt from the room and make sure he doesn't come into the kitchen and find them, but just as I turn, I spot Tammy.

She's standing by the fridge, frozen in place while she watches her husband do another woman.

Fuck, that's another woman.

Tammy's eyes are bright with tears, and you can tell she wants to run from the room, but when she starts to edge for the doorway, Hudson looks over his shoulder and snaps, "No! You stay! You watch!"

Tammy covers her mouth and starts to jerk with sobs. Then she looks right at me, and her eyes are screaming at me. "*Help me! Get me out of this!*"

Anger bursts through me in a rush so fast, it's nearly blinding.

I lunge for Hudson with a vicious growl, but when I go to grab him, my fingers fly straight through his shoulders.

He grunts, pounding on the woman a little harder, while I spin to look at Tammy in confusion.

"Please," she begs, and I hold out my hand, ready to pull her away from this mess, but her fingers fly straight through my palm.

No. I need to get her out of this.

We need to go.

We need to—

Hudson grunts, his moan changing pitch, and I swear he's about to come.

"Baxter!" Kai appears in the doorway, his face morphing with shock as he spots his father behind me...

.   .   .

"No!" I sit up with a jerk, breaths punching out of my chest as the horrifying images fade into the background of my mind.

"Fuck," I whisper, resting my head in my hands and muttering a string of unintelligible curses.

The bedsheets have twisted around my body, and I struggle to throw them off before getting up to splash some water on my face and recover from that nightmare.

Resting my hands on the edge of the bathroom sink, I stare at my reflection and swear that dream is going to haunt me forever.

"Unless you do something about it." I scrub a hand down my face, then give myself a firm look. "Go get her, man. Go right fucking now."

CHAPTER 58
TAMMY

As much as I'd wanted to bolt from the house, my practical brain was smart enough to make me pack a few things and get organized. Kai trailed me like a shadow, as if he was afraid I'd leave without him or something.

Hudson moved downstairs with his whiskey bottle. The volume on the TV was turned up to obnoxious, and I gritted my teeth, rushing to grab the last of my stuff.

I didn't bother saying goodbye as I left the house.

It felt so wrong.

Even though I was ready to end this farce of a marriage, I didn't want to do it like this.

By the time I'd packed up the car, tears and snot were streaming down my face, making the simple task of buckling Kai into his booster seat nearly impossible.

"I got it, Mommy." His little hand brushes my tears away before he takes the buckle from me, showing me how to make it click.

I smile down at him. "Love you, baby." Kissing his forehead, I move to the driver's seat. I'm still running on adrenaline, but that will soon fade; a caffeine kick is probably necessary. So, I stop at a gas station just outside Chesterfield and buy myself the biggest coffee I can. Kai has already fallen asleep, which is a blessing.

We hit the road again, and I play quiet music, wanting to stay awake and alert. Nolan is too far to make it in one drive, so I'll need to start thinking about a motel eventually. But right now, I just want to get some distance.

Nearly two hours in, Kai wakes up disoriented and starts crying and whining, wondering where we are and what's going on.

The sun is rising in my rearview mirror. I've been up all night, and it'd be stupid of me to keep driving because the thought of stopping and having to function like a normal human being is too much.

I need to find a safe place and get some decent shut-eye. Taking the next off-ramp, I pull into the first motel I see. It's obviously popular with travelers, and I'm guessing each room is filled with someone who is on their way to someplace else.

The reception office is just up ahead when I slam on the brakes, the air whooshing out of my lungs as I spot the tall man running down the stairs. He has a bag flung over his shoulder and is looking anxious as he hits the parking lot and runs straight past my car.

He glances at me, raising his hand to obviously thank

me for letting him pass. Then he does a double take and spins to gape at me, the bag slipping from his fingers and thumping onto the ground.

"Baxter." I breathe his name more than say it, but as soon as the word has left my mouth, Kai sits up in his seat, straining to see out the window.

With a little gasp, he frantically unbuckles and jumps out the back door.

"Kai, wa—" But then my voice is lost as I watch my little man race toward the towering hockey player with his arms outstretched.

Baxter crouches down, catching him in a flying hug and scooping him against his chest.

Kai's little arms wrap around his neck, and Baxter cradles the back of his head, smiling at whatever my son is saying to him.

It's a gentle smile, soft and beautiful... and then his eyes land on me, and I forget how to breathe.

My heart is pounding as I turn off the engine and slowly step out of the car.

"What are you doing here?" I grip the door, needing it to help me stand.

His gaze softens even more as he drinks me in and rasps, "I was coming to find you."

"What?"

"I was coming to get you." He pulls in a breath, trying to lean away from Kai, who is refusing to let him go. He quietly laughs and rubs my son's back before looking at me again. "I've let you walk out of my life so many times already. And I know you're married." He winces. "And maybe I shouldn't be saying this, but Tammy... if this marriage is hurting you, you need to leave him." He blows out a breath, his gaze taking on a sharp clarity as his voice rises with confidence. "You need to leave him... and you need to be with me."

My lips part, and for some reason, my voice has stopped working.

Maybe it's because my heart is lodged in my throat right now.

"I know I can't offer you vast amounts of wealth. I can't buy you a nice car or a big house. But I can love you. And I can protect you, and make you laugh... and play games with you." He winks, his smile a mixture of sexy and adorable before his expression turns to one of pure sincerity. "I'll listen to whatever you want to tell me, and I'll hear you." His eyes start to glisten. "I'll see you, Tammy. Every day, I'll see you and appreciate you."

It's impossible to fight my tears as his words soak into me. Like rain on parched soil, I can feel them filling me up from the inside.

"Please, choose me. I'll be the best partner and stepfather I can. I'll look after you guys. And I'll love you with everything I've got."

Covering my mouth, I try to hold back the sob that's rattling my insides. My stomach is jerking, and I'm still fighting for air.

Baxter moves around the car, his large arm enveloping me as he kisses the top of my head.

"It's okay," he whispers when Kai starts to cry too.

I sniff, pulling myself together and rubbing Kai's back. He turns his head, resting it against Baxter's shoulders and looking at me with his worried, tear-filled eyes.

"Mommy's okay, Kai. These are happy tears. Promise."

He swallows, his little lips quivering as he sits back and stares down at me.

I swipe the tears off my cheeks, my smile growing as I let out a shaky breath. Wrapping my arm around Baxter's waist, I nestle against him, then pull Kai toward me for a group hug. His little arm squeezes my neck tight, and I start to laugh as my face gets squished between my boy and a wall of muscle.

"Okay, okay." I pull back, keeping my hand on Kai's arm as I look up at Baxter. "You're not going to push me away when things get hard, are you?"

"Never," he whispers, pain flittering over his expression. "I will never do that to you again."

"Good." I sniff and nod. "Because I love you."

The words are so simple, yet so true.

And the look on Baxter's face is one I want to remember for the rest of my life. His lips part, this awestruck surprise taking over his expression.

"I love you," I say again, laughing as I rise on my tiptoes and kiss his perfect lips.

It takes him a second to respond, and then he's all in, gripping the back of my head and holding me against him, prolonging our kiss until Kai quietly asks, "Are you guys nearly done?"

The question makes me laugh into Baxter's mouth. He joins me, and then Kai starts to giggle, though he probably doesn't know why.

A horn beeps behind us and I flinch, whipping around to notice a car has just pulled into the lot.

"Sorry!" I raise my hand in apology and quickly get behind the wheel, pulling into the closest parking space.

Baxter is still carrying Kai and walks around to open the door for me.

I climb out, rubbing my forehead and glancing over my shoulder at the reception sign. "Have you checked out already?"

When Baxter doesn't respond, I turn to glance at him, and he shakes his head. "I was about to." His eyebrows dip. "I was going to drive to Chesterfield and..." He shakes his head. "What are you doing here?"

"I've been up all night, and I really need some sleep."

"No." He cups my face with a gentle grin. "I mean, why aren't you... home?"

My eyes burn, my voice wobbling out the words. "Because it's not my home anymore." I glance at Kai, who's staring at me like he's worried I'll change my mind. Giving him a brave smile, I lightly squeeze his leg and look back up at Baxter. "We were on our way to Nolan, actually. I'm hoping there's still a spare bed at Ponderosa?"

Baxter's smile could power a city right now.

I laugh, leaning against him when he pulls me into a tight hug. "There'll always be a place for you. I'll never let you go again," he whispers into my ear, and my chest sizzles with that promise, hope starting to bloom as all the dried-up deadness inside me starts to blossom with fresh life.

CHAPTER 59
BAXTER

Tammy spent the day sleeping at the motel, and once Kai woke up from a very long morning nap, I took him out for lunch at a local diner. By the time we got back, Tammy was showered and looking bright and playful. She let Kai have a little screen time, pulling me to the edge of the room and wrapping me in a tight hug.

"Are you okay?" I ran my hands up her back, molding her against me and wondering how I'd ever let her go again.

"I just read your email," she whispered, shuddering, then pulling back to smile up at me. "Thank you."

I kissed her. It was the only response I had in me, and if Kai hadn't been in the room, I would have done a lot more. I was desperate to show her everything I was feeling, but we hadn't had a chance yet.

That afternoon, Tammy pulled out Kai's Halloween costume, and we ended up booking another night at the motel so we could drive to the nearest town and do a little trick-or-treating with the rest of the kids.

It was a fun way to spend an evening, and I'd never felt more like a dad as Kai, the hockey player, walked up various pathways and knocked on different doors. I stood back with Tammy, my gaze watchful of the bigger kids as Kai did his thing. Tammy leaned her head against my arm as "our" boy went nuts over candy.

Getting him down that night became an impossible mission, and in the end, we all piled into the same bed. He finally fell asleep halfway through *Aladdin.*

The next morning, we headed back to Nolan. Kai rode with me for the first half, then changed his mind at lunchtime, and we arrived at Ponderosa Villa just before dinner.

The second Kai saw Casey coming down the stairs, he jumped out of the car and ran at him like an excited puppy. The two of them tussled on the cold lawn while Fezzik jumped around them yapping, his tail going crazy as he tried to lick Kai's face and tell him how much he'd missed him.

Then the little pup spotted me, and I got a very friendly greeting as well.

I swear I can still feel dog saliva on my face. I rub my cheek, frowning at my fingers while Tammy shifts her empty suitcase and tries to create a little space in our new room. I've created a few spare drawers for her, but we've got some work to do in here.

The villa is opening this weekend for the first exclusive guests, which means all of us are piled on the top floor. Casey's still in the pool house, thankfully, and Kai's been squished into the room next to ours. It was originally going to be a storage room, but we spent today clearing it out and putting a single bed in there. He's barely got room to move, and my mind is already ticking over with future plans. There's no way we can raise him here, which means we're going to have to find us a little house nearby. Maybe a small rental in Nolan. Tammy's already checking out schools for him... and I asked her this afternoon if she'd like to attend college.

She stopped short, blinking at me. "College?"

"Yeah." I nodded. "Now that Kai's a little older, he'll be starting school soon enough. I'll be around to help out when you're busy. This could be the perfect time to get that degree you always wanted. Early childhood teacher, right?"

She nodded, her eyes rounding like I couldn't possibly be serious.

"I mean, if you still want it." I shrugged, thinking it wasn't that big of a deal, but she gaped at me like I was handing her the world.

"I could go to college?" Her voice pitched, and I swear I fell a little harder as I watched that really sink in. Her face was so freaking beautiful as she let out a surprised laugh. "I could go to college! Wait, can I afford to go to college? Maybe we—"

"Shhh." I pressed my finger to her lips. "Don't spiral,

TT. We'll work it out. There'll somehow be a way for you to do this."

"What about you?"

"What about me?" I frowned.

"Well, don't you have a job you really want or…"

I skimmed my fingers down her cheek. "As long as I get to be with you and Kai, I'm happy doing anything. I've got work here, plus the coaching job. It doesn't pay much, but if I need extra, I'm sure I could find some. Maybe I could start up my own handyman business or something. I'm sure Nolan could use a jack-of-all-trades." I winked at her.

She threw herself into my arms, then kissed me like she meant it.

Shit, I could spend forever kissing this woman. And I want to kiss her right now, but she's still on the floor, sorting boxes.

"Do you need a hand?" I go to rise off the bed.

"No, I'm basically done. I just…" Her voice trails off as she opens a box, then starts looking through the top of it.

"Tammy…" I pat the bed. "Really keen to play some Baxter Says, if you're up for it."

She doesn't respond, and I worry my lip, wondering what's got her so hooked.

This time I actually get off the bed, hitching my pajama bottoms. "Or we could play Tammy Says. I love both games equally."

She sniffs, and my insides pitch. Shit, she's crying.

Racing around the bed, I crouch down behind her.

"Baby, what's wrong? What—" She's holding my journal, the page open on the poem I wrote her. Shit, why had I bookmarked that thing? Seriously.

I frown.

"I'm sorry. I know I shouldn't be reading this without your permission, but it caught my eye..." She looks over her shoulder, staring up at me with a glassy smile. "Did you write this?"

I nod. "I used to journal." Then I cringe. "I still do."

"I love that," she murmurs, then brushes her fingers over my words.

"When did you write this?"

"In high school," I admit. "It's not great."

"It's perfect," she whispers, looking at me with the sweetest smile. "Is it about me?"

I swallow, taking the journal from her and placing it back into the box. "Yeah," I rasp, my skin catching fire.

She swivels, rising on her knees so we're eye level. Taking my face in her hands, she brushes her thumb over my bottom lip. "I'm sorry it took me so long to see you. To see how you really felt about me."

I cringe, dipping my head. "I should have told you. I was just scared you wouldn't want me in that way. I didn't think I could handle losing you."

"You'll never lose me." Her brown gaze drinks me in. "I know that our situation is messy and complex. I know that I'm always tied to Hudson through Kai, and that's going to be really hard sometimes." Her hold on me tightens, like she's desperate for me to understand this next part. I run my hands down her sides, lightly holding her hips. "But I'm yours, Bax. From now on... yours and yours alone. You're the only man I want to be with."

My voice drops to a husky whisper as I catch her against me and rise from the floor. "Then be with me, baby."

CHAPTER 60
TAMMY

The back of Baxter's knees hit the bed and he flops down, bringing me with him. Straddling his waist, I pull him in for a kiss that hopefully amplifies everything I just told him. Because I mean it. I mean it so freaking hard.

I'm his forever.

And maybe I always have been.

Because kissing him like this feels so right.

I'm home now. My soul knows it, and my heart is starting to believe it too.

It won't be an easy road. My parents won't let this be smooth sailing, and neither will Hudson. He may have told me to go, but once he sobers up and gets an earful from his parents, he'll no doubt be chasing us down again.

But I won't let it scare me this time.

I deserve to be with Baxter, and if there's a fight coming, then I know he'll stand by my side. And so will everyone in this place. Because that's what family does. That's what family is. They support each other. They stick together no matter what. There are no rules or conditions. It's just love—plain and simple.

Baxter's hands start to travel across my back, lightly squeezing my neck before drifting down to my ass. He gives me a firm, suggestive squeeze as the ember that's been waiting for him flares to life.

I giggle against his lips when I tip my hips, grinding against the shaft in his pajama pants.

"Wanna play?" Baxter swipes his tongue into my mouth before I can respond.

I moan against his lips, tugging at his shirt and quickly ridding him of the fabric. Within seconds we're both naked, skin-on-skin contact in full effect as he continues to paint pictures with his fingers and drive my body to the point of insanity with his warm touch.

"Tell me you love me," I whisper in his ear.

He sucks my neck, licking a path to my chin before murmuring against my skin, "I love you."

His sexy voice sends tendrils of pleasure firing through me as I lean back and gaze into his eyes. "I love you too." I kiss his mouth. "And you were right..." I kiss his chin, rising higher on my knees and wrapping my fingers around his cock. Lining us up, I wait until he's perched at my entrance before saying, "Cupid did know what he was doing."

I sink onto him, his groan vibrating through me. Tight fingers grip my hips as I take him all the way. I clutch his shoulders, whimpering with pleasure, my head tipping back. He licks my throat, and I start to ride him—slow, languid strokes that fill me to my core.

"I love you," I whisper again, like they're the only words I know.

It's all I can feel as he takes me past the point of ecstasy.

I cling to him, scraping my teeth across his broad shoulder, then crying out when his thumb finds my clit and stars scatter across my vision.

There are no words to describe how good this feels, so it's lucky we don't need any. I lean back, staring into his face and seeing everything he wants to tell me, finally understanding that look in his eyes, knowing what his every touch means.

We instinctively pick up the pace, creating a perfect rhythm as our breaths and moans blend, composing music that's all our own.

The orgasm crescendos inside me, my eyes snapping shut as I stop breathing, my body going taut just before that electrifying release. Baxter groans, his fingers digging into me as he thrusts hard, and we hit that high together.

It's pure magic—new and thrilling and wondrous.

Because Baxter Brown... is the guy I was meant to be with all along.

CHAPTER 61
BAXTER

It's been nearly two years since Tammy and Kai moved to Nolan.

It's definitely had its ups and downs. Hudson tried to get that court case pumping after Tammy sent him the divorce papers. He was out to hurt her for leaving him and he did pretty well too. She cried buckets throughout the process. He got nasty, accusing her of all kinds of shit she never did. Thankfully, Asher's family hooked us up with a kick-ass lawyer and Hudson got put in his place. They were able to settle within the year.

Hudson now sees Kai once a month in Gladstone. Well, his parents definitely do. Hudson doesn't always make it, much to my annoyance.

It means we have to travel back to our hometown the last weekend of every month, but it's a good chance to see my dad, and we're making it work. Kai and Hudson stay with the Clarks while we stay with Dad, and Tammy pops next door to visit with her folks. Not sure I'll ever be invited over there myself—Kai and Tammy do a special Tan dinner just before we fly back each Sunday evening.

Her dad did wave to me over the fence last time I was raking leaves on Dad's lawn, so that's a win, right?

But I still haven't heard back from the message I left on his voicemail last week. "Mr. Tan. I just wanted you to know that I'm planning on asking Tamara to marry me. I'm not asking for your permission, as it's her decision, but it'd be so much easier and more joyful for her if we could have your blessing. I've loved your daughter most of my life, and I promise that's not going to change. We make a great team, and I'm really hoping you and Mrs. Tan can get behind us on this. Tammy deserves for this to be the happiest time in her life."

I was going to wait until I heard back from him before popping the question, but it's been six days, and I have to ask her tonight.

Tammy's due home from her summer job at Busy Bees Daycare any minute.

"She's coming!" Kai's voice pitches as he rushes into the kitchen and starts jumping by the counter. His energy levels have skyrocketed since starting school. He's going to be a big first grader this year. I honestly thought kindergarten would tire him out, but Nolan Elementary has awoken his boisterous side. He's made awesome friends, and on the days I pick him up from school, he talks so fast that I can barely keep up with him. I listen with a smile as we drive to hockey practice or the grocery store or whatever else needs doing. We've found ourselves a happy routine. Tammy loved her first year of college and is practically counting the days until summer break is over—craziness.

But I get it. She's finally getting to do all the things she couldn't before, and I'm happy for her.

With Asher's help, I've started up a handyman business and have a steady stream of work keeping me busy. Word of mouth is my main marketing tool, which is a relief because thanks to losing a bet with Mikayla (I should have known better, right?), my small company is called Baxter's Got You Covered.

I wanted to go with something simple like BB Repairs, but no, apparently that was boring and dumb, and Mick tricked me into this stupid bet. Now I've got business cards with a cheesy cartoon of me in my tool belt doing the thumbs-up with a speech bubble that reads *"No matter the problem, I've got you covered."*

Ugh.

The front door clicks, and I ping straight, Kai doing an excited little dance at my feet.

"Okay, chill, lil' dude," I whisper, resting my hands on his shoulders to calm him while nerves fire through me in a frenzy.

"Sorry I'm late," Tammy calls through the house. "I was just at the..." Her voice trails off when she walks into the kitchen, pushing up her sleeves and instantly knowing something is up. Her eyes narrow as she crosses her arms. "What's going on in here?"

Kai laughs and runs behind me, pushing me forward until I nearly stand on her.

"Oomph." I catch her around the waist and fight a smirk. "Sorry about that. He's excited."

"I can tell." She grins. "What's he so excited about?"

"Well..." I guide her to the back of the house.

Kai races out ahead of us, opening the door to our little backyard... which we spent all afternoon decorating with fairy lights and candles.

Tammy gasps. "Oh, it's so beautiful!" She smiles, her mouth opening with delight. "You guys did all this?"

"Yeah, we wanted to surprise you." Kai's impish grin is going to give everything away, but I've gotta admit, I love his enthusiasm.

I hold her hand as we walk down the steps, and she starts to laugh. "Seriously, is there like a birthday or anniversary I'm forgetting about? What is all this?"

"I wanted to celebrate with you."

"Celebrate what?"

"Well..." I take her hand, my throat suddenly feeling thick and gummy. "It's July Fourth tomorrow and... on that day, however many years ago..." I let out a nervous laugh. "I fell in love with you."

She sucks in a soft breath.

"I can still picture it all so clearly. You had red ribbons in your hair, and you were wearing this Stars and Stripes T-shirt. And..." I smile, brushing my thumb down her cheek. "You winked at me... I was a goner."

She grins and winks at me again, sending my insides into a frenzy as I slowly drop to one knee.

"Oh my gosh." Her fingers are trembling as she presses them against her mouth.

"Tammy Tan… I love you. And I want to spend the rest of my life doing that."

"I love you too," she squeaks and then starts sniffing, laughing and crying in the same breath.

"Will you marry me?"

"Yes." She doesn't even make me wait a beat, and I catch her against me, kissing her when she plants her lips on mine.

"She said yes!" Casey shouts from the bushes, and then our Hockey House family appear from their hiding places.

Tammy pulls away from me with a delighted gasp, laughing and greeting everyone as they form a circle around us. Everyone starts cheering behind me, and I hear the clinking of beer bottles as they celebrate this win.

Perching on my knee, Tammy spins so Kai can present the ring to her.

"It's so beautiful," she gushes.

"I helped pick it out." He's so proud as he slides it onto her finger, and I share a grin with him.

"I love it." She looks between us. "I love you guys!" Wrapping her arms around our necks, she pulls us into a family hug, and then Ethan's big arms come around us all.

Soon, we've got a Hockey House pile on our hands—and I wouldn't have it any other way.

I love these people. They're my favorite, and I can't wait to see what else life throws at us while we all do this thing together.

Thank you so much for reading Baxter and Tammy's romance. Watching them finally come together was such a joy, and my insides are bubbling as I think ahead to their future, which, yes… you're going to get a snapshot of.

From the very beginning, I always wanted to write an epilogue novel for these characters. And I'll be fast-forwarding three years down the road. You'll get to see each couple as they're met with new challenges in the world outside college. I don't want to give too much away, but get ready for: a wedding, a proposal, a pregnancy, a foster kid, and a marriage crisis that I promise will get resolved.

Bring on those happily-ever-afters in THE FOREVER GAME.

And if you're in the mood for some more romantic goodies, keep reading for a special Mikayla and Ethan bonus chapter… and the announcement of which Nolan U Series I'll be releasing in 2025!

MIKAYLA & ETHAN BONUS EPILOGUE

MIKAYLA

Hockey season is in full swing, which means I haven't seen my boyfriend in... oh... forever!

With him living in Centennial and me still at Nolan, our time together has been seriously slashed. Yes, he made the pros and is now a proud member of the Colorado Avalanche ice hockey team. Casey made it, too, and they both live near each other in apartments close to the sports center where their team trains.

But it's miles away from Nolan U, and with me in the throes of my senior year, I've been enduring this long distance shitshow with growing resentment.

Actually, that's not true. It's mostly fine. We text every day and video chat whenever we can. Between our busy schedules, we're doing our best... and this year, we've made a game out of trying to surprise each other. So far, neither of us has fully managed it because there are too many whistle-blowing whisperers among our friend group.

He's tried a few times, but I've always had my suspicions after a few shifty looks from Liam, and Casey being the worst liar ever. He actually outright told Ethan I was coming last time, even after I'd secretly made all the arrangements. He scored a solid punch in the stomach for that one, there was no justification good enough.

"He beat it out of me!"

"Bullshit," I'd grumbled.

That's the last time I ever ask for Casey's help.

I'm determined to surprise Ethan this time, which is why I haven't breathed a word to anyone but Jack. I trust Ethan's dad as much as my own, and I know he won't have given anything away.

Shifting in my seat, I stare out the bus window and feel my nerves skittering. I'm gonna kiss Ethan tonight. It'll be our first mouth-on-mouth action is six whole weeks.

Six weeks!

Thanks to him traveling and my weekends being full of extracurriculars, plus work, this has been our longest stint apart, and it's damn near killed me.

Skipping afternoon classes to come down here was a no-brainer. I'm gonna go watch him play, and then he can take me back to his place for the weekend and do whatever he wants with me. And then I'll do whatever I want with him, and we'll part fully sated before having to say goodbye again.

My stomach roils at the very thought of it, but I close my eyes and focus on what's happening now. Tonight, I'm surprising my man!

Jack is picking me up from the bus station, which will be fun. He's even offered to drive me back to Nolan on Monday so I can spend the entire weekend with Ethan. Super cool of him. And lucky for me that my Monday morning class has been canceled. It's like the universe is giving me a little bonus reward for pulling this thing together.

My workload this year has been intense, but I've only got a few months to go, and then I can start my internship at Hermes Sports Management in Denver. Once there, I'll only be a forty-minute drive from my boyfriend, which means we could probably move in together and I can just commute. I haven't pitched that idea to him yet, but I'm pretty sure he'll be into it.

Hermes is taking me on for the year so I can learn the ropes. I worked a little for them last summer, just to dip my toe into the pool, but it was on a volunteer basis. If I pass this semester with flying colors, then they'll take me on as a paid intern. Booyah!

My phone buzzes with a text, and I fight a grin.

Captain Hero: How's my lil mouse today? Will I get to see you this weekend?

It takes everything in me not to spoil the surprise, and I bite my lower lip, smiling like an idiot as I type back.

Definitely. Make sure your phone is charged and ready to go. I'm gonna video chat your ass off.

Not a total lie. We might at some point during the weekend be separated while he goes to get takeout or whatever. I can video chat him the whole way.

His GIF of a man sobbing into a huge handkerchief makes me laugh out loud, and I get a weird look from the lady in the aisle across from me. I smile at her and go back to my phone.

Captain Hero: If I didn't have this thing with my dad, I'd come up. But it's his birthday, and I can't go bailing on the guy. You sure you can't come down? I'll drive up and get you.

Now I'm getting batting-eyelashes and pleading-hands GIFs.

You're not spending your weekend being my chauffeur. Besides, I've got that stupid study group thing, and they'll kill me if I bail, and then I've got work on Saturday night.

Okay, now I'm outright lying to the poor guy. I'm pretty sure he'll forgive me the second I jump into his arms, though.

He'd better.

I get another sad-face GIF, and I reply in kind. Then we exchange crazy GIF messages for a few minutes. Our usual deal. I love that we still do this. Even after three and a half years of being together, he can still make me laugh like no one else can.

What can I say, I love the guy. I always will.

The bus finally pulls into the station, and I jump off, running into Jack Galloway's arms for a big ol' hug.

"How's my girl?" He squeezes me tight, and I love that I'm his girl. He's been treating me like a daughter ever since Ethan and I got together, and I'll forever love him too. "You ready for the big game?"

"You betcha." I grin. "Ready to surprise my man too. He has no idea."

"I've been really good. You'll be so proud of me. It's been so hard not to spill the beans." He shakes his head. "Lying to my kid does not sit right."

I wince.

"But it's for a good cause." He winks at me.

I jump up and kiss his cheek. "Thanks, Jack."

"Can't wait to see his face."

"I know!" I laugh as I loop my arm around his waist, and we walk to his car.

The arena is packed for the Avalanche home game, but we've got great seats. We could have gone in the box, but then we would have had to let Ethan know, so we're sitting in the crowd. And just between you and me, I actually prefer being in the thick of it, surrounded by die-hard fans.

I shout and cheer, launching to my feet and yelling things like I always do. I get fully absorbed in the game, and Ethan doesn't even see me. He doesn't know to look for me, which is why he walks out of the arena after their epic win and is oblivious to the fact that I'm watching him.

I loiter near Jack's car, not wanting to reveal myself too early. Thanks to some bitchy online articles when Ethan first joined the team last year, I've done my best to stay right out of the spotlight. I don't need some reporter telling me I'm distracting the team's new star player. Like it's my fault he missed that goal. What the fuck?

I also don't need them commenting on my serious lack of fashion sense and questioning whether I'm the right girl for the godlike man who is now gracing Centennial streets. I was pretty dark after that one. And even though I'll never admit it to Ethan, it hurt. So, I've stayed out of the way when he's in public situations like this.

The cameras start flashing as the team leaves the arena, and I bounce on my toes until he's clear of the interviews and walking away from the crowd.

"Go, girly, go." Jack pushes me into view just as Ethan's strolling toward his truck.

As soon as he sees me, he jerks to a stop, then blinks like he's hallucinating.

"You're not imagining this." I laugh, then start running for him.

He drops his bags and scoops me up, kissing me like

he hasn't had a decent meal in weeks and I'm his only source of sustenance.

His tongue sweeps across mine, filling me as I wrap my legs around his hips and cling like a spider monkey.

"Missed you, baby," he murmurs between kisses.

"Missed you," I mumble back, tipping my head to the side so he can lightly suck my neck.

"Did you see the game?" he asks.

"Of course we did." Jack walks up behind me, putting a stop to our vampire routine.

Ethan straightens, his lips still glistening with saliva. I wipe his mouth with a laugh, and he gives his father a dazed look. "I didn't even see you guys. I thought you couldn't make it. I thought..." He frowns at me. "Study group? Work? Is that all bullshit?"

I give him a catlike grin, and he narrows his eyes at me, fighting a smile as he pokes me in the side. I yelp and squirm, but he holds me tight.

"You little liar," he laughs in my ear.

"We didn't want to distract you during play," Jack cuts in before Ethan can start kissing me again. "And Mick here was dead set on surprising your ass, so..." He drops my overnight bag on the ground. "Hope you don't mind having yourself a guest for the weekend."

"As long as it's her." His smile is so warm with affection, I can literally feel my heart melting. My chest buzzes as I pull him close, resting my chin on his shoulder and just absorbing him—his broad chest, his strong arms, his solid body.

"Well, I'll catch you two lovebirds later."

"Thanks, Dad." Ethan gives him a wave.

"Thanks, Jack!" I call over my shoulder but keep my eyes on Ethan as he walks me to his truck.

We forget our bags and have to run back for them, but we laugh like idiots as we rush to his truck.

Then we grin like idiots as we drive to his place.

And soon we're stumbling like idiots as we flop through his front door, laughing into each other's mouths while messily yanking off our clothes.

He tugs my shirt over my head, catching my earring.

I trip against the doorframe, whacking my hip.

He swings me around and we lose our balance, tumbling over the couch and onto the floor, a mess of naked limbs and hungry kisses.

His lips cover every inch of my body while I rest my foot on his coffee table and scrape my fingers through his hair. My cries of pleasure are uninhibited, like we're the only two people on Earth.

When he plunges into me, filling me whole, I lose all sense of time and place.

He *is* the only person on this earth. I roll us over, sitting on him, threading our fingers together and riding him until he starts panting, "I'm coming. Fuck. Fuck." He's breathless, barely able to speak. "My beautiful... little... mouse." The last word turns into a strained moan as he clenches my hips, jerking inside me, then thrusting deep and strong.

We fall asleep on the floor, then wake with groans

and aching muscles around 3:00 a.m. Crawling into bed beside my man, I let him cocoon me in his arms, and just as I drift off, I feel his whispered words against my cheek.

"Can't believe you got me, baby."

My lips rise in a sleepy smile. "Couldn't pass up surprising my man."

"I'll get you back."

I snicker. "You can try, but you haven't managed to surprise me yet."

"Just you wait, lil' mouse. Just… you… wait…"

I drift to sleep with that promise ringing in my ear.

ETHAN

I think I made love to Mikayla on every surface in my apartment this weekend. We had to take a short sex break and drove to Denver for my dad's birthday, but as soon as we walked back into my place, I threw my keys on the side table and started stripping her naked again.

I took her against the wall, the painting behind us knocking in time to our heady rhythm. We spent the rest of the day playing cards, eating snacks, watching Netflix, and snuggling—no clothes required.

Fuck, it was perfect.

By the time I return to practice on Monday morning, my muscles are chewed gum. Skating across the ice with a lazy smile, I trap the puck and dribble it across the rink.

It's still early, and practice hasn't officially begun.

I've done my light workout to warm up, and now I'm just waiting for Coach, the rest of my team... and Mikayla.

She's gonna swing by and say *adios* before Dad drives her back to Nolan.

My stomach jitters, nerves prancing through me like fucking ponies. She doesn't think I can surprise her? Oh, she's gonna be surprised all right.

I flick the puck, and it fires into the net like a bullet.

"Nice, Galloway." One of the assistant coaches claps, capturing my attention before flicking his head behind him. "I let her in like you asked, but she's gotta be gone before practice starts, okay?"

"Got it." I skate for the edge of the rink and grin at my girl as she shuffles into the bench area and leans against the barrier.

"Hey, you."

"Hey." I kiss her lips, then grin down at her. "Thanks for coming."

"Can't leave without saying goodbye." She pouts. It's not a look I'm used to seeing on her. Mick is my strong, feisty, take-no-bullshit woman. She doesn't tend to feel sorry for herself and will hide emotion at all costs.

So, to see that sad, vulnerable look in her eyes... it fucking hurts.

After our epic weekend, having to say goodbye feels like some kind of torture.

It's killing me, too, but maybe a little less than her because... I know something she doesn't know.

"We'll see each other again soon." Pulling off my gloves, I cup her face. She shivers at my cool touch but doesn't back away from me. "As soon as you get to campus, look at your schedule and we'll lock something in. I'll come see you as soon as I get a free day, all right?"

"Yeah." She forces a smile.

"The season will be over soon, and then we'll get the whole summer together."

"I know." Her smile grows genuine at that idea, and not to sound like a romantic sap, but my heart feels like it's gonna burst right out of my chest.

Do it. Do it now, man.

"Five minutes, Galloway!" A call comes from across the rink as my teammates start clomping into the arena. I hold my breath and act before anything else can stop me.

"Hey, um..." I lick my lips. "Do you mind taking something back to campus for me?"

"Sure." Her eyebrows flicker with confusion.

"Thanks, baby." Pecking her lips, I dig out the box that's been wedged in my waistband and lay it down on the edge of the barrier.

Then, trying to play it as cool as I can, I murmur, "Surprise," and skate away from the wall.

I'm moving backward, so I can still see her face as she glances at the square box, then does a double take and gapes at it.

"What is this?" she calls to me.

I stop and grin at her. "Open it and take a look."

Her fingers are trembling as she reaches for it, popping it open and gasping, her eyes rounding as she stares down at the big-ass diamond I bought two weeks ago.

"Are you serious?" She's shouting at me now. Hilarious.

It's hard not to laugh as I reply, "You know I am."

She gives me a skeptical frown, and I roll my eyes.

Spreading my arms wide, I tell it to her straight. "Like I'm gonna live my life without you. Of course I'm serious!"

Her laughter is soft and breathy as she shakes her head, fighting a grin while gazing at the ring. It's unusual to see her so speechless, and I rest my stick against my thighs, my heart in my throat as I wait for that one little word—*yes*.

But she doesn't say it.

After what feels like a fucking millennium, she looks up and gives me a pointed stare. "So, you gonna ask or what?"

A relieved smile bursts across my face, and I skate back to her, dropping to my knee and gliding across the ice until I'm just in front of her. "Lil' mouse, will you marry me?"

Her eyes narrow with a dry look. "The name's Mikayla, tall man."

Damn, I love her so fucking much. Clearing my throat, I place my stick on the ground and hold out my hand to her. "Mikayla Evelyn Hyde, will you be my lil' mouse forever?"

She wrinkles her nose. "No."

What the shit?

The response is so unexpected, my jaw unhinges and my back twitches like I've just been tasered.

Did she just fucking say no?

"Your face right now." A soft laugh punches out of her as she climbs over the barrier and snatches my hand before slipping on the ice.

Her perfect ass finds a perch on my knee, and she rests her hand on my cheek. "I'll be your wife, Ethan. Not your mouse, your *wife*."

A thick beat of pure exhilaration travels through me. "My mousy wife."

"Yeah, right." She snorts. "Me? Mousy?"

"Well, you are in size, but personality-wise? Good point." I nod. "Okay, then. You can be my wifey mouse."

She huffs. "Why do mice even have to be involved?"

"Aw, come on, Mickey, you know."

Her horrified gasp makes me laugh, and I cinch her around the waist when she tries to bolt off my knee. "You did not just call me that in the middle of a marriage proposal!"

I can't help laughing at her incredulous expression.

"You suck at this." She slaps my arm while I try to pull my shit together and stop laughing.

She's funny as fuck and... "I love you. I love you so fucking much." Pulling her in for a kiss before she can argue with me, I cup the back of her head and make her stay until she melts against me.

As her tongue slides across mine with a wistful sigh, I know I'm gonna get the answer I want. Pulling back, I brush the tip of my nose along hers and softly ask, "So, is that a yes?"

She gives him a dry glare. "Like I can live my life without you."

A smile takes over my face. "That's a yes."

"That's totally a yes." Her smile is the most beautiful thing I've ever seen.

As she wraps her arms around me, a loud cheer rises from the other side of the arena. "She said yes!" Casey shouts, and my other teammates all start hooting and whistling while I kiss my fiancée, then pull away to murmur, "I got you."

She shakes her head. "You got me good, Galloway."

"You got me for forever, lil' mouse." I wink at her, then crush my mouth against her smile.

Enjoy some more of these two in THE FOREVER GAME!

Releasing October 29, 2024

And keep reading to find out which Nolan U Series is coming next...

SPECIAL ANNOUNCEMENT

Thank you so much to the readers who signed up to vote for which series is coming next in the Nolan U world. I am very excited to announce that in 2025...

NOLAN U FOOTBALL will be releasing!

I am so excited to work on this series. I loved hanging out with the Football Frat boys in *The Love Penalty*, and I can't wait to see more of them.

Here are some of the tropes you can look forward to:

<u>**ZANDER'S ROMANCE:**</u>

Second-chance romance / Secret baby / Football daddy vibes / High school sweethearts / Against-the-wall kisses / Irresistible chemistry

CARSON'S ROMANCE:

Bad boy/Good girl / Coach's daughter / Protective guy / He falls harder / Grumpy/Sunshine / Forbidden romance / Spicy lessons in the bedroom... and not in the bedroom 😊

WILY'S ROMANCE:

Nerd/Jock / Wallflower / Tutor / Curvy heroine / Dancing in the rain / Breaking the bed

---

GRADY'S ROMANCE:

Brother's best friend / Bad girl / Stranded/Forced proximity / Only one bed / Guy getting over a breakup

---

TYRELL'S ROMANCE:

Friends to lovers / Trauma bonding / Protective guy / He's trying to help her find the perfect guy (little does he know... it's him!)

I hope there's something there that's getting you excited. Keep an eye on my website and social media for updates.

Voting showed that readers are keen to have a delayed release so that the books can then come out one month after the other, so the first Nolan U Football novel will be releasing in April/May 2025.

But I've got plenty of surprises planned between those times, including special editions of the Nolan U Hockey series, plus a teaser novella for the Nolan U Football series and another Sports Digest, filled with interviews and articles, so that you can get to know some of the Football players before the series comes out.

Eeeeepppp! So excited for all of it!!

If you have any questions, feel free to email me: **katy@katyarcher.com** or message me on Instagram: **@addictedtocollegesportsromance**

NOTE FROM KATY

Dear reader,

I never planned to write a romance for Baxter, but I had so many readers asking for one, that I decided to go for it. Shae, one of my lovely readers, was the first to ask. She helped me brainstorm some ideas and I started getting super excited to discover who this mysterious, quiet, Baxter Brown was. And I quickly fell in love with him. So, I want to give Shae a special shout out for loving the hockey bros so damn much and having to have a romance for Baxter too 🤍

Writing this one was interesting, and by that I mean it was joyful *and* challenging. Tammy and Baxter were so obviously meant to be together, but they had some pretty big obstacles in their way. Baxter had to get over himself and learn to speak his mind while Tammy had to find the courage to leave an unhappy marriage. And that hit really close to home for me. Because I know how much courage it takes to walk away from a marriage that is chipping away at your soul and disintegrating all your self-worth. I know how scary that is. I was lucky enough not to have a kid in the mix, who knows what I would have done if that had been the case. But I managed to walk away—it was brutal and painful and I knew I ran the risk of never meeting anyone else. A few months later, much to my surprise, I was falling in love with the man I was meant to be with all along. The universe had my back—God was just waiting for me to step out in faith. So maybe that's why writing this story was so interesting... because it brought back all the emotions I went through during that time in my life. And it also reminded my how truly blessed I am 🤍

Life is a big ol' journey, isn't it?
And that's partly why I wasn't satisfied ending Nolan U Hockey without a special epilogue novella. I can't wait for you to see these couples doing the adulting thing. There's some tough stuff coming, but they all have each other's backs and you know I'm gonna give you an HEA, because even though it doesn't always feel like it... life is full of happy beginnings *and* happy endings.

If you enjoyed *The Only Goal*, I would so appreciate you

leaving an honest review on Goodreads. Even just a star rating is helpful. You don't have to write anything if you don't want to. But star ratings and even short reviews really help validate the book, letting readers know it's worth a shot. It also tells book retailers that this novel is worth shining a spotlight on. I know there are a bunch of readers out there who love college sports romance just as much as we do. If you can help me reach them, then that would be freaking fantastic. Thanks for the assist!

I'd also like to thank a few key people who have been instrumental in helping me prepare and release this book —Megan (for another stellar cover), Kristin (for a mistake free manuscript - hopefully!), Beth (for sound story advice), Kieran, Lauren and Tina (for your honest opinion on the story and how I can make it better), Rachael (for always doing whatever I ask), Melissa (for telling me not to give up when the chapters got too hard to write). I love and appreciate you all so much. Thank you 🤍

My review team—your enthusiasm spurs me on. I love all of our email interactions and messages. Thank you for all the lovely reviews and high praise for my books. I couldn't do this without you.

My readers—thank you! Thank you for trusting me to give you a good story. Thank you for taking the time to check out my work. There are so many amazing books out there, and you've chosen to read mine. Wow - that is humbling and so freaking epic!

My husband—thank you for being exactly what I needed. Thank you for making me smile and laugh every day—for being so kind and sweet. You are a true cinnamon roll hero and I wouldn't want to do life without you.

My beautiful sons—thanks for being my favorites.

My God—thank you for holding me close when life got so hard I didn't want to face it anymore. Thanks for giving me the courage I needed. And thanks for filling in all the spaces of my heart with your abundant love.

xoxo
Katy

BOOKS BY KATY ARCHER

NOLAN U HOCKEY
Hockey House V-cards (prequel)
The Forbidden Freshman
The Heart Stealer
The Game Changer
The Love Penalty
The Only Goal
The Forever Game

NOLAN U FOOTBALL
The First Play
The Forever Play
and more releasing in 2025...

NOLAN U BASKETBALL
Releasing in 2026
In development

CONTACT KATY

I love to hear from my readers, so feel free to email me anytime. You can also find out more on my website.

EMAIL: katy@katyarcher.com

WEBSITE: www.katyarcher.com

And if you want to connect with me on social and see pretty reels and teasers from the books, you can find me Addicted to College Sports Romance on...

INSTAGRAM
@addictedtocollegesportsromance

FACEBOOK
@collegesportsromancebooks

TIKTOK

@katyarcherbooks